LAUREN CONNOLLY
Award-Winning Author

FORGET
THE
PAST

Resist
ME

RESIST ME

LAUREN CONNOLLY

CITY OWL
PRESS

This book is a work of fiction. Names, characters, places, and incidents either are products of the author's imagination or are used fictitiously. Any resemblance to actual events or locales or persons, living or dead, is entirely coincidental and not intended by the author.

RESIST ME
Forget the Past, Book 3

CITY OWL PRESS
www.cityowlpress.com

Cover Design by MiblArt. All stock photos licensed appropriately.

Edited by Yelena Casale.

For information on subsidiary rights, please contact the publisher at info@cityowlpress.com.

Print Edition ISBN: 978-1-64898-208-8

Digital Edition ISBN: 978-1-64898-207-1

Printed in the United States of America

To my brothers, you are both awesome dog dads.

A Note to Readers

Content warning: This book contains scenes depicting a toxic relationship, kidnapping, gun violence, physical violence, and emotional abuse. There are discussions of child neglect and bullying.

Chapter One

LUNA

"A week ago, I wouldn't have been able to pick Delaware out on a map."

"That's not something you should be proud of." I glance to the passenger seat where my younger brother rides shotgun. Dash stares out the window of our rental car as we cross from Pennsylvania into Delaware.

"I blame our public school education," he concludes.

He's not wrong. There are a lot of reasons I hold a grudge against our grade school, and I don't mind adding sucky geography lessons onto the pile.

As the silence stretches, I try to find a response. A joke or witty comeback to maintain the light-hearted banter between us on this last leg of our journey. But nerves shut down my vocal cords. As our destination looms, I fight off the panic trying to convince me that this was a horrible decision. That in the next hour I will obliterate all the secret dreams I've kept tucked in a back corner of my heart.

We approach our destination as quiet as the manicured streets our car rolls down. This neighborhood lacks the personality of our childhood block in New Orleans. There was a wildness to that place. A dangerous edge. Here is all well-maintained safety. The former made me a survivor.

But this suburb might have made me happy. If only I'd known family lived here.

Following the GPS, I pull up to a house with a neatly trimmed lawn. There's a meticulously organized garden on the south side of the house, and despite its orderly rows, the small patch of agriculture gives the house more personality than the cookie-cutter palaces sitting equally spaced down the rest of the street.

"Mom grew up here?" Dash stares up at the massive house. The home isn't a mansion or anything, but it's at least three times larger than the shotgun house we were raised in.

"Maybe they moved after she left," I suggest, trying to connect our mother to this upper-middle-class dream house. The pieces don't fit. "Or maybe I got the address wrong."

Our mother, Vivian Lamont, does not give off middle-class vibes. She gives off born-without-wealth-and-one-day-expecting-to-fly-on-a-private-jet vibes. No matter how delusional that last belief is. I always imagined she grew up in some shack even shittier than the house passed down through my father's family.

"Doesn't hurt to check it out." Dash climbs out of the car, and I follow. A shiver creeps through my nerves, and I'm not sure if the sensation comes from the fall weather or some disquiet about this task. Still, as we head up the front walk, I take the lead. Like I always do.

As my finger hovers over the doorbell, I offer my brother another glance. A final chance to warn me off this course.

Dash just offers a tight smile and a quick nod.

Guess we're doing this.

I press the button, listening to the echoing ring of the bell. Long enough goes by that I'm considering ringing again when the dead bolt clicks and the door inches open wide enough to reveal the face of a woman.

We meet eyes easily, with her coming in at the same height as me. And the similarities don't end there. *That's my nose*, I can't help thinking. Straight with just a touch of a dip at the end. I've seen that nose every day in the mirror and all throughout my childhood whenever I looked at my mother's face. This woman also has the same hooded eyes as my mother, my siblings, and me. She uses them to watch us with sharp attention.

"I don't want any," she snaps, adding a jerk of a head shake that has her slate bob brushing her cheeks.

Those are my cheeks, my brain declares.

"Any what?" The question is all I can manage as I try to deal with the fact that I'm talking to a member of my family. An entirely new member I never thought I'd meet.

"Whatever you're selling. No solicitors. See?" She taps the sign hanging on her door. "Try the next house." The woman goes to shut the door, but I stop her, pressing my palm flat on the wood.

"Wait. I—"

"What are you doing? Trying to break into my house? No!" That's when this woman, who must be pushing seventy, gives me a mighty shove and slams the door in my face.

Behind me, Dash snorts. I throw a glare over my shoulder. "You want to take over?"

My brother backs away, hands raised in surrender.

Facing the door, I knock again.

"Go away! I'll call 9-1-1!" The barrier muffles her words, but the threat is still audible.

Shit. My eager hope twists into desperation as the situation falls out of my control. If she calls the authorities, we have to leave. Immediately. Dash doesn't need a run-in with police when he just finished his parole.

In my imagination, I always pictured bringing up this topic delicately. Sitting down together at a table and using a careful tone as I explained the circumstances.

But when has delicacy ever been how my family dealt with the world?

"I'm your granddaughter!" I yell, tilting my head back, trying to give the words enough power to pierce through the building between us.

She meets my shout with an extended silence.

"Maybe we should write her a letter or something." Dash offers the suggestion carefully. "Give her time to process."

Sure, he makes sense. But I didn't fly from Nashville to Philadelphia to have a door slammed in my face.

"Is your daughter Vivian?" I holler, not caring if all this ruckus brings her rich-ass neighbors out of their houses to give us dirty looks.

"No. That is *not* my daughter's name. See? You're lying to me."

At least I know she's still listening to me.

"I have a picture. Is this your daughter?" I hold up my phone toward the peephole. Mom loves posting on social media, especially pictures from when she was in her early twenties. A time she did a superb job at pretending she didn't have three kids.

"I'm not opening my door!"

I try not to growl in frustration. This is not going at all how I'd imagined.

Pulling on a special piece of knowledge, I bring up the name I saw on a hidden birth certificate. The one that led me here.

"Is your daughter Tsai Mei-ling?" Good bet I butchered the pronunciation.

Another stretch of silence.

"In her defense, that info is probably public record. Anyone trying to scam her could look it up," Dash whispers.

I grit my teeth and then relax my jaw, acknowledging the truth of his statement.

"How about a man named Bill Lamont?" I bark. "Do you know him?" My voice loses volume as my hope for this situation dwindles.

The door wrenches open.

"Bill Lamont is the devil," she hisses.

"Then consider us his demon spawn," I snap back, holding up my phone again now that there's nothing dividing us. "Is this your daughter?"

Eyes still full of distrust, the woman at least leans forward to squint at the picture. I found one of the few images Mom posted with us kids, all the Lamonts looking downright happy at the zoo. The type of outing a normal family does regularly.

We went once and never again.

"That's her," the woman answers, her voice losing the sharp edge of a moment ago. "That's my Mei-ling." Still, she doesn't step out of her doorway to invite us in. Her age-marked fingers grip the wood harder. "But that's not proof."

"Hi," Dash says, waving from his spot on the stoop but not moving closer. Probably worried his over six-foot height will only add to the discomfort of the situation. "We brought some documents that might be helpful." He holds up a folder, then passes it over.

I already know what's inside. Copies of our birth certificates. But our mother is listed as Vivian Lamont, and since we weren't sure if this woman would know that name, Dash also snuck a picture of our mom's license. That was his fiancée's idea. Paige works as a book editor and is good at picking out holes in information that would have someone questioning the validity of what they're reading. Or being told by a stranger.

The woman takes her time looking at the documents, her stare tracing over the printouts, then flicking back up to our faces.

"Your licenses?" she eventually asks.

I decide to take her not slamming the door again as a good sign. Dash and I pull out our IDs and pass them over. When she gives them back, I notice a slight quiver in her hand.

"I have a patio. Behind my house. You walk around there. I'll be out in a moment."

Then she shuts the door again.

"That could've gone better," I mutter.

"Could've gone worse." Dash gestures to a pretty stone path leading around the side of the house. I'm disappointed the walkway goes in the opposite direction of the garden, but we follow it and come upon an orderly yard with a larger garden than the one out front. This one also seems to be filled with food plants rather than vibrant flowers.

We settle into padded chairs in the afternoon sun, and I try not to fidget. Eventually, she reappears, carrying a tray holding a pitcher of colorful liquid and glasses. Dash jumps up and helps her settle the heavy load on a table. When I accept my glass of the drink, I take a sip and find myself enjoying the rich flavor of a fruity tea. Until this second, I didn't realize how dry my mouth had gotten.

The woman I believe is my grandmother settles into her own chair, not taking a drink.

"You are Tsai Shu-fen, correct?" I lean forward in my chair as I ask, hoping Google Translate helped me pronounce her name correctly.

She offers a short nod. "Why visit me now? Why wait?" Suspicion traces deep lines in her face, and with Dash's earlier observation still lingering, I don't blame her. I've heard of scams played on old people. Hell, that's what keeps the whole telemarketing industry afloat.

Still, I'd had this fantasy in the back of my mind where I'd find my grandmother and she'd recognize me immediately when she saw me. Then she'd pull me in for the kind of hug my mother had never bothered with.

But that was naive.

Life taught me the only way to get something good is to struggle for it. And even then, you shouldn't be surprised if the thing you wanted all along kicks you in the teeth.

"Our mom has been going by Vivian Lamont." I set my glass down as the sweetness turns sour in my gut. "But I saw another name on a birth certificate she'd hidden. I hired a private investigator to find you."

The woman blinks, all expression clearing from her face. I wonder if the change is a good thing or if she's going to try to shoo us away again.

"You're saying you're my grandchildren, but you didn't know about me? Mei-ling never talked about me? About her father?"

I grimace, knowing exactly how bad that sounds. Lingering behind my fantasy of a loving reunion, there exists a small worry my mother had a legitimate reason to cut off contact with her parents.

Maybe if Vivian Lamont was someone I could trust, I wouldn't have gone hunting.

"We don't know anything about her life before we were born," I explain. "She doesn't talk about it."

Tsai Shu-fen shifts her stare to the distance, as if Dash and I glare brightly like the sun, burning her vision whenever her gaze lands on us. "Tell me about what you know then. About you. About her."

Not my favorite topic of conversation, but between Dash and me, we give her an overview of our lives growing up in New Orleans. Bare facts. None of the hard or dark stuff.

My grandmother just sits and listens. Eventually, when our words trail off, she refocuses.

"I have a lawyer. I'll need to speak with him. Find out if you are who you say you are."

Dash clears his throat. "Then it's best you hear it from me. I spent some time in prison for stealing cars. I'm done with that life now, but I understand if you'd rather not be around me. But please, don't hold anything I did against Luna. She's better than me."

"I'm not better than you. I'm more stubborn." I turn to the older woman, suddenly defensive on my brother's behalf. I want to get to know her, but not if she's going to make Dash feel shitty about himself. "If you know anything about Bill Lamont, then I guess it's not hard for you to believe he's involved in some shady shit. Our father had no qualms about dragging Dash into them."

Her mouth tightens the way it has every time I've mentioned my father so far, but a spark alights in her gaze. "You don't like the man."

I snort. "*Not like* is an understatement. Hate is a better word."

Strangely, it's this, more than the documents and the pictures and our childhood stories, that relieves a slight hint of the tension in her shoulders.

She nods. "I believe you. But I will still double-check. How long are you here for?"

Dash and I share a silent communication before I answer. "We can stay for a couple of days."

Tsai Shu-fen rises from her chair. "Come back tomorrow. I will make dinner. A meal from home."

The single sentence clenches around my heart.

"Could I—" I swallow a blockage in my throat. "Could we come early enough to help you cook?"

The woman tilts her head. Then I earn my first smile.

Chapter Two

LUNA

One year later

"I need to get married? Are you fucking with me?"

The lawyer coughs as if my profanity chokes him. "No. You do not need to."

"But that's what you just said."

"Not exactly." He traces his finger over the legal documents in front of him. "No one can force you to get married just by writing it in their will. What your grandmother has done is set aside an inheritance for you that you can only claim if you are married by the age of thirty. There are other stipulations, but that is the main one. If you do not meet it, you simply do not get the money."

Dash snorts in his seat next to me, and I fight the urge to glare at him.

"Whatever. I'm not hard up for cash." Sure, the three hundred thousand the man just quoted me would be amazing to have stowed away in my savings. Get a nice interest rate, and no need to worry about my retirement. But I have a steady stream of well-paying clients providing me a comfortable life in Nashville. I don't need the money. Not enough to marry someone in the next five months before my thirtieth birthday. "We can skip the stipulations and move on to the next section."

"Well. There is one more thing Tsai Shu-fen has made it mandatory I inform you of before reading anything else."

Gritting back a sigh of impatience, I still can't keep the bite from my voice. "Just read it already."

The lawyer frowns, then continues. "If the benefactor, Luna Lamont, does not fulfill the requirements set forth to gain her inheritance, the money will pass on to Bill Lamont."

Blood fueled by denial roars through my ears.

"What?" Dash asks the single word screaming in my mind.

The man with his slicked back hair and perfectly tailored suit rereads the section slowly, but I heard him the first time.

"That's a mistake. Our grandmother hated our dad! She thought the man was a demon who stole his daughter away."

Which he sort of was.

"I'm merely conveying the contents of the will. There's no further explanation. I can, however, inform you I acted as witness when Tsai Shu-fen last updated this document, and she was of sound mind and body."

Not fucking sound enough if she decided to hand over six figures to my bastard of a father. And certainly not of sound body, seeing as how she passed away four months after signing this document.

Dash smirks at me. I don't understand how he can find any of this funny. He had the same messed-up childhood I did.

"What?" I snap.

"She hates him just as much as you do."

I wonder if the lawyer will kick us out if I kidney punch my brother. "Exactly. Why would she leave him any money?"

"To back you into a corner. Wai Po's tricky." Dash uses the title our grandmother insisted we call her. The word for grandmother in her native tongue. A gift she gave us once she started to trust us. "She's tricky like you."

"You've got to be fucking kidding me." The light bulb flicks on in my head. Just took me a moment longer than Dash.

This is how badly Wai Po wanted to see me married. She probably knew my first reaction to the money would be that I didn't care about it. We talked about my job and my paycheck. By our second visit, she began pestering me about how my line of work could crap out at any time. How I'd be safer in a relationship. A marriage.

I waved her off back then.

But now there's this money. I know this cash isn't a bribe to get me to do what she wants.

It's a threat.

If I don't find a spouse, then I'm handing the man I hate a fortune. My grandmother's money.

"Damn it!" A fancy pen rattles on the wood surface of the table as I pound my fists in one definitive *thwap*, earning myself a glare from the lawyer.

"Do you need a moment to compose yourself?" The man tilts his chin a fraction so he's looking down on me.

Who talks like that? Does he want me to take a little lie down on a fainting couch or something?

"No," I grind the word through my teeth. "I'm fine. And I'm not getting married."

Which means the money will never be mine. Hell, I can see the expression on my father's face, clear as if he's standing next to me.

Shock, then greed, then smugness.

Because the asshole will only need a second to convince himself he deserves every cent.

"There's no way to divert the inheritance to a charitable organization? Maybe smudge a line or something in the document?" I lean forward, eager for a way to fix this. The lawyer rears back, drawing the will with him.

"No. These are your grandmother's final wishes. Even if that means nothing to you, I will not allow alterations to be made to a legal document."

Means nothing to me?

All the anger drains out of my chest, leaving a gaping hole behind.

"You know, I do need a minute. To *compose* myself." I shove up from the cushy chair in this lawyer's plush office and storm into the hallway. I head down the hallway without a direction until I spot an exit sign over a door indicating stairs.

The stairwell is the opposite of the lawyer's office. All cement and practicality instead of plush leather chairs and brass fixtures that scream, *my clients make a lot of money and so do I*. When I first walked into the place, I'd thought we'd gotten the address wrong. Then the receptionist greeted us with a wide smile and said Dash and I were expected.

I knew my grandmother had some money. Her house was a decent size, and her designer clothes and pristine manicures spoke of a woman who lived comfortably.

But I didn't know she was rich.

No wonder Wai Po was distrusting of my brother and I when we first found her. Took some time for her to accept we were who we said we were. Once that happened, she was determined to get to know us.

The same way I was set on learning everything I could about her.

But I guess she didn't trust me enough to share her diagnosis. To warn me our time was limited.

"Damn it." My words bounce back to me off the stark industrial walls. I sink down to plant my ass on a step and bury my face in my hands.

There is not much in this world that can force tears out of me. Crying means vulnerability, and vulnerability means someone can hurt you.

I don't let people hurt me.

But damn it, this hurts.

To find family and then to lose them, all in a single year.

And that stuffy, stick-up-his-ass lawyer thinks I don't care?

"Fuck him," I mutter.

The click and squeak of the heavy door to the stairwell opening has my head swinging up. I quickly swipe away the few tears that muscled their way out of my eyes. Dash lets the door swing shut behind him and joins me on the stairs, his long legs bending at a dramatic angle on the short perch.

"You okay?" His gentle question has my chest tightening again, but I force myself to stifle the hurt. Of course, that only leaves the anger.

"It's complete bullshit. I can't believe she's giving all her money to Dad just to try to get me married."

Dash adjusts his seat. "Not all her money."

"What?"

"I'm getting the same deal as you. Three hundred grand when I'm thirty if I'm married."

I scoff. "Of course. Well, that's easy enough for you to fulfill." Dash is all set to marry the love of his life in two months. "Just don't mess up with Paige and you're smooth sailing." The truth of my words hits me, and a small spark of...not happiness exactly, but something like it brings a smile to my face. "That'll be nice, huh? No more wealth imbalance between you and her."

His fiancée's family has way more money than we've ever hoped to see.

Dash shrugs. "I got over that a long time ago." He drags his fingers through his already messy hair. "I'd rather have Wai Po."

The sober mood returns, and we fall silent, sitting together but working through our own grief.

"What are we going to tell Mom?" he asks after some time has passed.

Of course, Dash still considers her in all of this. His relationship with our mother was never as toxic as mine.

"When was the last time you talked to her?" I ask.

He fidgets. "It's been a while."

"What's a while?"

"A year."

My head jerks back. "Really?"

Dash nods. "It was soon after we found Wai Po. I wanted Mom to meet Paige. I thought if things went well, I could tell Mom about our visit. I invited her to lunch. Just her. But she brought Dad."

Our father would ruin any meal.

"What did he do?"

The skin around Dash's mouth turns white, and I start making plans to pay my father back for whatever wrongs I'm sure he committed.

"Tell me," I push.

After a long exhale from his nose, Dash relents. "He talked about

Paige like he does Mom. You know? Like she was a pretty object I brought with me. Then he started talking about Uncle Mike and how I should come to work for the family business. And all the while, Mom is smiling like she's having the best time. Like it was a reunion. Neither one of them asked Paige a single question." He shakes his head. "I told Dad to stop bringing up Mike. That I'm never working for him again and the lunch was about Mom getting to meet Paige, not some criminal recruitment. He flipped. You know the way he does. One second he's trying to charm me, the next he's making threats and claiming—" Dash's clenched jaw cuts off his explanation. After a stretch, he forces the rest of the words out. "Claiming the uppity bitch I'm dating has me by the balls if she won't let me do real work."

That seals it. Bill Lamont will get served a dish of piping hot revenge.

"We walked out. Haven't seen either of them since." My brother's fingers lace together, so tight his knuckles go white. "Mom doesn't know about the wedding. Or the engagement."

"Are you serious?"

Dash nods, untangling his fingers only to shove them into his hair again. "If it was just her, then I'd tell her. Yeah, she wasn't a great mom. I know that. But it's not like she ever hurt any of us."

Oh, little prince. Sometimes I have a hard time remembering my brother is a grown man. Especially when he says anything in defense of the woman who gave birth to us.

Doesn't he know? There are more ways to hurt a person than just by laying your hands on them.

Not that I'd ever want him to deal with that pain.

He continues to explain, unaware of my thoughts. "But it's like she can't do anything without Dad's permission. Or presence. And can you imagine him showing up to anything with the Herberts? With Paige's dad?"

"Judge Herbert, you mean?" The idea brings back a smile. If an evil one. Mr. Herbert is an intimidating man, but not in the way my father always tried to be. Bill Lamont relies on his fists to inspire fear. That works fine enough when the person you're going against is weaker than you. But Paige's dad has a presence that leaves you wondering what you've done wrong and if he can discover your fuck-up just by looking at you. After getting over my initial defensiveness toward him, I realized I liked the man. "You think Dad would have the balls to show up?"

Dash shrugs, and I reach over to rub a reassuring circle on his back, finding my own sense of comfort in taking on my classic role of big sister. Ever since we were kids, I've always been his protector.

Well, me and Leo.

Until my twin decided to join the dark side.

Doubt he's in the will.

"But this isn't about the wedding." Dash brings my focus back to the current tragedy. "It's about Wai Po. Mom needs to know."

As much as I hate what will come of my next words, I force them out. "I'll tell her."

"Luna—"

"Shut up." I soften the reprimand with a pat on his knee. "You cut off contact for a reason. Stick to that. I'll tell her. I was going to anyway."

"Really?"

"Yes." *No.* But no way am I going to let my brother step back into the quicksand of our family if I can help it. "I'll tell her. You and Paige keep your distance for as long as you want." Forever, if I have things my way.

Dash stares at me then, no doubt trying to figure out what's going on in my mind.

Good luck.

"I love you," he says. The intensity of his statement has me rearing back. But I can't go far because suddenly his long arms capture me in a tight hug. "I wish I'd said that more to Wai Po."

"I'm not dying," I mutter, moving to return his embrace.

But I understand the gesture. The panic that lingers from our grandmother's passing and how the hurt bleeds into worry about the mortality of others.

Suddenly I'm the one holding onto him tighter.

If I die, Dash will have Paige to hold him through the pain.

But I don't have that.

Without my brother, I'm alone.

Chapter Three

CHARLIE

When I get married, I will require all aspects of the ceremony take place on dry land. Nothing better than solid ground under your feet when making any kind of commitment. Or when doing anything for that matter.

For instance, this yacht is doing its best to hinder my ability to perform the simplest of tasks. Like walking.

The instant I stepped from the relative security of the dock onto this luxurious watercraft, my legs forgot how to stay steady. Perpetual sea legs. Or land legs. Whatever the problem is, I know it won't go away. I stumble to the closest seat I can find, which turns out to be a booth in the boat's interior near the buffet.

"Hey!" Paige settles beside me. My best friend brushes aside a stray blonde curl as she stares into my eyes. "How are you doing? Have you been falling over? Do you have bruises yet? I'm sorry about the boat. Since this party is mainly for all Mom and Dad's friends I didn't want to invite to the actual wedding, I figured I'd let my parents choose the place. I never thought they'd pick a boat. Mom and Dad wanted to surprise me with the location, and they must not know what these things do to your inner ear."

No, they wouldn't know. I love Paige's parents like an aunt and uncle, but most of the time Mrs. Herbert has her head buried in a car engine, and Mr. Herbert doesn't give off a warm cuddly air. They care about me, and I know they always wished Paige and I had ended up together. Still, I've never had a heart-to-heart with them about my vulnerabilities.

Including my aversion to boats.

"It's fine. Seriously. My balance has improved." Under other circumstances, I'd be honest with Paige, letting her know I'm worried I might tumble out of this seat at any second. But today we're all here to celebrate her engagement. None of this party should focus on me.

Still, my friend gives me a skeptical look. "Charlie—"

"Miss Herbert, there you are." A woman with a fancy camera hanging around her neck approaches our table. "I thought now would be a good time for pictures of you and your fiancé. Wedding party too? The view off the bow is magnificent! Will make for a perfect background." The bearer of bad ideas grins down at the two of us.

Paige glances my way. "I don't—"

"Sounds like a plan!" I wave my friend out of the booth so we can both stand. No way am I going to let my unsteadiness hinder any part of this party. With a strategic grip on the tabletop and locking my knees, I'm able to stand, making the move appear almost smooth.

I can tell from the way her brows dip, Paige is readying to mount a protest, but I spot the best distraction.

"Dash!" My shout catches the attention of the dark-haired man who just passed by our window. His head swivels toward us, then he backtracks, grinning wide through the glass. He gives me a nod of hello, then smirks at his fiancée as she waves and tries to mime taking pictures at the front of the boat. Dash feigns confusion, giving an exaggerated shrug, then points at his ear and mouths: *I can't hear you.*

"I know you can't hear me, you impossible man," Paige huffs. "That's obviously why I'm doing charades." She turns to the photographer. "I'll round him and the Best Woman up, and we'll meet you at the bow in five minutes." Paige steps away, then glances back at me. "You sure you're okay?"

"Promise. I'll meet you out there."

Finally, she and the photographer leave.

Five minutes. I utilize every second to shuffle my way to the front of the boat, grabbing on to anything that appears to be welded to the yacht in the process.

This is not my first time on the wild sea rodeo. When I was ten, my family went on a cruise, and for an entire week I stumbled around that ship like I'd broken into the all-you-can-drink bar. We were supposed to ride the cruise for an entire month while my mother worked as a musical act. I'd tried to white-knuckle my way into walking a straight line but just couldn't manage it. When my parents realized my balance was an unsolvable problem, my dad and I disembarked in the Bahamas and we flew home to New Orleans.

The guilt that came along with our early departure ate at me. Mom and Dad had never gone more than a long weekend away from each other, but I made them spend three weeks apart.

Suffice to say, she never took another cruise gig until I left for college.

I will not let my aversion to boats ruin another important moment for someone I love.

When I reach the bow, Paige and Dash are already in the midst of their shoot. They stand with a beautiful sprawling view of Lake Pontchartrain in the background. From the way the two gaze at each other, it's no surprise they're days away from making a lifelong commitment.

"Great! Now let's get a smile toward the camera." The photographer adjusts a lens before raising the camera back up.

But I guess that was too long of a pause for Dash.

"Mr. Lamont, if you would look at the camera?" She calls out again.

Then a second later. "Mr. Lamont, eyes my way, please."

Barely a moment passes before—

"Mr. Lamont—"

"Dash!" Paige growls as she cups his cheeks in both her hands. "Stop staring at me and look at the camera!"

The groom only smirks and leans in to kiss her deeply. The photographer shrugs and starts snapping what's provided.

"He's hopeless," a wry voice mutters just behind me.

When I turn to find the speaker, I have to grab onto the railing with my second hand, and this time not because of the water.

There's a woman. A striking woman.

She has a sharpness to her. Maybe from her neatly cut hair or the straight line of her brows. Or possibly from the piercing way she stares at the couple across from us.

"Love makes you goofy, I guess," I offer, wondering what it might be like to have her intense focus on me.

Searing. That's the sensation when she turns her head, meeting my gaze.

Even with all the angles to her, the ones that warn me I might get cut if I step too close, there's nothing foreboding about her smile. And with that soft expression, I spy her curves. The way her lower lip is fuller than the top. The nicely sculpted curve of her biceps that alerts me to who would win in an arm-wrestling contest.

Her. No doubt.

And then there's the round sweep of her hips, the shape emphasized by the vibrant red jumpsuit she wears. Plenty of people wouldn't call the one-piece outfit provocative, with fabric reaching down to her ankles and a top sporting thick, flowing sleeves. What has my mind floundering is the knowledge that all the pieces connect, which means the outfit comes off all at once.

Fantastic. I'm officially a creeper.

"How do you know Paige and Dash?" The tempting woman runs her own appraisal over me. I wonder if I meet any of her dating criteria.

"I'm the Man of Honor. Paige's best friend." That's got to give me some credit, right? That a woman as awesome as Paige likes me enough to include me in her wedding party.

The stranger's head tilts, and this time her eyes trail over me at an even slower rate, truly taking in every inch of my body.

"Charlie Keller." My name on her lips should be a best-selling song. I want to play it on repeat.

"Yes." I almost choke on the agreement, eager to find out how she knows me. If she wants to get to know more. "And you are?"

"I'm Luna." The woman extends a hand, and I detach one of mine from the railing to return the handshake. "Dash's sister. And Best Woman."

The second after she says it, I know I should have realized. For one,

Paige told me Dash's sister would be here and that she's basically a shorter version of her brother.

My best friend needs to work on her description of people.

Yeah, I can see the resemblance between Luna and Dash with their sharp cheekbones, dark brown—almost black—hair, and hooded eyes.

But Dash's dark brown eyes aren't beautiful and guarded like his sister's. And the guy's mouth isn't perfectly made for long, languid kissing. And his body is not merely a taller version of his sister's strong, curvy form.

"Nice to meet you," I manage to say in a normal tone of voice, without drooling.

"Good thing I wore heels." She nods down to her feet, which are sporting some strappy shoes with a spiked heel.

"Huh?" The awkward word is all I can manage when I get distracted by her red-painted toenails.

"Because you're so tall." She reaches up to tap the top of my head. "While I can walk under most limbo sticks without effort. At least this way they can take a picture of us together and both our heads will be in the frame." She smirks, and I grin in return.

"Oh, good. You're here. Let's get some shots with the wedding party." The photographer waves Luna and me over. Luckily, I'm able to shuffle along the railing to reach the happy couple.

For the next few minutes, the four of us stand grouped together for unending photos. Paige does her best to keep an arm wrapped around my waist when the opportunity presents itself, no doubt worried I'll face-plant if she doesn't lend some support.

"That's great. Now just the Man of Honor and Best Woman." The photographer messes with buttons on her equipment as we rearrange.

When Paige and Dash stroll off to the side, hand in hand, I try not to show how eager I am to get close to Luna again.

"You know, with those titles it sounds like this event is all about us," I murmur to Dash's sister when she's at my side.

Luna snorts, but then her body gets all kinds of stiff as she faces the photographer.

"Okay, these are just some casual shots. Feel free to relax into them," the woman directs.

I do my best to not appear to have a stranglehold on the railing, and I watch as Luna moves her hands around awkwardly, as if they're inflated with helium and she can't figure out how to keep them down.

The smile the photographer aims at the two of us is all strained patience, and I pity her. Models we are not.

"What if we do some funny ones?" I suggest, getting a genuine smile of relief from the professional.

"Funny how?" Luna's skepticism is clear in her voice.

"Like...oh my god! Is that a whale eating a shark?" I point wildly to the empty water, and Luna whips her head to the side, shielding her eyes, then glances back at me with a wry smile.

A click sounds. The candid moment caught.

"Got me." Her strong hand grips the rail beside mine. "What next?"

"Piggyback ride?" I offer, apparently because I'm in active pursuit of pitching face-first onto the deck.

Luna's lips twist in contemplation. "I'm giving you one," she announces.

"What?"

But the short woman is already hunching over, presenting me her back. "Come on, Man of Honor. I'm stronger than I look."

The situation takes some clever maneuvering and a lot of laughter from Paige and Dash. I'm not sure the shot of me, all long limbs draped over Luna's compact body, is wedding album material, but the silly pose breaks some of the tension of two relative strangers posing together.

My awe of Dash's sister multiplies exponentially when Luna not only lifts me off the ground but performs the feat in heels on a swaying boat.

This woman is a beast.

When we're back to standing, Luna wears a thoughtful expression, getting into the silly exercise.

"If I sit on the railing, our heads might be level." She taps the metal bar, measuring with her eyes.

"Sit on the railing? Are you kidding?" My disbelief squawks out in an unfortunately high pitch.

Luna gives me a grin that sparkles, and I swallow my vocal box.

"I've got outstanding balance. You just lean back. I'll climb up and use you to steady myself. Come on, it'll look..." She pauses, then rolls her eyes as she laughs out a sigh. "Cute."

I get the sense that Luna doesn't often let herself do cute, silly things. The fact that she thought this pose up herself means there's no way I can turn it down, even if the idea of her putting herself in a precarious position makes my stomach roll worse than the waves.

"Okay. Where do you want me?"

Luna proceeds to torture me by grabbing my waist and using her hold to back me up against the railing. Her guiding hands maintain my balance while causing me to fight off an embarrassing twitch below my belt. To keep any unwanted things from arising, I try to remember exactly what the roadkill opossum I spotted on the drive here looked like.

Not a thought I expected to bring up at my best friend's engagement party.

When the railing presses into my back and I've got a firm grip of the metal with both hands, Luna scales the rungs with nimble grace, setting her butt on the bar at my hip height. She doesn't seem unsteady in the slightest, but I give into the urge to wrap my arm around her waist, moving close to her side and providing support.

The photographer offers a thumbs-up, then clicks away. I throw a quick glance at Luna's face and once again watch a stiff, unnatural smile crease her tempting lips.

Tilting my head closer to hers, I whisper, "When I was fourteen my parents took me to Disney World, and when I met Princess Ariel, I got a boner and had to hide it behind my cotton candy while my mom insisted I take a picture with the mermaid."

Luna barks out a laugh just as the camera clicks, and I hear another flash of the shutter when she grins down at me.

"You would be a difficult person to blackmail, Charlie Keller. Telling all your embarrassing moments to the world like that."

"Ah, but I didn't tell the world though. I told you. And now you can hold that knowledge over me for the rest of my days."

She chuckles again, and I know the pictures have to be amazing, because there is no way that smile doesn't glow on film. Somehow taking my eyes off of Luna, I look ahead again to see Paige and Dash watching us. My friend has an encouraging smile, but her fiancé glances between Luna and me as if unsure about something.

"Got it!" The photographer lowers her camera and glances around. "Now let's get some shots of the parents. First the bride's, then the groom's."

Luna goes stiff against my arm, and I glance up in time to watch all the humor from a minute ago drain away, replaced by a carefully neutral mask.

Dash clears his throat. "Uh, no parents on the groom's side. Let's just stick with Paige and the Herberts."

"Give me a hand," Luna commands. I extend my palm, helping her easily leap down from the perch.

"That's silly," says a familiar voice from my childhood. Ginny Herbert steps forward, approaching her daughter. "We already have plenty of pictures with just Paige and the two of us. We want all four of us to be in the shot." She opens her arms, gesturing the couple forward.

"I don't—" Dash begins.

"You're our son now," a stern, take-no-shit voice says. Another I heard growing up. Mr. Herbert, in all his intimidating, looming power, steps up behind his wife. "You'll be in the picture."

Though the commanding way he spoke the words don't sound like a heartwarming sentiment, I can't help noticing how the declaration affects the gathering. Paige rubs a comforting caress over Dash's chest as he blinks rapidly. Mrs. Herbert beams up at her husband. And Luna's hand, which still rests in mine, clenches hard. When I glance her way, she has her lower lip pinched in her teeth.

Of course, it's during this touching exchange that the boat plunges nose-first into the wake of a speedboat, causing the slightest shudder in the yacht's swaying. Barely enough for anyone on board to notice, but way too much for my equilibrium to stay in check. Suddenly, I'm stumbling backward, losing hold of both Luna's hand and my footing.

Then the world tilts and spins as I topple over the railing.

Chapter Four

LUNA

Charlie has a strong freestyle stroke.

Good thing, because I was about to strip off my heels and dive after him. Now I get to admire the view while not messing up my hot-as-hell outfit.

Luckily, the boat's motor is off, so we don't leave Charlie in our wake.

"Shit shit shit," Paige mutters as she sprints toward the back of the boat where there's a low deck that people can dive off. If this was that kind of party. Which unfortunately for Charlie, it's not.

I grab the arm of a server, who is still gaping over the side.

"You got any towels on this thing?"

The guy focuses on me, then nods in a distracted manner before hurrying off.

I jog to catch up with Paige, just in time to watch Charlie climb up the ladder hanging off the back of the boat. If he'd been wearing swim trunks, the sight would've been hypnotic. All that dark mahogany skin on display, beaded with water and glistening in the afternoon sun.

In reality—not sexual fantasy land—Charlie's exit comprises sopping wet clothes and a squelching soundtrack of waterlogged dress shoes. Waterfalls spill off him, cascading down his suit jacket and dress pants.

With a grimace, he slips his phone out of a pocket and fiddles with the device.

I can imagine how this next bit will go. If we're lucky, he'll react like Dash would, getting sulky and silent as he suffers through the indignity.

At worst, Charlie will resemble my dad, muttering or shouting curses, demanding someone take the blame for what was an accident. Maybe he'll aim his ire at the boat captain or the Herberts. Maybe at me for being the one standing next to him when the tumble took place.

Either way, I brace myself and prepare my defenses.

"Oh my god," Paige moans. "I'm so sorry."

My defense immediately switches to offense. If the guy tries berating my future sister-in-law, he'll have to go through me.

I move to step forward when a sudden sound stops me.

Charlie chuckles.

At first the sound is a small thing, but then the laughter takes over his entire body, booming out. The server approaches with a towel, and Charlie accepts with a thanks before swiping the terry cloth over his face, grinning all the while.

"It's okay, Pancake." Charlie uses a silly nickname for Paige. "Should've seen this coming. I'll just sit out in the sun until I dry off."

"No way." The bride-to-be turns toward the front of the boat. "We'll talk to the captain and get this yacht turned around. I'm sure we can get back to the dock in just a few minutes."

Charlie grabs his friend's hand to stop her departure. "No. This is your party, and I'm not about to let my lackluster sea legs ruin it. So what if I'm a little wet? It's no big deal. I swear."

Paige stares up at him, her steady gaze searching. "You swear?"

"I do."

I bet he's lying, but I appreciate him putting up with the discomfort for Paige and Dash.

My future sister-in-law gives a definitive nod. Then she toes off her shoes, and in one smooth motion she tugs her green sundress over her head.

While everyone on the back deck comes to terms with the fact that we're suddenly seeing the bride in her underwear, she steps up to the edge of the diving area.

"If you swear, then what's stopping me?" she asks.

"Paige—" Both Charlie and Dash rush forward, hands reaching to stop her. But the blonde has the advantage of surprise, diving into the lake before anyone can stop her.

A second later Paige's head pops up from beneath the gentle waves, a wide smile on her face. "You're right! Not bad at all!" Then she does a lazy backstroke, as if she isn't beside a yacht full of stuffy business types here to celebrate her pending nuptials.

Dash sighs, then leans over to unlace his dress shoes.

"You're not going in too?" Charlie watches Dash with wide eyes.

My brother shrugs as he loosens his tie before going to work on his shirt buttons. "That's my future wife out there. Can't let her go it alone."

The groom strips down to a pair of boxer briefs in front of his in-laws and does an elegant dive off the back of the boat.

Impressive. Dash has grown up since those days we spent at the community pool together. Doesn't have to pinch his nose closed to dunk his head under the water anymore.

The memory has me smiling as I unstrap my heels, setting them far away from the edge of the boat. My soles enjoy the relief of resting flat on the deck. With the sun beating down on us, I start looking forward to this next bit. Everyone's attention stays fixed on Paige and Dash as the pair splash around in the gentle waves. Which means I don't have an audience when I reach back to unzip my jumpsuit. After carefully folding the fabric, I tap a server's shoulder, the same guy I'd talked to earlier about the towel. The bafflement on his face skyrockets when he sees me in nothing but my red bra and panties. I pat myself on the back for wearing a matching set today, almost as if I knew there'd be an opportunity to strip down.

"Would you mind putting this somewhere safe? Thanks."

He accepts my outfit with a wordless nod.

The sound of my question brings Charlie's eyes around. Now I have the Man of Honor's full attention.

"Luna?"

I grin at him, wanting to borrow some of his lighthearted nature, if only for the day. "You coming?"

"You're going in?"

"Someone has to fight off any alligators trying to eat the happy couple." I pat his chest as I stroll by. "Good thing I didn't go commando today," I throw over my shoulder, enjoying the shock that slackens Charlie's face for a single breath before I cannonball in after my brother.

Chapter Five

CHARLIE

Paige is in her kitchen when I walk in the back door. Normally, I'd knock first, but Paige said not to bother when I texted I was heading over.

Pumpkin gives a warning bark and scrambles off her dog bed in the corner.

"Pumpkin, sit. Friend." Paige uses a confident tone she never had when we were younger, and the pit bull pays attention. The dog's butt hits the ground, and her barks peter off. Extending my hand slowly, I let the sweet girl sniff my knuckles. Pumpkin snuffles, then licks my palm when she recognizes my scent.

"Pumpkin, free," Paige says, and the dog trots back to her dog bed.

"You all did a great job training her," I offer as I move to the counter, searching for any sign of coffee.

"Shocking, right? Since I was flirting with the trainer the whole time, you'd think we never would've gotten a thing done," Paige teases.

I grin over my shoulder, matching her expression. She met Dash at the dog rescue when she adopted Pumpkin and basically bribed the guy to get him to agree to help her with training.

Later, my friend found out some of Dash's hesitance came from his attraction to Paige and thinking he, an ex-con, would not do well lusting after a judge's daughter.

Luckily, the guy got over his hang-ups because Paige deserves to be happy.

And Dash makes her happy.

Hence, the whole wedding thing happening in a few days.

"I managed." The former dog rescuer and current mechanic strides into the kitchen. He gives me a nod before pulling a box of cereal off the top of the fridge and dumping the Frosted Flakes into a bowl.

"Is that your way of saying Paige sucked at flirting?"

My friend chucks a dish towel at me as her fiancé smirks.

"She wrote her number in a romance novel and gave it to me. Real kinky stuff."

"You love that book! Plus, I landed you. Obviously, all of my efforts worked." She leans over to kiss his shoulder. "You're welcome."

Dash's smile widens as he pours milk into his bowl. "Thank you."

Damn. They're just too adorable. So sweet I feel like I'm drinking syrup straight from the bottle.

Enough to make my chest ache for a similar connection. A partner of my own. But maybe that just stems from the general disquiet I've had with my life lately.

Falling in love would be nice, but it won't fix anything.

Pushing the introspective thoughts aside, I return to my caffeine mission.

"Coffee?" I ask as Dash shovels down his breakfast at record speed.

"Oh. Sorry." Paige holds up her half-full mug. "I made myself a latte, and Dash doesn't like to drink coffee before work because it makes him horny."

"Paige," Dash groans around a mouthful of cereal. I press knuckles against my lips, trying to smooth away a smile.

"What?" She stares at him, actual confusion on her face. "It does."

Dash pushes away from the counter. "I know," he mutters, wrapping his arms around her waist. "But Charlie doesn't need that information." He presses a kiss to her cheek before stepping back.

Paige glances between the two of us, then stage-whispers, "Sorry."

Dash shakes his head, but I can see the grin on his face as he passes me by with a pat on my shoulder.

"You two have fun. I'll see y'all at dinner."

Once he's out the door and we hear the engine of the car start, I turn back to my best friend.

"Why does coffee make him horny?"

She takes a deep sip of her latte. "He says I smell like coffee. And not bad coffee breath either, which would've been mortifying."

"Ah. Well, if I promise not to get a hard-on, is it okay if I brew myself a pot?"

Paige chuckles and opens a cabinet to pull out some ground coffee and a French press. "Go for it. I'm going to take a quick shower and get dressed."

"No problem. I'll just bond with Pumpkin." The dog in question lies on her back in her bed, snoring heavily.

"Have fun with that." Paige places her mug in the sink and leaves me alone in the kitchen.

With or without people, the room is small but somehow not cramped. The same way I'd describe this entire house. A perfect size for two people. And a pit bull, of course. I helped Paige pick the place out a couple of years ago. She was happy to be buying a home of her own.

And now I'm envious. Not of Dash. I'm not pining for my best friend.

The two of them are perfect for each other.

What I'm really after is my own version of the happiness she's found.

These thoughts trickle slowly through my head as I heat water in the teapot and scoop the ground coffee into the press. At the sound of footsteps approaching, I call out, "You sure you don't want another cup? I can make a bigger batch."

"Yeah, I'll take some," says a slightly husky voice. A voice that does not belong to my friend but is familiar all the same.

Trying to not appear too eager, I rotate on my heel and meet a set of decadent brown eyes that have me pondering a piece of dark chocolate melting on my tongue.

"Luna." *Shit, what's wrong with my voice? What sound was that? A dying rodent?*

The corner of her mouth teases up. "Hey, Charlie. How's it going?"

"Good. Great. Really, really...awesome."

Luna's smile widens at my ramblings, which is just unfair. She looks amazing this morning. Not that she's all dressed up like at the party. In fact, she has an outfit from the opposite end of the spectrum on. Athletic shorts that show off a set of muscular legs, paired with a loose T-shirt that has a Red Cross blood drive logo half worn away on the front. Her short hair is a finger-combed tangle around her face. Just as my eyes catch on the inky strands, she gathers them up, pulling a hairband from her wrist and fashioning a messy bun on the top of her head. The movement has her breasts pressing against the fabric of her shirt, which is how I'm almost certain she's not wearing a bra.

The whistle of the teapot cuts off my gawping.

I turn my back on the wonderfully sleep-mussed sight of Dash's sister and focus on the simple task of coffee.

"You said you'd like a cup?"

"Yeah. If there's enough to spare."

"Plenty." Silence descends as I carefully pour the boiling water into the press, then place the top on. Problem is, now there is a wait time for the coffee to brew.

"Are you and Paige hanging out today?" she asks.

With a deep breath to steady myself, I turn around to meet Luna's eyes. Only she's not looking my way, her head in the fridge instead.

"Yeah. Yes. We're going to get brunch and catch up." Without thought, I start cracking my knuckles. A nervous habit I thought I got over years ago. Forcibly, I relax my hands and try to keep the hopeful note out of my voice. "You're welcome to join."

Luna turns toward me, carrying a yogurt container and a banana. "Thanks, but I can't. Have some business in town to take care of."

"Right. Yeah. Of course."

"How long are you States-side? You live in Germany, right?"

"Uh, yeah. For now."

"For now? You moving soon?"

I wish. But then I'd need some destination in mind.

"No immediate plans. Just pondering things. But I'll head back to Germany a few days after the wedding."

"What's your job?" Luna settles at the table and opens her yogurt. But all the while her attention rests on me.

"Salesman. Fabric sales. The company sells fabric." How many more ways can I babble out the same information? Good thing I'm not such a mess when talking to customers. Then I would definitely be moving soon because I'd be out of a job.

"You're into fashion?"

"We focus on durable materials for outerwear. Not normally what shows up on the runway. And I'm just good at selling things."

"Do you *like* selling things?" Her piercing stare digs into me, and I find myself spilling out truths I haven't even admitted to myself.

"I'd like it more if I was selling something I cared about."

She nods. "Hence, the pondering."

The timer goes off, giving my hands something to do. I slowly push down on the press, watching the fragrant brown liquid swirl on the other side of the glass. One mug already sits out on the counter, and I fill the thing up, intending to give the cup to Luna and grab another for myself.

Her willingness to help is where everything goes wrong. The moment I turn to find another mug, she's there offering one, having transported from the table to right behind me. At the sight of her so near, my body jerks as I battle the urge to get closer, stay where I am, or jump away. The miscommunication sends my top half teetering and arms flailing.

Flailing is not recommended when holding a French press.

"Shit!"

Hot coffee hits my chest.

LUNA

Charlie stares at me, mouth agape, eyes wide and pleading, as if he's begging me to tell him he didn't just commit a wild blunder.

Again.

But I can't. The man dumped a good portion of coffee on his blue button-down. The best I can do for him is stifle my laughter and try to get the fabric off his body to keep the heat from burning his skin.

"Here we go. It's okay." My fingers tug at his buttons, parting the fabric. I'd push the shirt entirely off if he wasn't still clutching the French press. "Put that down."

Charlie blinks once. Twice. Then moves robotically to place the coffeemaker on the counter. His hands now free, I guide the shirt off his shoulders and toss the ruined clothing to hang over the side of the sink and grab some paper towels, wetting them down with cool water.

The next part is where things get odd. I should've handed Charlie the damp towels so he could wipe himself off.

But no. Instead, my hands gravitate toward his chest, and the next thing I know, I'm running the paper towels over his pecs and down his flat stomach. As if making sure his body is squeaky clean is my responsibility.

There's a grunt, and I glance up in time to watch his teeth dig into his plump lower lip.

Damn, that mouth is pillowy. Wonder what he can do with it.

The second the dirty, teasing thoughts pass through my mind, they're followed up by a logical one.

Bad idea.

Charlie is a good man and my soon to be sister-in-law's best friend. Not anything like the bang-and-leave guys I normally hook up with. The ones perfect for a single night, parting ways in the morning, no questions asked, no awkward conversations. And by morning, I mean a few minutes after we're done fucking.

I don't do sleepovers.

Charlie, with his kind smiles and goofy mishaps, has the words *Life-Long Sleepover* tattooed across his forehead. Because he's the best kind of guy.

Time to stop touching the sexy man.

"Guess you should be the one doing this. Sorry. I got so used to bossing my brothers around that I can't help myself with other people." I hold out the paper towels for him to take, and after hesitating, Charlie accepts them.

While he no doubt tries to come to terms with my odd behavior, I quickly pour myself a cup of coffee and put the distance of the small kitchen between us as I settle at the table and peel my banana.

Charlie moves in a dazed manner as he finishes wiping himself off. Then his eyes go to his shirt. He picks the thing up, stares at the giant brown stain, then drapes the shirt over the back of a chair. Like he plans on letting it dry.

Gah, I can't let it happen. Not when he looked so good in it. Allowing the shirt to be ruined would be like acting as an accomplice to a crime.

"No, wait. Come here." I'm up from my chair and ushering him over to the sink. "You need to run cold water through the back of the fabric, and hopefully that'll get it all out. But if not, you need to rub the spot with dish soap or laundry detergent and cold water. Just don't let it dry."

After basically raising Dash on my own, I learned the tricks to remove every kind of stain from clothes. Our clothes needed to last. We didn't have the money to just go out and buy a new wardrobe whenever we wanted.

Not for us kids anyway.

Charlie follows my instructions while I hover at the sink, biting off chunks of my banana and keeping my eyes on the fabric in his long-fingered hands rather than allowing my eyes to wander up to his exposed chest.

"I'm sorry," he mutters.

"For what? I'm the one who got in your way and potentially cost you a shirt. Then I stripped you down."

Charlie chuckles. "Can't seem to keep my clothes on around you."

I smirk, remembering the way he divested himself of a few layers after climbing back on the yacht. And then, in his black, tight-in-all-the-right-ways boxer briefs, Charlie dove back into the water beside our impromptu swimming group.

"You're lucky you look good wet."

Charlie grins at me, and the odd tension between us breaks. There's a subtle sound of footsteps on hardwood just before Paige enters the kitchen. She stops, staring between the two of us. Then her brows drop.

"I think I'm missing some key pieces of information in this situation."

Instead of answering, I bite off the last chunk of my banana and wink at her.

Paige tilts her head, much like her dog does when confused, just before a hopeful little smile curves her mouth. "Charlie is single, you know?" she offers, unprompted. "And multiple women have said he's very good in bed."

The banana was a mistake. Paige's words have me sucking in a surprised breath, which means I breathe in more banana than air. I choke on the thing, trying to cough the yellow mush out of my throat.

I'm successful, only my aim is lacking because I spit the half-chewed fruit straight onto Charlie's shirt where it rests in the sink.

The two of us stare at the new mess as I pant. "Shit," I gasp out, losing my standing as the smooth one in this kitchen.

Charlie abandons his shirt and places a hand on my back. "You okay?"

I nod, then glare at Paige. "Don't say stuff like that when I have a full mouth."

"What? It was a simple fact."

If my brother didn't love her so much, I might strangle Paige. "And blue whales are the animals who have the largest penises! That's a fact! But you don't see me trotting it out during dinner with your parents, do you?"

"Well, they're not very interested in animal genitalia. I don't see why that fact would be relevant to the situation."

A snort at my side has me redirecting my scowl. Charlie bites into his goddamned lower lip again. Still, he's not able to hold back the laughter for long. One second the man stands tall above me, then next he's sliding down to the kitchen floor, holding his stomach as he roars in laughter. Pumpkin trots over to him, tail wagging as she licks the side of his face.

I want to be mad. I want to be furious.

But the sight before me is so joyful that I fight my own smile.

"Please do!" Charlie eventually forces out. "Please tell Mr. H about whale penises. And please do it when I'm there. I will give you all my money."

I glance at the woman who's soon to be a member of my family. Paige shrugs, an affectionate smile gracing her pretty face as she watches Charlie dissolve on her kitchen floor.

"I will do no such thing," I mutter with absolutely no heat.

"Do you need a shirt?" Paige asks. "You're the same size as Dash."

Charlie nods, wiping tears from the corners of his eyes. Then he grins up at me, and my stomach twists in a strange way that combines pleasure and discomfort.

"Sure you don't want to get breakfast with us? Since you just spit out all of yours?"

Funny thing is, I do. The idea of spending more time with Charlie Keller is tempting.

But that's a sensation I shouldn't explore.

"Can't. Busy." I move to escape the kitchen and the heat of his attention. But I lose the battle against the urge to glance his way one more time.

Mistake. Watching the smile fade from Charlie's face as his eyes focus on the floor, I wonder if this is what it's like to walk away from an adorable puppy at the animal shelter my brother used to work at.

He's not a puppy. He's a man. And you don't need one of those.

I never have and never will.

Chapter Six

LUNA

Parking on the familiar street has my muscles tensing. Ready for a fight.

But I don't let anything as unacceptable as fear register in my mind. Surviving here means wearing a tough exterior at all times. No hesitating. I climb from my car and head up the cracked sidewalk, my confident stride fueled by my need to have this encounter over as quickly as possible.

The door seems smaller than it used to be, as if the wood is a dying thing that slowly decays as the years pass by. The color is different too. A surface that used to be brown is now a faded blue. I've been gone long enough that things had time to be new and grow old. There's no sound when I press the doorbell. I rap out a pounding knock with the side of my hand.

Still nothing, but that doesn't mean no one is home.

"Hey!" I yell as I knock louder. "It's Luna! Open the damn door!"

This time when I drop my hand, I hear movement on the other side. Not sure what kind of greeting I'll get, I take a few steps back and make sure my piece is easy to reach in my waist holster. I've never had to use the thing other than in a shooting range, and I hope today isn't the day that track record changes.

The door whips open, and the woman framed in the entrance stares down at me, distrust on her face.

In that moment I can't help comparing her to Wai Po, recognizing the similarities in their faces. Confusion wrinkles the same sharp brows my grandmother and I share with Vivian Lamont. As if she doesn't recognize me.

Do I look that different?

My mother always insisted I keep my hair long because men want a girl who looks like a lady, not like a boy. The first thing I did when I went to college was shave every inch off. My first year, I rocked a freeing buzz cut. But maybe I kept some of my vanity because I tired of the minimalist style and let everything grow back as far as a short bob that now frames my face. A face that looks more like hers than like my white dad's. He's all blond-haired, blue-eyed, Anglo to a T. Dash, Leo, and I take after our mom with our dark hair, hooded brown eyes, and skin sporting a golden undertone. For the longest time all I ever had of my Asian heritage was my looks. Mom was stingy with details about her past. I didn't learn I was Taiwanese until I found Tsai Shu-fen.

"Luna?"

My first instinct is to snap back at her. *No, it's the tooth fairy, duh. Definitely not your estranged daughter.*

But I smother the rebellious urge, holding on to civility as best I can. "Yes. It's me." I sound like a robot wearing her daughter's skin suit, but I can't seem to infuse any kind of affection into my voice.

"Why're you here?" She leans a shoulder on the doorframe and braces her hand on the other side, barring entry with her entire body. As if I'm begging to enter the sanctum of her home.

Missed you too, Mom.

"I have something to tell you. It's not really front porch talk."

For a second her coolly dismissive exterior cracks, eyes wide in panic. "Is it Dash? Is he okay?"

Would she have that reaction if my baby brother came here and told her something was going on with me? Maybe Vivian Lamont cares about me, somewhere way down deep. But I don't know that there's anything on this earth that could bring motherly affection for me to the surface. It never rose before.

"Dash is fine."

Tension drains from her in response. "Don't scare me like that."

Not like I was trying. If I wanted to hurt her, though, I could. I could tell her what's going on with Dash. Tell her he's getting ready for his wedding and didn't bother sending her a notification about it. I could tell her the way Paige's mom loves Dash like a son, the two of them working on cars together. Legally.

I could inform my mom she's not the most important woman in her little prince's life and never will be again.

But starting a fight is not why I'm here today. Petty revenge will have to wait for another time.

"Can I come in?"

She looks me up and down, as if I'm covered in bed bugs and just asked to take a roll in her sheets. But she steps back, walking into the house, leaving the door open as a silent indication I should follow.

Instead of storming back to my car and driving away like I want, I bite down hard on my anger and step into my childhood house.

No way will I ever call this thing a home.

The layout is as familiar as a worn pair of kicks, but the shiny new electronics are like neon laces added to old dirty sneakers. Only distracting for a moment.

I stride through the living room, straight back into the kitchen. Vivian leans against the counter, sipping some fruity cocktail as she watches a reality show on the TV mounted over the sink.

If we had a normal mother-daughter relationship, I might ask if she's tried K-dramas. My roommate in college turned me onto them, and now I'm just slightly addicted. For a time, I wondered if maybe I was Korean. But when I finally found Wai Po, I learned about my Taiwanese heritage. Not that the discovery dampened my adoration for South Korean dramas.

When Vivian sets her glass down, she doesn't acknowledge me, just reaches for a bottle of nail polish and shakes it hard.

I wonder if she's imagining my face when she does that.

My mom blames me for the fact that we don't have a relationship. I blame her ability to gloss over parts of reality she'd rather not acknowledge. Parts I'd started pointing out to her when I got tired of playing her dress-up baby doll.

"So," I begin, "about a year ago—"

The sound of the front door opening cuts me off.

"Mom?" The voice is deep and familiar.

"In the kitchen!" she shouts back, and her beautiful face splits into a wide smile when my brother strolls in.

"Leo." I say my twin's name in greeting with as little emotion as I can manage.

"Luna?" He stops mid-step, every bit of his shock showing on his face. The man is a terrible poker player.

"Wow. You still remember my name. I'm flattered."

He regains the ability to move and rolls his eyes, then throws a quick glance behind him before moving further into the kitchen.

"There's leftover pizza in the fridge if you're hungry, baby." My mother scoops her drink up and gestures with the glass before taking a sip.

Of course, she didn't bother asking me if I wanted pizza.

"Thanks, Mom." Leo dodges around me, heading straight for the food. Not acknowledging in any way that it's been close to two years since we last saw each other. It takes everything I have not to pick at him as he settles his ass at the kitchen table without another look my way.

Now that I'm back here, I can't help noticing the strange difference between this house and the Herberts'. Take away the actual appearance of the places, and you get down to what makes a home. The people. In Paige's home, which I have an open invitation to visit whenever the whim takes me, you'll find everyone joyfully, if frantically, in the midst of wedding preparations. It's been that way for months, with Mrs. Herbert working to ensure the day is perfect for her daughter and soon-to-be son-in-law. And despite the stress that comes with all the planning, love fills every joke and bantering comment exchanged in those four walls.

Here, though, there's no sense of urgency. Neither of these people know about the massive life event taking place in less than a week. That the baby of the family has excluded them from his celebration.

Mom sets down her drink and strolls over to my brother, where he sits devouring the leftover pizza without heating it up. She claps her hands on Leo's shoulders and gazes at him with so much fondness I can guess at least half is a show for me.

That's my mother. Displaying affection to one child in an attempt to hurt another.

"Look at you! Still a growing boy even at your age."

I fight off the urge to mime gagging.

"Worked up an appetite on the job, huh? Uncle Mike better appreciate all the hard work you do."

Leo grunts, and I shove my clenched fists into my pockets. Yeah, I'm sure Uncle Mike has him real busy.

Before a comment can snap off my lips, the front door shoves open, and my nerves tighten to pure steel. I need the reinforcement to deal with the new arrival.

"Fuck, I'm hungry." A deep voice announces a second before the owner steps into the kitchen.

My father, ladies and gentlemen.

His blue eyes land on me, then widen, and when he paints on what other people have labeled as a charming smile, I just feel sick.

"Hey there, baby girl. Finally come home to your momma and daddy?" He hooks his thumbs in the loops of his jeans and stares down at me. Bill Lamont loves to stare down at people from his six-foot height. Loves pretending he's some kind of big man.

Not for the first time, I'm glad I look nothing like him. That I didn't inherit his pale skin, primary-color eyes, or yellow hair. That no one is ever going to point to me on the street and say, "There goes Bill Lamont's daughter."

I hate this man and the callous way he treated both me and my brothers when we were children.

But I hate him for what he's done to Leo most of all.

"I'm not home," I growl. Home is my house in Nashville. The place I bought with my own savings and filled with my own happiness.

He keeps his patronizing smile on. "Then why are you here? Need money? That fancy fighting you do not pay anymore? Maybe we could set up a bout down here for you. Put you in the ring with someone who knows how to hit."

There's so much wrong with his statement I don't know where to start.

"I came here to talk to Mom."

I don't add the rest even though the words already sit on my tongue.

I'd sell every one of my worldly possessions and still not ask you all for money. My job is about preventing fights, not starting them. Hitting your kids doesn't mean you know how to hit.

"She doesn't have the checks." Bill meanders to the fridge, pulling out a beer. "I do. And if you want cash, you'll have to work for it. Just like Leo." He claps his hand on my brother's shoulder.

Leo keeps chewing on his pizza like he can't hear any of what's going on around him.

"I'm not here for money." I barely keep my voice steady. There's one task I need to complete, and then I can get the hell out of here. "I'm here to talk to Mom. Let's go outside." I nod to the back door, hoping Vivian will pick up on my urgency. But my dad wraps a possessive arm around my mother's waist, keeping her in place.

"We don't keep secrets from each other." He sends a mocking smile my way before tugging from his beer. "But when you never visit, you forget things like that."

I barely suppress a snort. Why would I visit people who told me I was dead to them?

"Leo's here almost every day." Bill gestures toward my brother with his beer bottle. "Comes by after work just to say hi to his momma. And he's getting more responsibility at the shop. Doesn't need to beg anyone for a paycheck."

My brother keeps his stoic routine going as my mother lets out a happy sigh. "I'm so proud, Leo. Knowing you're part of the family business."

Shut up. Shut up. Shut up.

Am I chanting at her or myself?

Both. Definitely both.

"Leo is such a loyal boy, you know?" My mom beams between her son and her husband, as if they're the only three people in the room. I'm only here to be the audience for the show. "Hardworking and loves his mother so much. It's nice to have a child who does. Who cares."

The hypocrisy is too much, and that's the only thing I can blame my complete lack of tact on. Certainly not my constant need for petty revenge.

"Tsai Shu-fen died."

All three faces turn toward me, finally fully acknowledging my presence.

Leo has his brows dipped in confusion.

My mom looks like I threw a glass of water in her face.

My dad's cheeks and neck flush red. "What did you say?"

"I found out about Tsai Shu-fen. My grandmother. I met her. She passed away three weeks ago because of cancer." Focusing fully on my mother, I let all my disappointment and anger show in my face. Drip from my voice. "I thought, as her child, you might care."

As my parents both grapple with this info, I march up to my brother, determined to get more out of this visit than just the hollow victory of shocking Bill and Vivian Lamont.

"Hug me or I'll put you in a headlock." I stand next to Leo, arms spread wide, glaring to keep them from seeing how vulnerable I am in this moment. How much I need this single sign of affection from my brother.

One glimmer of hope that this man is still someone I know.

Leo snorts, but then rises from his chair and envelops me in a tight embrace. The hug feels like hope, and with us standing close, I'm able to whisper one more thing to him without our parents hearing. When I step back, my twin has wiped all emotion from his face, giving me no sign of whether he'll follow my whispered directions.

I can only hope.

CHARLIE

"You left this to the last minute, huh?"

My mother glares at me over a display of blenders. "Hush now. You going to help me or shame me?"

"Both?" I offer her the cheeky smile that always melts her glare away.

"You're lucky you're my only child or I'd ship you straight back to Germany. Lord knows there was less sass in my life before you came around." As she grumbles out the words, her lips start to curl at the edges.

I whistle an innocent tune as I tuck my hands deep in my pockets and stroll down the next aisle. Passing by cookware, I let the happy glow of the day infuse my entire being. In the past, shopping with my mother would have ended up low on the list of fun activities. But now, after being away for so long, I'm enjoying myself.

Doesn't hurt that I just finished eating delicious brunch with my best friend, and before that spent more time in Luna Lamont's presence. I conveniently gloss over the part where I once again made a complete fool of myself.

Overall, this is shaping up to be a great day. Which puts into stark contrast how few of those I've had lately.

I wince at a stab of shame.

How could I think that? I have a great life.

I work for a company with a good atmosphere and reasonable hours. They've set me up with a position in a foreign country, just like I told them I wanted when I was first hired four years ago. Over those years I've built up a group of friends in Germany, getting drinks with them at least once a week and traveling all through Europe.

Some might say my life is charmed. For a while I thought so too.

The dissatisfaction came on slowly, with small dips in my mood that lasted for a few days. I'd press the snooze button a few more times and find myself gazing at the clock, trying to will the workday to pass by faster. Then there were the spikes of anxiety that gripped my chest whenever my supervisor gave me a new project. My mind shied away from spending any more brain capacity on fabric sales.

All of those signs I forced myself to ignore, accepting them as normal among all adults in the workforce.

But then one night when I was chatting with Paige about her latest editing project, I blurted out the question.

"Does your work ever depress you?"

On my phone screen, Paige blinked wide eyes. "Depress me? I mean, some of the authors write about hard topics. They craft the scenes so excellently that I feel what the character does. Their sadness. Is that what you mean?"

"No." I'd searched for a way to explain the creeping shadow descending over the hours I spent at the office. "I mean, does the idea of doing your job ever…I don't know. Do you wish you could get away from it? Just keep sleeping through the day or something."

My friend stared at me, and I let her. The moment was important. The first time I'd shared the ache no painkillers could correct.

"Martin." Paige announced her cheating ex's name like it was the solution to a brain teaser I'd given her. I flinched at the sound, my dislike for the asshole rooted deep in my bones.

"I'm not talking to that motherfucker about my work problems if that's what you're saying," I growled.

But she was already shaking her head. "Sorry. Meant to say more words. What you described, work never made me feel that way. Martin did. Our relationship. I should've gotten out of it long before he cheated on me. You should break up with your company. Not that I think they're going to cheat on you. How would a company even do that?"

And just like that, my friend had me laughing, my anxiety forgotten for a time.

But never gone. Especially with her advice lingering long after we hung up.

You should break up with your company.

Easier said than done. I can't just serve up the "It's not you, it's me" line. My employers are good people. How can I leave a career with great benefits when I don't know what I want to do in my life? I've spent many evenings trying to figure out what my passion is, but nothing falls perfectly into place.

"None of these are right," my mom says, unknowingly echoing my inner monologue. She's stopped in front of a variety of sheet sets.

Slipping my phone from my pocket, I pull up the web page we consulted before coming into the store. "These are on the registry." I tap a slate-gray set and try to imagine my friend gravitating toward the neutral color.

"You and I both know Ginny cobbled that together when her

daughter forgot. Neither Paige nor Dash are the ask-for-gifts type." Mom passes on the boring sheets.

"Well then, what do you want to do?"

"I want to get her something with *love* in it."

The emphasis she puts on that four-letter word has me backing away, hands raised. "Sorry, Momma. I draw the line at going to an adult toy shop with you."

"You devil!" She barks through a laugh, then chucks a pillow at me. "I can't take you anywhere."

"I'm not the one throwing things in the store." With a mocking amount of carefulness, I place the pillow back on its shelf.

"You're a bad influence." She meanders away, smoothing her hands over the purple silk scarf wrapped around her head, as if the brief moment of immaturity might have knocked the fabric loose.

That's Regina Keller. One moment the image of elegance, the next as mischievous as a teenager.

I've missed her.

With the ease of travel, flights coming and going all the time, New Orleans shouldn't feel far away. But I can't help feeling panic that I'm missing precious time with my parents. During my childhood they traveled all over the world, and I always went with them. Now I'm lucky if we see each other twice a year.

Sometimes, when the homesickness of missing my parents hits hard, I'll play through one of my mother's albums, letting her voice lull me into believing she's by my side. But I can only ever trick myself for so long.

Just like this visit will only last for a limited string of days. The thought sends a familiar spike of anxiety through me, and before examining the urge, I cross the few feet between me and my mother and scoop her up into a hug.

"Charlie?" Her tone is half-curious, half-worried, and all-loving. Her strong arms wrap around me, returning the hug. "What's wrong, baby?"

"Nothing." I set her down and make sure a reassuring smile is in place when she sees my face. "Just missed you is all."

"Okay then." Doubt sits heavy in her voice, and she cups my cheeks, the tips of her acrylics just brushing my skin as the familiar scent of cocoa butter surrounds me. The attention brings to mind the word she said earlier.

Love.

This is love. This is what my mother wants to gift to Paige. An embrace that shows all the support and affection and hope that the Kellers have for my friend.

"I thought of a gift." The triumph in my voice has her lips twisting.

"You gonna share your insight with me or do I have to guess?"

"Isn't it obvious?" No matter how much I missed her, the urge to wheedle her can never be eradicated.

"You sound like your father. *Isn't it obvious?*" She affects a deep voice, mocking her husband in a way she'd be just as happy to do to his face. Mom steps back, planting fists on her hips and giving me a scorcher of a scowl. "No, it's not obvious. Tell me already."

I pause just a second longer, for dramatic effect. "Give her a song."

"Charlie." My mother speaks my name with surprise that morphs into a sweet dismissive expression. "She hears me sing all the time."

"But not *for her*," I insist. "You know Paige would like that more than a random item bought from her registry."

Mom waves a hand as if my words buzz around her face. "They're starting a life together. They need more than a song."

Sometimes I want to grab my mother by the shoulders and shake her until she realizes how much her art can mean to a person. Sure, when Mom takes the stage, she knows how her talent can hold a room. At times, she's proudly proclaimed her diva status. But around the people close to her, Regina Keller sinks into a humble state. As if she thinks her voice is a showy illusion, and the people who love her see right through it.

She's wrong.

"Then give her a check along with the song. But I'm telling you, if you get on that stage and sing, Paige will feel every ounce of love you want her to."

My mother doesn't respond right away. She turns away, pretending to browse the bath towels. I follow behind, acting like the well-behaved son for the moment. After picking up a peach towel that Paige would be just as likely to use for her pit bull, Pumpkin, as she would for herself, my mother tosses the fabric to the side and strides toward the door.

"Fine. A song it is. But you're picking it out and playing the guitar with me. And your father is going to dance with her. There we are— family gift. Plus, a check. A really big check."

I hide my grin behind a hand, trying to smooth the cocky expression away before she sees.

"Paige will love that."

My mother huffs as if frustrated with me, but the sound only makes me want to hug her again.

One more week. The internal countdown clock to my departure sucks away all the happiness of the moment.

What if I want to stay?

Chapter Seven

LUNA

The bar smells like stale beer and fried food. Not my first choice, or even my tenth, but I thought Leo might back out if I chose to meet in a halfway decent spot.

He's petty like that sometimes.

The bartender frowns at me. Great customer service, right there.

"I'll have a ginger ale," I tell him, which only sets his frown in concrete. Then the door opens, flooding late afternoon light into the bar and stealing attention away from me. My twin brother strides in, all confidence in a room like this. A room he's used to.

How I wish we were used to different rooms.

He spots me at the bar and strolls over.

"Shot of tequila." Leo wraps his knuckles on the bar once when he orders, but the bartender doesn't seem to mind. Still, he scowls when he slides my soda to me, as if the lack of alcohol offends him.

"You're drinking a shot?" I ignore the surly man, focusing on the person I care about. "You celebrating something?"

Leo drapes himself over the stool next to me, doing his best to wear a condescending smile. "I'm a busy man. I've gotten used to drinking my poison quickly. No time for sipping."

Keeping my eyes locked on his, I purse my lips into the smallest pinch I can manage, then take the most minuscule sip of my drink.

The cockiness in his expression bleeds into true—suppressed —amusement.

"Aah." I smack my lips. "Refreshing."

"Drama queen," he mutters with a smile.

"Butt head," I say back with a smirk of my own, hiding the pang in my heart.

This is it. These minor exchanges are enough to keep me hoping.

Leo is a dick. I know that. He does immature shit and says mean things. But there's this constant nagging in the back of my mind that tells me something is off whenever he flings one of his barbs. A whisper of a voice begging me not to give up on him. And then I get a glimpse. Maybe it's a genuine laugh or a throwback to our childhood together, and I wonder if there's still some parts of my brother worth saving.

The bartender sets Leo's drink down, and I watch him throw it back like water.

"What's up, Loony? You need help or something?" He stares at me, calculating.

And just like most things with Leo, there are layers. Would he help me if I had a problem?

Probably. Maybe.

Would he judge me?

Probably. Maybe.

Would he charge me for help?

Probably. Maybe.

But I've never asked him for help. Because when we were kids, I never had to ask. He knew what Dash and I needed, and he did his best to get it. Then a switch flipped, and it was just me taking care of things.

Leo turned into someone I fought against to keep Dash safe. Which meant I brought none of my problems to my twin, and he stopped trying to solve them on his own.

"I don't need help." I sip more of my ginger ale and study my brother, looking for more hints. For more cracks.

Leo flexes his shoulders and kicks the heel of his boot against the barstool, agitation in all the lines of his body.

"Like I said. I'm a busy man. Want to get to the point?"

"Do you know why I'm in town?"

I watch him lose every hint of aggression in an almost eerie display of mood switching. He lounges back against the bar, not a care in the world.

"I heard you in the house. Death in the family, huh? Old granny bit the dust?"

My teeth ache as I clench my jaw, and I stare off to the side, blinking rapidly.

Damn Leo. Damn him and this bullshit front.

At least I know how to get through it, even if it means using words sharpened to hurt.

"You sound like our father."

Someone who didn't know my brother may have thought he wasn't affected.

But I see the tense muscle in his neck.

"You say that like it's a bad thing," he mutters.

Disgust. Pure and toxic, coursing through my veins at the idea that Leo wouldn't care if he grew into that man.

"Guess I shouldn't be surprised, with you working for Uncle Mike. Like father, like son. Should I watch what I say around you? Flinch if you move too fast? You going to show me how big a man you are with a fist to my face?" With each sentence my voice grows harder, and I stare deeper into eyes the same dark shade as mine.

"He doesn't do that anymore," Leo says, but his words lack conviction.

"Only because the coward knows he can't win." If Bill Lamont went for me like he used to, I'd break his arm. And maybe a few other bones, just to drive the point home.

I almost wish he would.

Leo closes his eyes, but I know he's listening to me.

"I'm in town for Dash's engagement party," I announce, loud and proud.

This time Leo can't hide his reaction. His whole body jerks, and his eyes flash open to glare at me.

"The fuck?"

"Yeah. I didn't think you knew."

And I wasn't supposed to tell him.

But the difference between my baby brother and me is that I haven't given up hope.

Maybe it's naive, but under Leo's asshole exterior I'm betting there's a sliver of a good man to be saved. And I'm willing to carve my nails into his soft underbelly if it means I can dig that decent bit out to the surface.

Leo's jaw clenches hard, and I watch as he silently commands his body to relax. But I have his undivided attention now.

"Our little prince is getting married. Or I guess I should say *my* little prince. Seeing as how I'm the only one he told. The only family member invited."

Leo's fingers clench around his glass, and I rejoice in the knowledge that I'm getting to him.

"Actually," I continue, "he asked me to be his best man. Or best woman, I guess. Whatever you call it. On the happiest day of his life, I'm going to be standing beside him." Leaning in, I drop my voice to a low, unforgiving note. "Where will you be?"

"What is this? You rubbing the shit in my face?" Leo waves for another shot and throws the alcohol back faster than the first.

"No." I straighten on my stool.

"Sure seems like it. You get off on bragging? Want to list how many of my exes you fucked next?"

That earns a bark of laughter out of me. My brother scowls my way, and I hit him with a smirk. "Sure you wanna know?"

"Fuck you," he mutters without real heat. All that's left is weariness. An exhaustion usually reserved for men twice Leo's age.

The guy is my twin, but sometimes he seems decades older. Other times I would swear he never made it past teenage nonsense. The back and forth must wear a guy out.

"I'm here because I'm confused," I admit. "And pissed off."

"You're mad at me now? Huh."

"Yeah, Leo. I'm mad." I pick my soda up and swallow half of it in one go, the carbonation burning my sinuses. I blame the sting in my eyes on that too. "Why are you still living like this? I don't get it. I can't believe you want to be a part of the life. That you want to be Bill 2.0."

"I don't," Leo growls, then presses his lips shut.

Finally. God, I could cheer just from that one small confession. That hint is all I need.

"Leave then." I strip my voice of every ounce of judgment and anger. All that's left is desperation. This choice is life and death. "I'll help. Whatever you need."

My brother shakes his head and waves for another tequila. "Leave it alone."

I tilt my head at an odd angle until I capture his eyes with mine.

"Never."

Leo snorts, then swallows the fresh drink. As if the alcohol took some of his openness away, he glares at me. "I don't need you. That's Dash. Go baby him." My twin laughs hard. "Or is that why you're here? He has a new woman to take care of him, and you're looking for someone else to baby?"

I ignore his words as I consider the problem.

Leo wants out, but he won't leave.

Why?

Is this him clinging to his comfort zone, or are his ties to our uncle's criminal organization keeping him in place?

"Are you staying because Bill is making you?"

"That fucker can't do anything to me anymore." Leo bites the words hard, showing more of his scorn for our father. "Not since we were sixteen."

I nod absentmindedly. That's around when Leo got big enough to hit back.

"Is it because Mom wants you to stay?"

"Stop digging."

That might be part of it. But I sense there's more.

Then the answer flares in my mind, so obvious, I should've guessed it first. "Uncle Mike won't give you an out."

Leo clenches his jaw and stares toward the exit. But he doesn't walk out. And I know deep down he wants my help. But he's never figured out how to ask for it.

Guess I have to shove it in his face.

Good thing I'm a pushy bitch.

"He let Dash go after he paid whatever price Mike quoted him," I point out. "I bet he'd do the same for you."

Leo mutters something, and I lean closer on my stool. "What was that?"

My brother sighs and rubs a hand over his face. "I've already asked."

"And he said no?"

"No."

"Then what did he say?"

"He gave me a number."

A number? That means hope, and the beacon flares scorching hot in my chest. "How much?"

This time Leo does get up from his chair, slipping cash out of his back pocket.

"I know you love me, Luna." His voice has lost every note of teasing and cockiness and exasperation. Now he just sounds tired. "But you don't love me that much. And if it's all the same, I'd rather not see your face when you realize it."

My brother heads to the door, shoulders bowed, hands shoved deep in his pockets, the false animation he'd imbued himself with run dry.

"Asshole," I mutter into my drink. He's naive if he thinks I'm letting this drop because he decided to throw himself a pity party.

Then I remember one more important task. "Leo!"

His heavy sigh could fill the entire bar. "Yeah?"

"What's Dad's number?"

That earns his full attention. Looking back over his shoulder, he shoots me a disbelieving eyebrow raise. "You want to talk to him?"

I scoff. "No."

"Then why do you want it?"

"Reasons."

He faces me, the embodiment of wariness. "What reasons?"

I meet his stare head-on, leaving every ounce of emotion out of my voice.

"Mine."

My brother watches me for a stretch of time before shaking his head. But as he resumes his departure, he calls out a string of numbers.

With his back turned, he misses my evil grin.

Chapter Eight

LUNA

"What the fuck do you think you're doing?" A young guy growls the greeting a second before the legs of his chair slam down on the concrete. I interrupted him playing that balancing game kids in school always did when they were bored and their chairs weren't attached to their desk.

Not the best position for a man keeping watch.

"I'm here to see Mike." Giving the guard any information is generous on my part when I could've easily brushed past him before he thought about standing. But I don't want to play a round of tag where this teenager might decide to win by pulling a weapon.

"He doesn't just see anyone. And you can't go in there." He shoves up from his seat, blocking the door in an unimpressive show of acting as a wall.

I sigh, shaking my head at this boy. Eager to be part of this criminal element but already messing everything up. He's clueless to the point where I'm tempted to correct his mistakes.

Don't relax on your watch.

Don't admit to a stranger that you know who they're talking about.

Worse, don't tell them the boss is in the building.

But I'd rather not start a habit of training people to be successful criminals. My real job revolves around teaching people to survive, and this kid seems to have a death wish.

"He'll see me." I feign a relaxed posture, leaning back against the wall with my arms crossed. He doesn't need to know that puts my hand in a perfect position to slip my gun from its holster. "Tell him Luna is here to talk."

The kid obviously doesn't like taking orders, his scowl deepening. "Listen, bitch. I'm not telling him anything. You better get the fuck out of here before I stop being nice."

I fight the urge to roll my eyes. Or to kick him in the nuts. I hate it when a boy calls a woman a bitch just because he's intimidated by her. It's like getting spit at. Not technically hurtful, but disrespectful as hell.

"Listen here, gumdrop. I'm not leaving until Mike tells me to. So you better let him know that Luna Lamont wants a word."

"Wait, what?" The guy blinks in confusion, and I wonder if the disorientation comes from my last name or the nickname I assigned him.

I've found that when I want to insult a man, I'm better off inventing a random insult than using the more common ones. If I were to call this boy pencil dick, he'd know right away that I'm insulting his junk, and he'd feel the need to retaliate. But gumdrop? He's too busy trying to figure out what that means to decide whether he's going to get mad about it.

Random candy items always seem to hit the right note.

Tootsie roll. Bubble gum. Junior mint.

Used them all.

But almost immediately, I'm bored with watching the ungreased gears slowly try to rotate in his brain. Time to hurry this up. The sooner I'm out of this building, the better.

"I am Luna Lamont. You may have met my brother Leo. Or, of course, my uncle. Mike."

The kid's face goes white. Yeah, now he gets it.

Just called royalty a bitch.

Not that I've ever been a part of this family business. Still, this guard is low in the scheme of things, I doubt he knows the politics.

"S-sorry. Yeah. I'll go tell him you're here." He scurries from the room.

As the clomp of his footsteps fade, I meander over to the chair he was sitting in, flipping it so the legs stick up in the air. As I wait for the criminal-in-training to retrieve my uncle, I pull out a pocketknife and methodically loosen the screws holding the seat together.

A stuttered *sorry* is not a good enough apology.

For all I know, Uncle Mike will tell the kid that I'm not part of the organization and to throw me out on my ass. Meaning, the boy will saunter back in here like the shit-for-brains he was just a moment ago.

Not that I want to be thought of as a member of the Lamont chop shop. I've hated the family business since I was old enough to understand what was going on with all the different cars my dad drove around in. Bill Lamont never cared what I thought, of course. I was his daughter, therefore I should automatically trust him and keep my mouth shut. I could never manage the first, but I did try with the second, if only for me and my brothers' safety.

Screws loose and my little revenge complete, I right the chair before returning to my lean against the opposite wall. Soon footsteps sound on the other side of the closed door. I brace myself for the shitty guard to burst back in the room spitting foul curses while dragging me out on my uncle's orders.

Not that I'd let him put his hands on me.

But when the door swings wide, a familiar figure looms in the entrance.

"Hey, Uncle Mike."

"Little Luna." The big white man gives me a grin that could charm weaker souls. I learned long ago how easy his good mood can vanish. "What brings you here?" Cold calculation sparks in his eyes as he tries to decipher the answer before I give it.

"Mind if we talk alone?" My gaze flits over to the guard and then back.

"Of course. Stay here, Troy." Mike waves the young man back to his post, then gestures for me to follow deeper into the building.

We walk down a long hall illuminated by fluorescent lights. Halfway down I hear a crash behind us and barely suppress my smile. Uncle Mike's brows lower, and he makes to move back the way we came, but Troy sticks his head through the door. The boy's face is creased in pain.

"Chair fell over. Nothing to worry about boss. Sorry for the noise."

Uncle Mike's jaw tenses, but he moves back in front of me, leading the way. One of the shut doors we pass no doubt opens to the garage where my uncle's crew dismantles stolen cars and readies the parts to be sold. I wonder if Leo is there now, working a job that slowly eats away at his soul and risks his freedom.

Mike finally opens a door at the end of the hall, revealing a staircase. We climb to the second floor, stepping into an open space with cubicles and offices. He points me into the first and settles behind the desk.

"Sit." He waves to the chair across from him.

I'd rather stand, but I can see this turning into some type of power battle that'll have to end with me in a chair because Uncle Mike has something I want and no real reason to give it up.

I sit.

"How are things?" he grunts. "You been by to see your folks?"

"You mean you don't know?" Legitimate curiosity colors my question. I thought my father reported everything back to his big brother. But maybe not.

Mike's brows dip, the only indication that he's in the dark. A place he does not like to be.

"I went by yesterday. My grandmother died, and I was the messenger."

"Ah. And you're here because you missed your family? Want to be close to us all again?" He smirks, knowing my answer. The cocky statement still comes out a second too late. I saw the burn in the man's eyes.

The anger that he was the last to know information about people under his rule, which includes my parents.

I'll have to remember that.

"I came here because I want to know something."

Uncle Mike tilts his head.

Trying not to let on how anxious I am to bring up this topic, I keep my voice steady as I ask, "Why'd you let Dash leave the business?"

My younger brother used to steal cars for our uncle, and he was good at it if I heard right. But no matter how good, he got caught. Him and Leo, at the same time, and the pair went to prison. Only when Dash got out, my younger brother started living by the law. Leo went straight back to our uncle.

Mike taps his knuckles on the metal surface of the industrial desk that takes up more than its fair share of the small space. He doesn't answer right away, seeming to ponder his response.

"We had a financial arrangement," he offers at last.

I knew about that.

"And his heart wasn't in it."

That's new. Not that Dash stopped wanting to steal, but that Mike cared.

"What does that mean?"

Mike glares hard at me. "Someone who doesn't want to be in this game is a risk to my business. I need loyalty, even if that loyalty is based off greed. Dash didn't care about money or driving anymore. He just wanted out. I told him as long as I got refunded all the cash he was worth to me, I'd let him go."

A small hope springs in my chest.

Could it be that easy?

"If you had someone else who wanted out, as long as you got your money's worth, they'd be able to walk away?"

Mike pinches at his bottom lip. "Possibly. But some people are worth more to my bottom line than your baby brother."

I lean forward, elbows on my knees, my eyes boring into his milky blue ones.

"How much is Leo worth?"

Chapter Nine

CHARLIE

Luna looks better in pants than I do.

My eyes track each of her steps as she glides up the aisle in her tuxedo pantsuit. Dash's sister puts every man in attendance to shame by the way she wears her suit and excels in it.

As the small string band warms up, Luna and I take our spots under the floral archway.

"You look handsome." The officiant pats down my lapel, and I treat her to a wide grin.

"As good as the CEO?"

Marianna Tweep smirks at me. "You've read my latest book."

I shrug but keep on smiling. Marianna is one of the authors represented by Paige's publishing company, but the two women became good friends outside of work. The author constantly graces the *New York Times* bestsellers list with memoirs about her eclectic life.

Who better to lead my best friend's wedding ceremony?

"Don't worry. I'm sure no one has figured out exactly which tech billionaire you had your liaison with."

Marianna smiles wickedly. "Especially because three separate ones have already claimed to be the man to the press." She leans in close to whisper, "All three are lying."

I chuckle, then glance up to find Luna watching the two of us. Her face is unreadable, and I find myself ravenous to know what she's thinking. I lean across the small space separating us.

"You ready to fulfill your position as Best Woman?"

Luna's lips twitch, and she sinks a hand into a deep pocket only to pull it out a second later holding a small velvet box that no doubt holds the wedding rings. But then she dips her fingers into the other pocket, extracting them and clutching a travel-sized pack of tissues.

"For you?" I ask.

She rolls her eyes. "For Dash. My bet is the second he sees her in that dress, he'll bust a leak."

I consider the stoic man and shake my head. "No way. He'll last at least 'til the vows."

"Is Paige wearing a veil?" Marianna asks. "If so, I will place my money on when he raises the lace up. That will shake the man."

"Five bucks?" Luna spikes a brow, and the three of us nod with conspiratorial smiles.

Just then, the groom appears at the door leading to the Herberts' backyard. Paige's parents earn enough money to afford a wedding at any one of New Orleans' swankiest venues, but my friend insisted she wanted to get married here, in her childhood home. She said that this yard is where she fell in love with Dash, and it's where she wanted to marry him.

I don't doubt her reasons, but I think another unspoken factor was her future husband's comfort. The less extravagant the better. I don't know the particulars of Dash's past, but I do know his family doesn't come from money, and the guy spent a few years behind bars. The fact that Dash is now marrying a judge's daughter is a certain kind of cosmic joke.

Another reason the backyard venue works better is the small size of the ceremony. Both sides kept the number of people they invited small, the entire party numbering thirty people at most. An intimate affair reflecting that the bride and groom prefer quality over quantity in their friends.

Plus, as far as I know, Luna was the only family member Dash invited. My curiosity continues to spike whenever the topic of Luna and the Lamont family arises. Don't they have another brother? And Paige mentioned once that Dash's parents live in the city.

Still, if they're not here it must be for a reason. A good Man of Honor knows how to keep his mouth shut and not stress the bride out by prying.

Dash hurries up the aisle, his face an emotionless mask and his shoulders tense.

Better not be getting cold feet.

"Everything cool?" Luna asks when her brother settles at her side.

He mutters something under his breath. From the way Luna and Marianna lean in, I know they didn't hear his response either and are just as interested as I am.

"What was that?" Luna prompts her brother.

His lips twist, then he raises his voice another notch. "Ginny said I jinxed it."

The Best Woman's brows dip. "Jinxed what?"

"My marriage."

Now the older Lamont sibling scowls. "What the hell? Why would she say something like that?"

The groom shifts on his feet, a guilty move if I've ever seen one. "I kept my eyes closed," he says, defensiveness coloring his tone as his face stains red.

Luna pokes her brother. "Explain what happened 'cause I'm about to go shake some sense into your soon-to-be mother-in-law."

"Don't do that." He reaches a hand up as if to comb his fingers through his hair, but Luna grabs his wrist before he messes up the already styled mass. "I hadn't seen Paige since last night. I just wanted to check how she was doing."

"And?"

"And...we ended up making out in her bathroom. Ginny found us and yelled at me to get out and said I jinxed everything." Dash huffs out an offended breath. "But I kept my eyes closed!"

A snort from my left has me glancing over to see Marianna covering her mouth as her eyes twinkle with laughter. I grin along with her. Paige found a good one if he can't go twenty-four hours without touching her.

A minuscule stab of envy pricks at me.

None of my relationships ever came close to the type of devotion Dash just displayed in his misstep. Sure, I've cared about all the women I've been with. Enjoyed our time together. In fact, I'm still friends with most of them. We exchange catch-up emails every few months or get drinks when we're in the same city.

But when we ended things, there was no passionate parting. Which is probably why the end came.

And isn't that just my whole life in a concise summary?

Passionless.

"You're impossible. Couldn't keep your hands to yourself for one day?" Luna has no pity for her brother, and the groom scowls back at her.

"It's an outdated tradition."

"Whatever. Mrs. Herbert will forget about it the second the ceremony starts. Stop pouting." Luna grabs her brother by the shoulders and maneuvers him into the proper position under the archway. "Now stand there and don't mess anything up."

"What would I mess up?"

Before the siblings can really get into it, there's a rising, purposeful note from the band indicating that everyone needs to shut the hell up. The gathering goes quiet as we all turn our attention to the house.

The doors open, and Mr. Herbert steps through first, tall and intimidating in his all-black suit. Most of the time that much dark, stiff clothing in New Orleans would be torture, but the day holds a comfortable coolness that we all appreciate. Pumpkin trots at his side, the brindle pit bull wearing a collar of flowers that matches the floral arrangements. Mr. Herbert unhooks the dog's leash, and I let out a short whistle my friend taught me. As Pumpkin bounds down the aisle toward me, petals someone must have sprinkled on her back flutter to the ground.

A four-legged flower girl. The small crowd coos and claps, and I pull a bacon treat and a short leash from my pocket. Most brides only want someone to hold their bouquet. Paige asked that I also hold her fur baby.

Ginny Herbert appears next, decked out in a floral gown. She pauses beside her husband, and a moment later their daughter joins them.

Paige hovers between the pair, beauty personified.

The impressive thing is her grace doesn't come from the flowing dress or expertly styled hair or professional makeup. Instead, every bit of her radiance glows from her smile.

Everyone in attendance knows this woman has no doubt in her mind. Paige gives an excited wave in Dash's direction as she glides down the aisle. I glance at the groom. Dash stands tall, biting his lip as a tear tracks down his cheek while he watches Paige float toward him.

Luna reaches a hand forward, circumspectly passing her brother a tissue, which he accepts without looking away from the vision of the woman he loves. As Luna retracts her hand, our eyes catch.

Five bucks, she mouths with a triumphant grin.

LUNA

After Paige reaches her spot beside Dash, I have trouble paying attention to the rest of the service. Not because I'm bored, but because their love is distracting. The way the woman stares at my brother, as if he's the sole root of all her joy, is both impossible to look away from and hard to watch.

Could I ever love somebody like that?

Even if that is a possibility, I don't have time to go searching for the perfect person to spend the rest of my life with.

I need a husband right now.

A quarter of a million dollars.

Mike's quote still has my mouth going dry and heart pounding hard. According to my uncle, Leo brings in such regular product that the business would take a hit if my brother were to walk out. But Mike would let my twin go for the price of $250,000.

I have money in my savings, but nowhere near that.

Unless I count my grandmother's inheritance.

Wai Po's money would more than cover that amount. But only if I get married before I'm thirty.

Well, married and a few other things. There were more stipulations the lawyer didn't bother to read after my dismissing that first crucial requirement.

Leo's face flashes in my mind. His hopeless expression when I told him about Dash's wedding.

Our little brother is speaking heartfelt vows to the woman he loves, and Leo is missing it because he can't get out from under Mike's thumb. Can't imagine a future where he's not living a criminal life.

But I could secure his freedom.

"Do you have the rings?" Marianna's question returns me to the present, and I reach into my pocket for the wedding bands Dash entrusted me with. The designs are simple, just a silver circle like Paige requested. But my brother asked the jeweler to add something extra. On the inside of the band sits a minuscule paw print.

After I pass him the rings, Dash holds them up to show his almost-wife. She lets out a delighted gasp, then eagerly shoves her hand forward.

Is there anyone in the world I would trust enough to let them put a ring on my finger?

After Mike spoke that astronomical number and I accepted that my grandmother's money was the only way to pay for Leo's freedom, I started cycling through all the people I've ever known, vetting them as potential temporary spouses. As long as one of the stipulations isn't that the two of us never get divorced, I don't see why I can't just get married for a brief time. Long enough to collect the inheritance legally.

Immediately, I ruled out everyone I met before the age of eighteen. Almost every single one I met through my parents, which meant they were more likely to steal the money for themselves than let a cent go for my brother.

There must be some level of trust in a fake marriage.

No one from my college days stands out in my mind. None that are still single anyway. Momentarily, I considered approaching one of my clients. Most of the people I work with have A or B-list stardom, mainly from the country music scene. They tend to make seven figures or more, so what would my inheritance matter to them?

The problem with that route is trying to convince a celebrity that the marriage is about me getting access to my money rather than theirs. I'd have to work hard to prove to them I'm not a gold digger or a fame hound.

I don't have much time.

"I now pronounce you Paige Lamont Herbert and Dash Herbert Lamont." Marianna's musical voice fills the backyard, ringing with joy. "You may kiss each other."

The gathering erupts with cheers, and I push away thoughts of my problems long enough to celebrate with everyone else. This day is about the happy couple. I need to focus on my role as Best Woman. Take note from my counterpart Charlie, who's rocking his role as Paige's Man of Honor.

He pumps his arm in the air as Dash dips Paige low. Petals rain down from the bouquet Charlie holds for his friend, and I appreciate how committed the man is. Never once has he shied away from responsibilities normally handed off to a female friend. Apparently, after their brunch, the two went to the nail salon together. I'm betting the guy would do anything for his friend.

Absolutely anything.

The thought snags on a sharp corner of my mind, and I stare at the Man of Honor as the bride and groom straighten, waving to their cheering audience.

Charlie is a good guy.

Anyone who spends any time around him would see it. He doesn't care about conforming to societal expectations of a man. He knows how to laugh at himself, instead of blowing up when a woman spills coffee and then chewed banana on his nice shirt. He literally fell off the side of a boat and refused to let that ruin Paige and Dash's pre-wedding party.

Plus, Pumpkin likes him.

All of these small things are ringing endorsements that I consider as I accept Charlie's offered elbow and the two of us walk side by side down the aisle behind my brother and my new sister-in-law.

"They're perfect for each other." Charlie grins down at me.

"Yeah. They are."

Dash and Paige are the image of what every married couple hopes to be. Wildly happy as they head toward the next chapter in their life.

That's not something I ever expected for myself.

I still don't. I need a practical marriage, not a picturesque one.

As my hand sinks into the stiff material of Charlie's suit sleeve, I imagine what it would be like for he and I to officially walk down the aisle together.

Could he be the solution to all my problems?

Chapter Ten

CHARLIE

Luna is staring. At me.

She's been staring since the vows.

Admittedly, I only notice her attention because I've been sneaking my own glances. But I can't help myself. Not when that suit fits her just right.

Why is she looking at me?

Do I have something on my face?

After they cut the cake, I duck into the bathroom to check.

Nothing stands out. I run my hand over my close crop and rub a palm against my jaw. Everything is in place, my face still clean-shaven from this morning.

Nothing spilled on my suit. Nothing untied or untucked.

All there is to stare at is me.

And that unnerves me all the more.

Maybe it's the bet. I haven't paid her yet, but I didn't think she was so hard up for cash that she needed my five dollars immediately.

Heading outside, I aim toward the table where Dash's friends Cole and Summer sit. Since Cole worked at the same animal rescue as Dash, the guy is on dog duty for the rest of the night. Pumpkin sits obediently next to him, and the two create an intimidating picture. A beefy pit bull beside a guy with more of his white skin covered in ink than not. But I know Pumpkin is soft as melted butter, and Cole is just quiet. Summer, his colorful, friendly girlfriend, also naturally softens Cole's edges with her eager smile.

"Hi, Charlie! You did great." Summer raises her wine glass to toast me, and I offer a bow.

"I try. Can't believe you're keeping Pumpkin so calm. I thought she'd be bored and causing mayhem by now." I scratch the pittie's blocky head, and she gives me a doggy grin, her tongue lolling out of the side of her wide mouth.

"That's all bribery. Cole's pockets are full of treats." Summer reaches into her man's pants, coming out a second later with a dog biscuit, and I pretend I don't see how Cole stares at his girlfriend with hot eyes.

Must be nice to have an adorable woman inadvertently brush your junk ever so often.

"Hey, Summer. Cole." Luna appears directly in front of me, nodding to the couple before training her focus on me. "Let's dance." She scoops up my hand and pulls me to a dance floor constructed in the middle of the yard just as a slow song starts.

Not that I needed any kind of forcing. I'm happy to be pulled along behind her.

Don't screw this up, I tell myself. *No more klutzy shit. You are smooth as syrup.*

Unfortunately, when I move to wrap my arms around Luna's waist, I somehow end up punching her in the boob instead.

"Ow." She cups the poor abused boob, and I wonder if I'm about to spontaneously catch on fire. Because I have to be in hell right now.

"Shit, Luna. I'm so fucking sorry. Are you okay? What am I saying? Of course, you're not okay. Do you need an ice pack? I bet I can get something from the caterers."

Luna grabs onto my arm, keeping me in place. "I'm good. Best if I refrain from icing my tit in the middle of my brother's wedding."

My face blazes hot with mortification, and I wonder if she feels the heat. "I swear I'm not trying to be this much of a mess around you. Did I hurt you?"

"No." Luna lets go of my arm. "More like surprised me. I don't often use my boobs as punching bags."

"Of course not." My focus drops to her chest, then I realize I'm leering at her like a creep. "Well, I'm going to go find a hole big enough to bury myself in."

"Wait." Luna grabs onto me again when I move to leave. A smirk touches the edge of her mouth as her sharp eyes spear me. "You're not getting out of dancing with me that easy."

"Sure you want to? At this rate, I'll find a way to step on both of your feet. You'll leave this wedding on a stretcher."

"I'll risk it. You just need to loosen up." Luna clasps my hands and guides me in rhythmic swaying. My shoulders slowly relax under her instruction.

Gazing down into Luna's dark brown eyes, I loosen up more as her presence drives away the tension in my body. Finally, I register the music, the different instruments working in a familiar conversation I've known my whole life. Music soothes the soul, and it calms me.

"That's it." Luna slides her hold up my arms until her hands rest on my shoulders. This time, I'm able to set my palms on her hips without any incidents. "See? You're a natural."

"Well, music is in my blood."

"Oh, really?"

"Yeah. I guess with all the excitement on the boat, you didn't get to meet them." Applying a small amount of pressure to her strong body, I turn us until my parents come into view. "Mom and Dad. She's a jazz singer. I grew up with more than just lullabies."

My parents notice my attention and raise their wine glasses my way. I nod back, wondering how goofy my grin looks now that Luna is in my arms.

"They look nice," she offers.

"They're the best." Her warmth soaks into my palms where I hold her. "I'll introduce you later."

Then, showing the first hint of intelligence this evening, I stop the question I'd almost spoken aloud.

The one asking about her parents. That would have been a bad move. Luna's parents are Dash's parents.

The people who live in this city but were not invited to the wedding.

Whatever the story is, I'm betting the mood won't be improved by bringing them up.

"Do your parents live here? In New Orleans?" Luna asks before I come up with a different route to take the conversation.

"Yeah. They still travel for Mom's gigs, but not as much as they used to."

"Do they visit you in Germany?"

"At least once a year. Still, it's hard living far from them." Though the beginning of the dance was a clumsy mess, now the two of us move in perfect sync. Like we were made to dance together. Or maybe I just like to imagine we were.

"Are they why you're thinking about changing things up?"

I shrug. "It would be nice to live closer. But my company doesn't have any open positions States-side. Not ones related to my skill set anyway. I can't quit. Not without another thing to go to."

Luna nods, gazing over my shoulder, other thoughts I'm not privy to flitting through her eyes. Maybe she's planning on relocating here from Nashville.

One more reason to come back home.

Even though I live on a different continent, I can't help wanting to ask Luna out on a date. She's intriguing, with the powerful way she carries her small body and the observant quality she has. I'm betting she knows every exit in this yard and the Herberts' house, exactly how many people are at the wedding, and who is most likely to cause trouble.

She'd probably make a good federal agent. Or a spy.

Paige mentioned Luna teaches self-defense. Her students are lucky to have someone so badass showing them how to stay safe.

"What's your living space like in Germany?"

The question throws me off-balance, and I lose the groove of our dancing. Luckily, Dash's sister uses her strong arms to guide me back into the rhythm before I can injure her toes.

"Sorry. Uh, my place is nice." *Do you want to visit?* "I rent the upper floor in a house. Have my own living space and kitchen and everything." *Come and stay as long as you want.*

"Do you cook for yourself?" The tone of her voice coaxes my curiosity. I get the sense this is more than idle small talk.

"Most nights during the week, but they have great pubs over there. And their Hefeweizen is unmatched."

"Are you a clutter person or pretty clean?"

Odd. Still, I enjoy the randomness of the question. As if Luna is interested in the small details that make me who I am.

"I'm neater than most. We traveled a lot when I was a kid. Easier to pack if I didn't throw my stuff all around."

She nods, back to staring at me, her intelligent gaze measuring.

"What about you?" The urge to get to know her better, get closer to her, has my fingers inching closer together on her lower back. "Do you like living in Nashville?"

Luna's brows pop up, and I get the sense she didn't expect the questions to be turned back her way.

"Nashville's great. Especially now that I'm established. Business is good. My house is comfortable."

That doesn't sound like she wants to move to New Orleans.

"And the music scene?" I press.

Her eyes spark, a wicked grin curving that plump bottom lip. "Unmatched."

An image forms in my mind then. Luna and I like this, surrounded by music all the time. Sometimes dancing. Sometimes relaxing. Always exploring and listening.

Always together.

If we were different people, I'd shoot my shot. Knowing that if she said yes, we'd only spend a few nights together before both going our own ways. Still, those few intimate moments would be better than nothing.

The band switches into a faster number, and our arms slide away from each other. But I don't leave the dance floor, not ready to give up my time with her.

Luna keeps her focus on me as she bobs along to the beat. None of her moves are particularly seductive, but I'm still having trouble thinking of a woman I've ever found more tempting.

But she's my best friend's sister-in-law, and I can see the risk of a fling gone wrong between us.

Probably on my end.

Even without a kiss, I'm in danger of falling for Luna Lamont.

Chapter Eleven

LUNA

This is a job proposal, not an actual marriage.

With that reminder to myself, I watch Charlie closely as we walk through New Orleans Animal Rescue. Judging every move and decision he makes as if this is the only chance I'll get to figure out if he's the man I want to spend the rest of my life with.

Not the rest of my life, just a little over a year.

When I decided that going the marriage and inheritance route was a real possibility, I got back in touch with the lawyer to finally learn all those stipulations. One of the most important was how the inheritance would be paid to me. Apparently, Wai Po was thorough. She dictated that the money would be distributed in monthly installments over a year as long as I continued with the marriage requirements. If I tried to duck out early, I could keep some money for my troubles, but not all of it.

And to pay off Leo's debt, I need as much as I can get.

Which means this can't be a quick wedding, quick divorce. Whoever I convince to hitch themselves to me has to be ready for a long-term commitment.

"When you approach a dog's kennel, let them sniff your knuckles. Then offer them a treat but slip it through your fingers when your hand is in a fist. So you don't lose anything important." Cole demonstrates his directions by giving a milkbone to a shaggy black dog who whines in happy excitement at having people approach him.

One of the many eager animals in this rescue.

With Dash off on his honeymoon, he worried the shelter might be short volunteers this week. My brother used to work full-time here before becoming a manager for a local auto shop. Now he gives his time to the animals pro bono, paying back the place that took a chance on him when nowhere else would hire a parolee.

Wanting to give Dash the chance to truly relax, I offered to go to the shelter in his place. It's not the first time. When Dash worked here, I always made sure to stop by on my visits to New Orleans.

Still, I always forget how loud the place is. Dogs howling and barking and whining, the chorus bouncing off tile walls. Charlie strolls at my side, seemingly unaffected. Overall, the guy has a laid-back nature.

Also, a helpful one, seeing as how he volunteered to come here with me.

Another mark in his favor that he's willing to spend some of his precious vacation time helping abandoned animals. That's only something a decent guy would do, right?

Problem is, I find it easier to expect the worse from people. I can't help playing devil's advocate with every argument my mind makes in favor of Paige's best friend becoming my future fake husband.

Admittedly, I'm having a difficult time with this one.

Maybe Charlie is planning on starting an illegal dog fighting ring and needs some contestants?

Just as the far-fetched possibility pops into my brain, the man kneels by a smaller crate containing a mangy chihuahua. In a deep tone, he coos to the animal about how adorable it is.

And I'm forced to admit that at least when it comes to dogs, he's a decent guy.

"Since this is Charlie's first time, why don't you walk a dog together?" Cole suggests. "This is Pig. She's sweet. Great with the cats." He leads us over to a kennel with a roly-poly pit bull. The dog's face practically splits in half with her wide, panting grin. She's a barrel on stumpy legs, her name apt.

"Will this fit around her neck?" Charlie eyes the slip leash, doubt in his voice.

Cole huffs out a laugh. "Her neck's not that thick."

When Charlie still seems unsure, I hold out my hand, and he lays the rope across my palm.

My brothers and I never grew up with pets, which is why I was surprised when Dash got a job here. Not that he had a lot of places to choose from. But then when I came by and saw him working with the animals, I was impressed. He's the one who first showed me the technique to perfectly loop the slip leash around even the most rambunctious dog's neck. Pig is easy compared to many I've walked in the past.

"That's a good girl," I murmur, leading her out of the kennel and toward the exit. Charlie follows just as obediently at my heels, and I wonder if he'd be as easy to train to be my fake husband.

Stop it, I hiss at myself. *Controlling someone won't work for this.*

I need a partner. Someone I can trust to stick with me for the year. And that's not something I want to get through manipulation. That risks the whole endeavor crumbling.

I only have one shot at this.

"You're good at that." Charlie watches me as I guide the pit bull out of the building toward a gated area. Once inside the fence, I slip off the leash, letting her off to run.

"I've done it before," I shrug. "And Pig is well-behaved. Give it a couple of tries, and you'll have it down."

Charlie's smile glows bright as the sunny day. "With you as my partner, I have no doubt."

The comment causes goosebumps to prickle over my skin. A surprisingly pleasant sensation. The same tingle that caressed my nerves when Charlie climbed onstage during the wedding reception, accepting a guitar and strumming an acoustic version of Anita Baker's "Sweet Love" while his mother crooned the song.

The warm sensation in my chest has to mean he's the right pick for this endeavor. There's no other reason I'd feel this way around him.

This is the beginning of trust.

And that's all this is, I tell myself.

. . .

CHARLIE

I discover Luna's hidden talent: befriending beefy canines.

One in particular.

Pig the pit bull. The name suits. The dog has a porkish build, and when she pants she snorts in through her nose. A very snout-like nose.

The bumbling dog adores Luna, fetching for her, sitting for her, begging for belly scratches from her.

"Here, Pig! Look, I've got a nice squeaky tennis ball!" I wave the neon yellow toy in the air, trying to attract the pit bull's attention and give Luna a break.

The dog barely spares a glance over her shoulder before going back to staring at Luna, stubby tail wagging in hopeful supplication.

I can easily see how the woman would inspire such devotion.

Luna grins my way. "Pig likes me more than you."

"I know when I'm beat," I agree, strolling across the fenced area to join them.

The dog plops down in the dirt, then starts rolling around as if grass is as the best back scratcher in the world.

"She's a sweet girl." Luna grins down at the silly puppy. "Hopefully, she gets to go home with someone soon."

"You should adopt her," I say, not thinking much about the statement other than the words feel right.

Luna jerks her head back, blinking up at me in surprise.

"Me?" she scoffs. "No way. I couldn't."

That's a bummer for Pig. "Your place doesn't allow dogs?"

"I own my house." Luna doesn't meet my eyes anymore, instead gazing the way of the shelter.

"Are you allergic?"

"Not that I know of."

"Then why not?" I ask carefully, wondering if I'm treading on sensitive ground.

Luna shakes her head, attention landing anywhere other than Pig and me. "I just wouldn't make a good owner." She rockets a squeaky football to the opposite corner of the fence, and Pig scrambles to chase after the neon toy. "I don't know how to take care of a dog."

Paige had a similar concern when she first adopted Pumpkin. But animals are resilient and easy to learn. "You're doing a pretty good job right now. I bet Dash could give you tips."

Luna keeps shaking her head. "I work too much. And I—" She laughs to herself, but not as if her thoughts are funny. "I'm just not good at taking care of things."

That's an oddly cryptic statement that I have to use all my willpower to keep from digging into. The problem is, I have this nagging longing to know Luna. Every detail under her hard exterior.

Why can't she take care of things?

What issues keep her separate from her family?

But more than that, I want to know the everyday things.

What is her morning routine like?

What snack does she have to have in the house at all times?

How did she get into her line of work?

What would she look like lying beside me in a bed?

The dog comes barreling toward us, sliding to a halt just an inch from Luna's shins. Pig offers the squeaky toy as if in tribute to the woman she only wants to see happy.

Guess Pig and I are in the same boat.

"Okay," I concede. "I get it. My life doesn't have room for a pet either. Still, it's hard to see all these animals in need and not want to do something."

Luna crouches down to pat Pig's full belly. The puppy gives a happy wiggle and grins up at Luna with her doggy tongue lolling out the side of her mouth.

Pig looks ridiculous.

Ridiculously happy.

I pray someone else walks into the shelter with the same magnetism as the woman next to me. Sucks to disappoint an innocent animal.

Luna slips the lead over Pig's neck before standing, brushing her hands off on her shorts as if that'll erase all signs of the affection she just bestowed.

"I learned a while ago you can't save everyone."

And with that cold statement, Luna turns back toward the building, Pig trotting obediently at her heels.

As I watch the two walk away, I fight a fierce urge to find a way to be her savior.

Chapter Twelve

CHARLIE

Don't you dare spill anything on yourself.

Normally I don't have to give myself a pep talk about the simple act of drinking a soda. But I'm waiting for Luna, and it has not passed my notice that my body malfunctions whenever she's in a ten-foot radius. Most guys only have to worry about not getting a boner when they're around a woman they're crushing on. I, on the other hand, have to worry about every limb in my body possibly betraying me.

I'm Superman, and she's my walking, talking kryptonite.

I spot her strolling down the street. With each confident step she takes, Luna's hair sways against her bare shoulders. Her tank top shows off sculpted arms and hugs tight against her torso.

Never before have I been envious of a tank top.

With aviators covering her eyes, I'm unsure if she sees me staring. Either way, I can't seem to do anything else.

Luna pauses at the hostess's stand, and I rise to my generous height, waving for her attention.

The way her mouth curves into a welcoming grin does all sorts of inappropriate things to my breathing. Good thing I wasn't drinking when she hit me with it.

"Hey, Charlie." Luna strolls up to the table and settles in the seat across from mine.

I'd stayed standing in the wild hope she might go in for a hello hug. No luck there. Careful not to hit the table with my knees, I settle into my chair.

"Hey, yourself. How's your last day in town going? Got any exciting plans?"

Now in the shade of the restaurant's awning, Luna removes her sunglasses. I expect to meet a casually smiling gaze.

Instead, I'm staring into a level of intensity I wasn't ready for.

"Talking to you is the biggest thing on my agenda."

That's both thrilling and ominous.

"Is everything okay?"

Luna sits in her chair with perfect posture. Suddenly, I get the sense that this lunch invite I thought might be something like a date is much more serious.

"Nothing dire has happened." She keeps her eyes locked on mine. "But I have something important to ask you about."

"Whatever I can do to help."

She's the sister-in-law of my best friend, a relatively tenuous connection when looked at in those simple terms. But I have this tug in my chest demanding I do whatever she asks. That I go to any lengths to make her happy.

"How much do you know about Dash and my family?"

The grimace claims my mouth before I can stop it, and Luna gives a quick nod.

"You know some at least." She doesn't fidget or avoid my gaze. Luna is not here to mess around.

"I know Dash served time for stealing cars."

Her jaw hardens, and I wish I'd kept my words to myself. But then she sighs and offers a tight smile.

"That's part of our uncle's business. Dash is out of it now though. In case you were worried."

"No. I know. Paige told me." My friend isn't one to hold past sins over a person as long as they show remorse.

Luna sets her folded arms on the table, opening her mouth to keep going, but a server shows up before she can speak. After we both order the gumbo and Luna asks for an iced tea, the staff leaves us alone. I lace my fingers together in my lap to keep from reaching across the table to her.

"My brother Leo never left the business."

I knew in a vague sense that Dash had another sibling, as well as parents who live in the city. But when none of them came to the wedding, I figured it had to do with his problematic past.

Sucks being right sometimes.

"I'm sorry."

Luna nods, then stays quiet as the server returns with her drink. After swallowing an aggressive gulp, she pushes on.

"Then there's my grandma." Luna spends the rest of the time before our food arrives detailing how she discovered her other living relation in Delaware, and how just as she was getting to know the woman, her grandmother passed away from cancer.

"I didn't know she was sick." For the first time, I witness a crack in Luna's confident, cool demeanor. Just a small quiver of her voice in that statement.

But hell does it hit hard.

Suddenly, this outdoor seating seems too exposed. I want to shelter her so she can grieve in privacy without the sun glaring down on her pain and strangers potentially overhearing her raw words.

But just like that, Luna's shoulders go back, and the vulnerability disappears.

"My grandmother added Dash and me to her will. Turns out the grocery stores she and my grandfather opened were pretty successful. She left us both an inheritance."

I nod. "She was trying to take care of you even after she passed. I'm sorry you've had to deal with that pain."

Luna blinks at me from across the table, and I replay my words to see if I said something wrong.

"It does hurt," she admits. "Mainly because of the time lost." The crack returns, and as if realizing this, Luna glares at her lap. I can imagine she's giving herself a silent berating for showing weakness.

I wish she was comfortable being vulnerable with me. But I get the sense that few men—few people—have given Luna a reason to trust them.

"Anyway," she pushes on, "the money. It came with stipulations. One of them was that I won't inherit unless I get married."

Good thing the outside chairs are made of sturdy material because I rock back hard at that revelation.

Is Luna getting married?

Under the table, I crack my knuckles.

"There were other things, but I didn't bother listening to them because that first one was ludicrous. Especially because I need to be hitched by the time I'm thirty. Which is in less than five months. Even if I have the urge to shackle myself to someone, I'm not about to do it that fast."

Just then the staff arrives with our food, and I mull over Luna's story as they arrange everything on the table.

A strange concoction brews in my chest. Relief that Luna's not about to commit to someone for the rest of her life. But also a pervasive melancholy at the dismissive tone she used to talk about a lifelong partnership.

And then there's sadness. That the one thing left to her by this woman she obviously loved is out of her reach.

"But then I talked to my brother." Luna's determined words bring me back to the conversation. One that isn't over.

"Dash?"

"Leo."

Ah. The one still in the illegal family business.

Luna swirls her spoon in her bowl, eyes on the brown broth. That's when I realize I haven't taken a bite. Making sure the gumbo makes it to my mouth and not my shirt, I briefly take my focus off Luna but keep listening as she continues.

"I know he wants an out. Of the business. Problem is that the work is like quicksand and he's buried up to his neck." She abandons her food for more tea. "There's one thing that'll get him out. A language they all speak."

I can guess. "Money?"

Luna nods. "Money. And I know how to get some."

I wonder if someone walked by and kicked out the legs of my chair because my brain whirls wildly off-kilter.

She can't be leading up to what I think she is.

With a clatter, I drop my spoon into the bowl. Brown droplets splatter on my crisp, white button-down, but for once I don't have the headspace to cringe at my clumsiness.

The fierce woman sitting across from me claims every iota of attention. "Why did you ask to talk to me, Luna?"

She sets her own spoon down with more control than I'd managed.

"Because, Charlie Keller. I want to know if you'll marry me."

Chapter Thirteen

CHARLIE

Things need to get messier before they can get better.

I try to believe this wisdom as I stare around my disordered living space. There are cardboard boxes and random piles of belongings and packing material skewed everywhere.

So much for being able to pack up my life quickly.

But I haven't relocated like this in a while. I'm not moving across town or to a place a couple of hours away. My possessions need to cross an ocean.

My phone buzzes on the coffee table.

Swiping it up, an excited sweat breaks out over my body when I read the name on the screen.

Luna.

"Hey!" My greeting comes out more enthusiastic than necessary. But I'm bottled up after the days I've gone without speaking to her. Without seeing her.

Last time was at that cafe in the French Quarter. When she proposed.

"Charlie. Hi. It's Luna." Her voice sounds stiff, and I wonder if it's our connection. More likely she's calling to back out of this whole thing. My hopes waiver on a cliff edge.

"Yeah. I have your number saved. How's it going?"

"Good as it can be. I'm calling because I talked to the lawyer again. The executor of my grandmother's will. I made sure I have all the requirements she set forth for me to receive my inheritance. Thought it would be good for me to lay everything on the table before you make any kind of decision."

"Yeah. Of course." I carefully place a handful of books in a moving box. "Definitely want all the facts before I decide."

"Here it goes. Also, I warn you, my grandmother was a smart, tricky woman. She left me no loopholes to jump through as far as I can tell."

"Okay. Lay it on me."

"First off, the marriage, obviously. But the wording is that I need to be married when I turn thirty, and the inheritance will be paid out to me in monthly installments for a year as long as I remain married during that time."

Married to Luna for a year. Not looking like a bad deal yet.

"And like I said, we can come up with a percentage of each payment you think is fair for you to receive. Or a lump sum at the end."

I wonder if I blacked out for part of the original discussion because I do not remember any talk of me getting paid. The idea has me itchy. I don't want to take Luna's money.

"Don't you need all of it for your brother?"

"If we stay together the full year, there should be fifty thousand that won't go to my uncle."

"I don't want your money, Luna."

A longer pause. "Sorry to have bothered you then. I'll find another way."

Panic ups my voice a few notches. "Wait! That's not what I'm saying."

The line is silent for a beat.

"Then what are you saying?"

"That you don't need to pay me to help you out. I'll do it with no money required."

I wish Luna and I were talking face to face so I could get a better read on what these stretches of silence mean.

"You don't know all the stipulations. You have to want something."

Yeah, more time with you. The vibrant, badass woman I haven't been able to stop thinking of since that damned yacht party.

"Why don't you just tell me what the rest of the rules are?"

A sigh. "Okay. We need to live together during our marriage. Now, this is the big one. And the only reason I brought this all up is because you said you wanted to move back to the States. I figured you can move in with me in Nashville and take the year we're married to figure out what you want to do next in your career." She huffs out a noise that sounds close enough to a laugh to ease my nerves. "I'll be your sugar momma."

Unfortunately, I was drinking tea during that last comment. Luckily, I was facing away from my books when I did a spit take, spraying some towels instead.

"My what?" I choke out.

"Your sugar momma. Like sugar daddy, but I'm the one supporting you financially."

I'm busy wiping spit and Earl Grey off my chin as I work through her words. "You're planning on supporting me? And paying me? How do you get any money out of this deal?"

"Creative budgeting."

That sounds like a lot more work than it's worth. Especially because I don't want a paycheck from this arrangement.

"Fine." I give in, but only for the moment. "What's the rest?"

"We have to do a hobby together from a list she has and provide video evidence of us doing the activity the length of our marriage."

I settle on my couch. "A hobby? Why a hobby?"

"My guess is her goal was for me to stay married even after the first year is up. I think this is her way of instituting bonding time. She and my grandfather took art classes together apparently."

"What's on the list?"

"Let's see." There's the sound of shuffling papers over the line. "Art classes are number one. Cooking classes. Dancing lessons. Couples' yoga. Tai chi..." Luna rattles off a few more leisurely activities. "We have until my birthday to decide."

"I'm good with any of those."

Once again a pause comes long and heavy. I realize then that Luna pauses like this in person too, but her gaze is so piercing that the conversation doesn't seem to end when her mouth shuts.

"You're making this too easy."

"Was I supposed to make it hard?"

"I guess not. But I called fully expecting to have to give you the hard sell and still get turned down. I'm not sure what's appealing about this deal to you."

You are, I want to say.

And it's true. Side perks are having someone finally push me to leave the job I'm not passionate about anymore while also giving me a living option closer to my parents.

But the true draw is Luna herself.

I know this entire thing—the engagement, the marriage, living together—is all a ruse to get the inheritance. But I can't help hoping that maybe her grandmother was on to something. That this could be a real chance to figure out if Luna and I are compatible. Show her that I'm someone she could fall for.

"I like adventure. This is just one more wild life choice I get to make. And you're not asking for eternity. Besides," I let my voice sink a note deeper, "I've always been on the lookout for a sugar momma."

That earns me a snort, and I can picture the cute way her nose wrinkles when she suppresses a laugh.

"Fine. It's an adventure." Luna's voice gets serious then. "If I don't claim this inheritance, then it goes to another benefactor. We could probably trick the executor on a few of these things, but I don't want to risk it. I'd rather whoever I do this with stick to the guidelines."

"Do you know who the other inheritor would be?"

"Yes. And let's just say he'll do anything he can to get this money. Luckily, he doesn't know about it."

I wonder who he could be. Not Dash. She already told me her younger brother gets the same payout when he's thirty. I doubt it's Leo, or else Luna would want the money to go directly to her twin.

I let the question go, not secure enough in my position to ask her. Which is strange because if we go through with this plan, Luna will be my wife. "Like I said, none of the rules you listed off seem hard to follow. If you're down, then so am I."

Again Luna hits me with a silence. Waiting for her to get her thoughts in order, I wander around my kitchen, making note of the items I'm particularly attached to. The mug Paige got me with a picture of us screaming on a roller-coaster drop. Always makes me laugh. I set it in the middle of the counter to be bubble-wrapped when I get off the phone.

"You mean it, don't you?" Luna's bafflement rings clear even an ocean away. "You'll marry me?"

"I will. How soon can I start shipping boxes to your place? I'll put in my two weeks' notice tomorrow, but I'll probably need three to get everything squared away here—"

"Charlie," she cuts me off.

"Yeah."

"You're...thank you."

I grin, staring out my window at the street below, starting my slow goodbye to my life in Europe. "We're in this together now."

"I guess we are."

"Now we've just got one more question to answer."

"What's that?"

"Are you going to be Luna Keller? Or should I be Charlie Lamont?"

Chapter Fourteen

LUNA

My future husband waits on the curb inside the terminal.

Might as well start calling him that now, I figure.

Other people might struggle to find their passenger, but mine stands a head above everyone else. It helps that he's not passing the time waiting by staring down at his phone. Charlie searches the approaching cars.

Looking for me.

I'm at the airport to pick up my fiancé. Never thought that would be a scenario I live out.

Through the windshield our eyes catch. Then Charlie hits me with his beautiful, wide grin that shines brightly in this dingy terminal.

Something in my chest does a weird flip-flop. Definitely not my heart though. That's not allowed.

I maneuver to the curb and throw my car in park before climbing out to help Charlie with his two massive rolling suitcases. Considering that he's moving his entire life across the Atlantic, I'd say he packed light.

"Hey! No need to get out, I've got this." He waves me off, but I'm not daunted by polite refusals of help.

"You get one, I'll get the other," I counter while popping open the trunk.

Charlie doesn't bother arguing anymore, letting me grab his other bag and heft the thing into my car.

Smart man.

Once we're settled in our seats and pulling onto the highway, Charlie shifts his body toward mine.

"How is everything?"

With traffic heavier at this time of day, I have to keep my eyes fully on the road, which means I don't get to stare at the attractive man in my passenger seat while we talk. Guess that doesn't matter too much. If everything sticks to the plan, I'll have a good year to ogle him.

No, I scold myself. *No ogling allowed. This is just business.*

"A lot of your boxes arrived, and none looked like they sustained damage. I have them all in my guest room. Well, your room now."

"No stipulation in the will about us sharing a bed?"

My heart rate accelerates faster than the speed of the car. "Did you think there was?"

Charlie's already dark skin grows darker with his blush. "N-no! Of course not. Just a joke."

I focus on the road and try to dismiss the stray thought of what it would be like to slide under the covers with Charlie. I wonder if he sleeps in a shirt and shorts. Or just boxers.

Or nothing at all.

I shove the thought from my mind.

"No. She didn't go that far. No proof of our marriage getting consummated is needed."

Awkward silence descends between us, which does not bode well for our marriage.

"This is weird, huh?" Charlie's question pulls me out of my head. "I mean, we're going from zero to sixty. Maybe more than sixty. I don't know what speed a fake marriage is, but it's definitely something that takes easing into." The laughter in his voice soothes my nerves, and I grin over at my new partner as we slow down for a stoplight.

"Yeah. Not sure how to prepare for this."

He squints at me. "You're telling me you have no prior experience with fake marriages?"

I struggle to keep a grin off my face. "Oddly enough, no. Zero."

Charlie reclines his seat a few inches, and I realize he's already slid the seat back as far as it'll go. The guy is like Dash: long legs.

"Sounds like we'll learn together then."

I nod, accelerating as the light turns green. "You know, everything my grandma is demanding we do, I think it comes from her idea that long-term associating and building shared interests will keep a marriage going. Since this isn't real, we could approach it as friend bonding. By the end of this thing, you and I will be best friends." I drum my fingers on my steering wheel. "Or we'll hate each other."

"I don't see how I could hate you, Luna."

That draws a dark chuckle out of me. "Just you wait." Wanting to get off those confusing topics, I switch us back to casual chatting mode. "How was your flight?"

"I got an emergency exit aisle. That was nice."

"Uh, because you're worried about a water landing?"

Charlie laughs as he leans his head back on the headrest. "No. I trust pilots and flight technology. No, I like them for the leg room." He pats his thigh, and I can't help noticing how his pants hug his legs tight.

Charlie Keller is a well-formed man on the lanky end of the spectrum. He's tall and lean, towering without being imposing.

Some women might enjoy the challenge of climbing him.

Not me. Nope. Definitely not his future wife.

"Still couldn't sleep though." He sighs. "It's going to take me a while to get off Germany time."

"You tired? You should nap. I'll wake you up when we get to my place."

"You don't mind?"

I glance over to see his lids already drooping. "Nope. Go forth and sleep."

Charlie reclines the seat the rest of the way, and in less than a minute he dozes off. As he slumbers beside me, I get an almost protective sensation. Like I'm keeping my future husband safe when he's at his most vulnerable.

More like I'm desperate to figure out a way to pay the guy back for this amazing favor he's doing me.

How could he not want money?!

The fact that he's continued to refuse me paying him drives my mind on a winding trip. Money is all my family ever cared about. How to make a buck off of anything.

Thank god, my father doesn't know about the inheritance. I'm not sure how much my life is worth to him, but I'm guessing it's less than $300,000.

A half-hour later, we pull up in front of the small, white house I bought with my own money two years ago.

The place isn't huge, but I like the cozy little structure.

And it's mine, which is the most important part. Earned every square foot of it.

The engine quiets when I turn the key. Charlie doesn't immediately rouse. I take a moment to examine him. He has a round face, but interesting angles appear when he smiles. And Charlie smiles a lot. Must've lived a charmed life to have so much joy in him.

I'm not jealous.

Well, maybe a little.

But I wouldn't want to take his happiness from him.

His hair is cut close to his head in a fade that darkens from his ears to his crown. I wonder if the contained cut is his preference or chosen for his corporate job. Maybe he'll let his hair grow over the next year, allowing some kinky curls to develop.

The idea of us spending an entire year together is wild.

If he agrees, that is. No signed wedding certificate means the deal is still in limbo.

If I were smart, I would have driven him straight to the courthouse and gotten this set in stone. No backing out.

But there's more than just getting his signature on a piece of paper.

Wai Po made sure of that.

I know this fake marriage scheme is ridiculous. I keep waiting for Charlie to tell me that Dash asked him to go along with it for long enough that my baby brother can find me some professional help.

But Dash doesn't know about this, and Charlie has literally shipped his life to my house over the past few weeks.

Just to test that this is real, I reach over and poke him.

"Huh?" Charlie blinks himself awake.

"We're at my house. Are you ready to come in?"

"Wha—" He cuts himself off, shaking his head to wake himself up. "Yeah. I'm ready."

Charlie unfolds himself from the car, and we each claim a bag. He doesn't bother arguing with me this time, and I hope we've cleared up that nonsense never to be dealt with again.

No stereotypical gender roles in this household.

Although I might give him the job of reaching for things on the top shelf, just so I don't have to bother with dragging my step stool out every time.

"This is it." Wow, I could sell used cars with that enthusiastic pitch. The front door lets us into a small entryway. On my long list of construction projects is knocking down one wall here to open things up a bit more. "Swear it gets better." There goes that saleswoman again.

When I glance up at Charlie, he's smiling back at me.

That's when I remember the job he just left—and assume he was good at.

Salesman.

Yeah, I'm not impressing this audience. Hopefully, my house can speak for itself. I have tried to make my home a comfortable space. Nothing like what I grew up in. I chose the furniture and decorations not because of their price tags, but more because they gave me a good feeling.

The whole place is one floor, and we need to cross through the living room to get to the guest bedroom. I'm pushing open the door when I realize I lost Charlie over by the coffee table. He reaches out a hand, sifting through the books I left sprawled across the surface. A collection of history books and memoirs, all holding facts and experiences related to a single country.

"Are you planning a trip to Taiwan?" Charlie glances toward me, fingers still resting on a title.

"Maybe. Someday. That's where my grandparents are from," I say, like it isn't a big deal. Like I didn't spend a chunk of my life wondering. Like I didn't just learn a year ago when I finally tracked down my grandmother and she told me.

The books, with their stiff, barely touched pages, mock me.

I'm not a historian. None of my interests deal with memorizing facts from textbooks. But after my grandmother died, the authentic ways I could learn about my Taiwanese heritage shrank.

The problem is that I don't want to have to learn the information.

I want to already know it.

The way I know how to hot-wire a car without setting off the alarm and how to climb out a second-story window using a drainpipe.

The way the smell of fast-food fries and boxed mac and cheese reminds me of dinners as a kid.

The way I know which streets in New Orleans to avoid after dark.

Endless Lamont teachings I never remember learning. As if I always knew them.

I wish my Taiwanese heritage was the same. That the knowledge was an essential part of my DNA.

But it's always going to be secondhand knowledge. Whatever I can pick up from studying or watching the news or taking a trip. I may look the part, but it's not a true part of me.

One more reason to be pissed off at my mother.

"They moved to America soon after they got married and had my mom here. But I guess she didn't get along with them. All I know is she left when she got pregnant with me and my brother Leo. Cut off all contact. Changed her name and everything."

Charlie straightens, keeping his earnest eyes on me. "But you reconnected, right?"

I turn back to the bedroom, not sure what kind of emotions will show on my face. "Yeah, I knew her. I found her a year before she died. So there's that, at least."

But I could have had twenty-nine more years. I could have had her love and my history.

And I could have had more than just her.

"Too late to meet my grandfather though. He died in the nineties."

Wai Po showed me pictures of a stern-looking man. Would he have been cold with me? Or could I have gotten him to smile the way I'd gotten my grandmother to those last few visits?

"I'm sorry. That's rough." Charlie appears next to me now, but despite his size, I don't feel crowded. His presence comforts me.

"I missed out on a lot of time with my family." Admitting that hurts, but Charlie needs to know how important this next year is for me. "I don't want that to happen with Leo."

"I understand."

Chapter Fifteen

CHARLIE

"You want me to what?" Luna gapes at me from across the pizza box.

I wipe my greasy fingers on a napkin and try to keep my voice lighthearted yet reasonable. Selling people ideas is what I do. This should be easy. Just another day at work.

"I want you to adopt Pig."

My knuckles let out a light series of pops as I crack them, trying to eradicate some of my nervous energy.

This weird requirement could implode the whole arrangement.

"It's been weeks," Luna points out. "She's probably already in a new home."

"She's not," I say with confidence, though not much happiness. "I texted Paige earlier. She asked Cole, and he said no one has claimed her. Pig still needs a home. Why not here?"

"This...why are you asking for this?" My future fake wife crosses her arms and leans on the table. I'm briefly mesmerized by the way her dark hair swishes forward in a straight curtain. "You can get a dog if you want to. I don't care."

"Pig doesn't like me," I point out. "She needs to be your dog. But I'll help you take care of her. Maybe she'll warm up to me at some point, but you need to be a part of this."

"You're not making any sense, Charlie!" Luna stomps to her fridge and comes back with a beer, screwing the top off with a quick flick of her wrist. "I'm asking you to devote more than a year of your life to me, and you don't want money or concert tickets or favors. You just want me to adopt a dog! Where is your head right now?"

Not completely sure, but when this idea came to me, it just felt right.

Like saying yes to Luna's proposal.

Still, this take-no-shit woman is not someone to let things go without an explanation, so I come up with one on the fly.

"Okay, it's like this. You may think this marriage thing is a burden for me, but it's not. I'm going to live in your house rent-free, no job, and just ponder my future. That's going to get boring quickly. I need some kind of responsibility. Some regular tasks to take care of during the day to keep from becoming a couch slug."

"Which brings us back to you adopting Pig. She'll be your dog." Luna takes a sip of her beer, and I try not to imagine tasting the hoppy liquid on her lips.

My mind scrambles for more reasoning. "No, see, what if on this journey of self-discovery, I realize travel is what I want? Or living in a different country? It's difficult to cross oceans with a dog." I meet Luna's gaze. "You bought this house. You've set down roots here. You want to stay in Nashville."

"Yeah, so?" she asks.

"Then you're more stable than I am. At the end of the year, Pig needs to be your dog. That way she still has a home when this marriage is over." I brace myself, hoping that Luna doesn't smell the bullshit I just dumped in front of her.

Because I don't want Pig to be her dog.

I want Pig to be *our* dog. I want to have one more thing tying the two of us together. Something to share. Something to keep us connected after the end date of our relationship.

The year hasn't started, and I'm already mourning the loss of her. I don't understand this instant connection, other than I've felt the pull once before.

With Paige.

Not that I'm pining after my best friend. We tried dating in high school, and I realized that was not what our relationship was. Luckily, we felt the same way, and our friendship only got stronger.

Now Luna Lamont stands in front of me, and I'm drawn to her like a hook sits deep in my gut and she's holding the end of the line attached to it. At the same time, she's talking about end dates. And I don't want whatever relationship we build to end.

From the way I've mentally replayed her stripping out of her clothes on the back of that yacht, it's clear I want more than just friendship. But that might be one-sided. If that's true, I can find a way to accept the platonic relationship.

But the idea of walking away from Luna completely?

Does not compute.

"Fine," she huffs, staring at the ceiling like she's mentally mapping out a new future on the white expanse. "Guess I'm getting a dog."

I did it? I convinced her?

Keeping my urge to whoop out loud under wraps, I allow myself a small but triumphant smile.

"Does this mean we're going down to New Orleans again? Because I love my brother, but I don't usually visit this often." The smirk on her face tells me she doesn't mind.

"I bet Paige would be willing to drive Pig up."

Luna groans. "Hell. Dash and Paige. What are we going to tell them? And your parents? I normally don't consider other people when I plan things."

That sounds lonely, but I guess that's the way Luna prefers her life. Or maybe it's all that's been available to her before now. Maybe I can show her that making plans with another person doesn't have to be painful.

"For the next year and however many months, we're partners." I hold her gaze, and make sure she hears how serious I am about the commitment. "That means I'm on your team. Tell me how you want to play this."

I'd hate lying to my parents, but I could probably have them believing Luna and I are in a roommate situation. Not entirely off base, other than the legal nature of our relationship.

"Truth," Luna declares. "We'll tell Dash and Paige the truth. He already knows about the inheritance. Hopefully, Paige doesn't hate me for taking advantage of you."

"She could never hate you." Paige isn't the type.

Luna shrugs as if that doesn't mean much to her. I get the sense that it does.

"I don't talk to anyone else in my family. If anyone at work asks, I'll tell them we got married. And if they ask after the fact, I'll just say we got divorced. They're all celebrities, so they're familiar with brief marriages."

Damn, that dismissive note in her voice has my stomach queasy. When I envisioned getting married, I always pictured it as permanent.

"What about your parents?" she asks.

"My parents?" I try to refocus on the discussion.

"How do you want to play it with them? You know their reactions best."

My parents are understanding. And supportive. But my mom is also just slightly desperate for me to fall in love. I'm not sure what their reaction will be, but I know for sure I don't want to lie to them for an entire year.

"I'll tell them the truth. And they'll probably want to have you over when the weirdness gets easier to deal with."

Luna nods absently, her eyes staring at the ceiling again. I glance up as well to see if our future together is projected there. If there's a way we can study the events for any possible missteps.

"Okay," she says quietly, then again with more conviction. "Okay." She strolls out of the kitchen and disappears down the hall into a room, reappearing with a notepad and pen and paper.

"We've covered your demands. Or demand, more like. And we know what we'll say to people. Now for the final discussion."

"What's that?"

The determined way Luna holds the pen both unnerves me and turns me on.

"The marriage rules."

Chapter Sixteen

LUNA

My entire childhood was a mess of ever-changing rules and no real structure. There was no way to know if I was doing or saying the right thing because my father would change his mind about what he wanted day to day, hour to hour, sometimes minute to minute.

So yes. I want rules. I want them written down and referable, that way we never question where we stand or how to approach this entire situation.

With these in place, I figure our chances of making it through a year can only increase.

"These are the parameters of our agreement," I explain. "Both of our expectations."

I settle at the table and poise the pen over the paper. "First rule, obviously, we must follow all the requirements set forth by my grandmother."

Charlie nods, settling in beside me.

"Okay. Now you."

Charlie takes the pen from my hand and slides the paper his way. Then he hesitates, brow scrunched, as if in deep thought.

"Seriously? You don't have a list already? How are you unsure about this right now?"

Charlie offers a confused shrug. "I don't know. I guess I thought we'd figure things out as we go."

Oh, sweet, naive man.

"Maybe in an actual relationship." I reach out to tap the paper. "But this is basically a business deal. Why don't you add the stuff about Pig to start?" I prod him in the side, still not fathoming my future fake husband doesn't have more hard limits at the ready.

Charlie carefully jots down a few sentences, then passes the paper back to me.

As if I have the right to add more.

I read over his scrawl.

Luna will adopt Pig, but Charlie will be the primary caregiver until the end of their marriage.

That's it.

"Okay, what about house rules?" Maybe if I lead him enough, the ideas will start flowing.

Charlie tugs on his lower lip, thoughtful. "I don't know. This is your house."

"Oh my fucking god. This is like pulling teeth. Be a little selfish. A little honest. What'll make you more comfortable here?"

He shrugs. "I'm an organized person. Not a fan of clutter or mess. You don't mind me cleaning your place regularly, do you?"

My forehead hits the table, and not too gently. "You're turning yourself into my live-in maid? What universe are we in right now?"

"Hey." Charlie's hand comes to my head, urging me up. "Cooking. I'm not great at that. How about you cook, I clean? Or you get us take-out if you're a shitty chef too."

"I'm a nutritionist. Cooking is in my wheelhouse. I'll handle the meals." At this point I'm desperate, so I write that rule down. "We can split the other chores. You don't have to clean the house."

Charlie shakes his head. "You're at work all day. I'll handle it."

"Charlie!" I shove up from my chair to pace. "I'm not marrying you to get a housekeeper! I'm supposed to be your sugar mamma!"

His teeth sink into his thick lower lip, obviously trying to stifle a laugh at my outburst.

"Luna." He takes on a gentler tone. "You are supporting me

financially for the next year. You're giving me the freedom and time to figure out my life's passion. This is not a one-sided exchange."

When I open my mouth to protest, he stops me with a raised hand. "How about this? We'll add a rule that if I'm ever feeling overwhelmed with the amount of housework, we'll talk about it and devise a new system. Okay?"

The deal still sounds like him creating an out he'll never use, but it's hard to argue with Charlie when he gives me those hopeful eyes.

"Fine."

My fake fiancé's shoulders relax, and he grabs the pen and scribbles on the paper. Then he pauses and I can tell by the edge he holds himself on that he's finally thought of something.

Thank god.

"What is it?"

"I just…" He trails off, then rubs an agitated hand over his skull.

"Come on. What rule do you want to add?"

He clears his throat once. Then again. "I know this isn't a real marriage, but…" Another throat clearing. "Commitment would be nice. For as long as this lasts."

Ah. That.

A year of celibacy shouldn't be hard. It's been six months since I was last with someone, and the experience wasn't worth repeating.

Then the image of Charlie entering the house some night with a strange woman wrapped around him appears in my mind. The thought has me queasy for a reason I don't want to dwell on.

"Yes. Fine." My words are terse. "We'll both abstain from dating other people while we're married."

Charlie nods and writes some more words down. I move to stare over his shoulder, baffled by the short list of items.

Is this how easy it is to fake a relationship with another person?

I thought we'd have a whole scroll of stipulations. Multiple notebooks. That we'd need a table of contents and a glossary.

"I guess we don't have to laminate this tonight. I kind of sprung it on you. You can take the next few days before we sign the marriage license to brainstorm whatever else you want."

"Sure," Charlie says, not sounding like he needs the time.

Is this why I gravitated toward him? Why I thought pitching this wild idea would have a chance?

The man is just so easygoing. It's strange for me to be around someone who doesn't seem even mildly anxious about what we're setting out to do. I'm not normally a worrier. Not anymore. I spent the last decade honing myself into a person ready to take on most any challenge.

But that was all physical stuff. Now I have this, a requirement to simply coexist, and I'm checking my arms to see if hives have broken out.

"Luna."

The way Charlie says my name, softly with a hint of wariness, as if he's concerned I'll sprint toward the door, lets me know how much of my disquiet I'm showing on the surface.

Time to bury that shit.

"Yeah?"

"This can be a good thing." A smile plumps his cheeks. "A fun thing. I don't want you to approach this marriage as a job." He nudges my hip with his elbow. "We're becoming friends, in some of the strangest circumstances possible. But I'm being honest when I say I'm looking forward to this next year. You know what…"

The way he trails off ratchets up my anxiety, but then he reaches for the paper and I calm a bit. More rules. More clarity. This is good.

Then I read the five words he pens down.

Have fun with each other.

"What does that mean?"

"It means what I wrote." In the face of my scowl, Charlie only laughs. "I want us to do fun things together. Show me what you love about Nashville. I'll come up with stuff too. We're partners. Let's be partners in fun!"

"Oh god. You're, like, super-dorky, aren't you?" The question came out drier than I meant, and I want to stuff it back in my mouth, hating that I might have hurt Charlie's feelings.

But he just stands from his chair, towering a good foot over me, and grins down at my upturned face.

"Hell yeah I am. What do you say, Luna Lamont? Do you agree to my rule? Will you have fun with your dorky husband?"

There's a whole range of sarcastic answers that pop into my mind. But every one of them borders on cruel. Even if I'm not a nice person, I don't want Charlie thinking I'm an asshole.

Besides, there's a simpler, easier answer.

"Yes. I'll have fun with you. Not sure I'll be any good at it."

"All I ask is that you try." He's still smiling at me, the expression sinking into something comfortable on his face. And there's a subtle heat to it that has me snatching the pen back.

"As two single people living in close proximity, I believe it is important we keep this completely platonic. An agreement between friends, which means no fooling around." I can't meet Charlie's eyes when I make this declaration, instead focusing on where the point of the pen meets the paper. "Agreed?"

A pause. Then, "Agreed."

"Good." *Good*, I repeat to my brain silently, to make sure it's on the same page.

Yes, Charlie is an attractive, kind man. But the end goal of this is more important than any brief pleasure we'd get from a hookup that would just end up destroying our carefully created partnership. We have to get through this year with our sham of a marriage intact if I want any hope of freeing my brother.

"Might as well add for clarification that this all lasts until May 11th of next year. Then you'll be free of me, off to live the new life you've decided you want."

When I glance up from the paper, having finished writing that sixth rule, I'm met with the sight of Charlie's back. Instead of facing me, he stares out the window into my backyard, seeming lost in thought.

"A year," Charlie murmurs. "Probably be over before we know it."

Chapter Seventeen

LUNA

"I'm here!" Charlie strides down the hallway of the courthouse toward me. I brace myself for when he gets an eyeful.

I'm not wearing white. Or a dress.

For maybe five minutes, I considered it. Getting something lacy with a bunch of frills. And I'd probably look good. But I wouldn't look like me, and there's enough insincerity in this ceremony already that I decided to dress up, but in the way I prefer.

Which is why I have on a suit. The cut fits me perfectly, and the ensemble is my favorite piece of clothing in my closet. I treated myself to a custom-tailored suit after I got my first official client. Probably should have put that initial paycheck in my savings, but for the first time in a long time, I gave myself permission to buy something completely impractical that made me happy.

And I don't realize until this moment how much it would crush me to see disappointment on Charlie's face. To watch him scan my outfit and twist his lips to hide a dissatisfied grimace. Because I'm not the model bride.

No matter that this is all fake anyway.

But now the real Charlie is in front of me, with his eyes consuming me, three-piece and all.

"That suit looks amazing on you. Hell, I've never worn a suit that well." My fake fiancé smooths a hand down his lapel, but from his grin I know he's not concerned about being outshone.

And I'm suddenly very glad I added that final rule to our contract because I have the oddest urge to climb Charlie and claim his grinning lips in a hot kiss.

Not acceptable thoughts about my husband!

It's probably the suit. His suit, not mine. Charlie paid me a high compliment when he said I looked better than him. Because damn, my future fake husband is fine.

Talk, dark, and handsome has never been a more apt statement.

Every inch of his suit is black. The jacket and pants, of course, but also the shirt and the long, thin tie. He must have gone to a barber because his fade is perfection, as is his close shave. And god, the way his ebony skin stretches over that strong jaw of his.

It's enough to have a fake fiancé wondering why we aren't doing this for real.

Stop it! The suits are to blame!

I shove away the unwelcome thoughts and put on my serious face.

"Are you having second thoughts?" I ask. "Is that why you're running late?"

Charlie's skin grows darker with a blush, but he steps in close, cupping my elbow with his hand.

"No. I'm in all the way. I just thought if we're going to be in this for more than a year, we might as well look the part." At that, Charlie slips his hand into his pocket as if searching for something. Finding the item, he spreads his fingers wide, revealing two slim gold bands.

"Charlie!" I gasp out his name, not because the rings are beautiful but because I can't believe how much he's committing to this role. "You didn't have to."

He shrugs, handing me the larger one. "I want you to know that I'm not about to back out a month into this thing. And you don't have to think of them as wedding rings if you don't want to. Think of them as partner rings." He holds up the smaller band, the one he plans to slip onto my finger in a few minutes. "When you wear this and look down at it, I want you to remember that I'm here for you. That you can trust me."

Swallowing becomes difficult, and the ceiling is suddenly fascinating.

"Luna?"

I clear my throat. "The rings are a good idea. Thank you." I was too busy with the online paperwork to consider if we should mess with more traditional wedding objects.

When Charlie smiles at me this time, there's a depth of sincerity that is also strangely arousing.

Damn these motherfucking suits.

When I realize we've been staring at each other for just a little too long, I step back.

"We should be able to go in soon," I tell him, my tone formal now. Back to business.

We settle beside each other on the hard bench outside the judge's office, and I try not to admire the way the high-quality material hugs his legs.

"Are you here to get married?"

At the sound of Charlie's question, my head pops up. Why would he ask something so obvious? But then I realize he's not talking to me. My fake fiancé faces an elderly couple sitting on the bench across from us. They can't be younger than seventy, but by the blissfully happy expressions on their faces, they might as well be teenagers.

"We are," one lady responds, clutching the hand of the woman at her side. "Forty years together, and we decided, why not?" The crystals on her glasses sparkle as she tilts her head toward us. "You too?"

Charlie slings an arm around my shoulders, and I don't flinch from the touch. Probably because it feels more like comradery than possessive.

"Yes ma'am. This is my fiancée, Luna. And I'm Charlie."

The women offer us soft smiles. "I'm Margaret, this is Tiffany. How'd you two kids meet?"

Charlie gives me a wicked grin before turning back to them. "Well, you see, we were on this boat..."

As he relates our first encounter, sparing himself no embarrassment, I can't help but feel awe at how easy he is around these strangers. Not that Margaret and Tiffany are intimidating, but there's an air of vulnerability to the way Charlie opens himself up. His genuine nature is probably what gets the couple to share their own story of a love spanning decades, sometimes hidden from public view, but now allowed to be on display. By the end, I'm battling a wave of shame that Charlie and I are entering into this marriage under false pretenses when people like our new acquaintances struggled for the right.

Not that Charlie and I would have had an easy time of it if we'd met and fallen in love during the same time period Margaret and Tiffany did. A Black man and an Asian American woman would've had plenty of shit to deal with forty years ago. I can imagine we'll run into some modern-day bigot nonsense over this next year too.

I wonder if our lack of love will make that kind of hate easier or harder to deal with.

Still, I chant to myself to push the doubt away.

For Leo. For Leo. I'll put up with anything to save Leo.

By the time the judge is ready, Charlie has offered for us to act as the witnesses of Margaret and Tiffany's wedding, and they've agreed to do the same for us.

One less thing to worry about.

Only when Charlie and I are standing in the chambers, facing each other with those two loving women watching us, I can't help thinking I need to commit to this ruse just a little bit more.

"Do you have rings?"

"Yes!" I triumphantly hold mine up, and Charlie chuckles.

My fake fiancé scoops up my hand in his warm palm and slides the tiny gold band onto my ring finger. I follow the same steps, experiencing a strange rush of ownership as I push the gold over his knuckles.

For the next year, Charlie Keller is mine.

CHARLIE

. . .

Luna is the most gorgeous fake wife a person could ever hope for. The plum color of her suit sets off a warm glow under her skin and somehow makes her hair appear even darker.

Add all that to the ring on her finger, and I know my mind will forever save this image.

"You are now husband and wife." Since we're in a courthouse, there's none of the usual flare, nothing like what Marianna put on for Paige and Dash's wedding.

But there is a contractual obligation.

One requirement Luna's grandmother dictated was that a photo must be submitted to the executor of Luna and her husband kissing on their wedding day.

I wish I could have met Tsai Shu-fen. She's a tricky woman, and I'd like to shake her hand.

My wife slides a cell phone out of her pocket and turns to Margaret.

"Would you mind taking a photo of us?" Luna clears her throat, then powers on. "Kissing?"

The two lovely women chuckle. "Of course. First kiss as a married couple is something you'll want to remember."

First kiss, period.

But I don't correct them. Instead, I focus on not getting too excited about this. About not reading too much into it.

This is fake. All temporary.

"Let's do this." Luna is all business, clasping my shoulders. She has on a set of heels that give her a few extra inches of height, which means I don't have to bend over as much.

"All ready!" Margaret calls.

Then Luna's lips meet mine.

The universe shimmers around me like a heat flare has hit this courtroom.

"Oh darn. I accidentally closed the camera. You two keep going! I'll have it back up in a second."

The flustered little old woman can take as long as she wants if the result is me continuing to kiss Luna.

No struggle here.

And to my surprise, Luna doesn't seem interested in stopping either.

My newly legal partner lets her hands creep up until she's wrapped her arms around my neck, pressing her body closer to mine. It's all I can do to keep from groaning. I want to be closer. I want to consume my wife. Without thinking, I let my hands slide from her waist to around her back, and then I'm standing upright. But I don't leave Luna behind. I pull her with me, lifting her entirely off the ground, clasping her flush against my body. All the while our lips meld together until we share breath. I smell her mandarin bright scent as I breathe deeply of her. Luna's as exciting as the fruit on my tongue, with a sharp, almost spicy flavor. And so damn refreshing.

As my individual thoughts trail away, every inch of my body rejuvenates and comes out on the other side cleansed.

Luna is joy and need and home against me.

"Got it! Bravo, you two! Quite a kiss!"

We break apart gasping, our wild eyes meeting each other and coming to the simultaneous realization that we did not just kiss like a fake husband and wife should.

But I'm probably the only one of the two of us who doesn't regret it. Trying not to reveal my reluctance, I allow Luna to slide down my body until her heels settle on the floor. She takes a step or two back, movements steady even as her eyes display a lack of balance.

"Here you go. You have a good one there." Margaret hands Luna's phone back to her and grins over at me.

"Thank you." I smile at the two women, then taking a chance, I scoop up Luna's hand and pull her to the side where we can act as witnesses for our new friends. Not that either of us can pay attention to the ceremony.

I don't know what thoughts are cycling through Luna's head, but from the way she stares at the ceiling, I know her brain is busy at work.

"Can I see the picture?" I whisper to her.

Luna starts, then she swipes through her phone, tilting the screen so we both can see.

Hell, it's glorious.

Margaret got us when I'd lifted Luna. One of her legs bends slightly, giving the lift a whimsical air. And with the way our eyes are closed, we both seem completely lost in the passion of the moment.

I know I was.

"Lawyer can't complain about this," she murmurs.

My happy excitement dims at her words. Of course. Naive of me to read more into the exchange than there was.

Luna was acting the part. Just like she said she'd do.

This is fake. This is all fake, I remind myself.

I turn my attention back to the couple in this room who are actually in love. The way Margaret and Tiffany gaze into each other's eyes is something from a romance novel. Pure and inspiring to observe.

My chest aches from watching it. From wanting it.

Could Luna ever look at me that way? Am I being unfair for hoping?

Maybe I should give up the fanciful notions I have about the two of us. Just fulfill the task of being her fake husband like I agreed to and not strive for anything more. That would be the honest approach.

But can I give up hope that her kiss—that amazing, ground-rattling kiss—meant nothing?

I don't know what to do with all these feelings that keep growing. The woman beside me is sun, dirt, and water for these emotions, and the roots are spreading deep into my chest, finding cracks and crevices in which to tether until I'm not sure I'll be able to uproot this longing.

"You are now wife and wife," the judge declares, and Tiffany gives a whoop before planting her own passionate kiss on her partner. Neither of them ask for a picture because their relationship is not for show. There's no ulterior motive.

Their connection blooms from pure love.

Just as I feel a dip in my lips, the despondence in my chest dragging away my joy, there's a sudden pressure against my palm.

And that's when I realize Luna has slid her hand into mine.

As we watch the two women celebrate their love, I give Luna's fingers a gentle squeeze, and she offers a firm press back.

Chapter Eighteen

CHARLIE

"Do you listen to country music?" Luna glances at me as we walk down a street in the heart of Nashville, side by side but not hand in hand.

Maybe I could convince her it's best for our ruse if we're touching at all times. If only she didn't have a perfectly honed bullshit detector.

"Sometimes. If the mood strikes me." My favorite genre changes practically moment to moment. "Safe to say I like all genres, but judge things song by song."

Luna lets out a gusty sigh like my answer was not at all what she wanted to hear.

"You sound like a music nerd."

"Is that a thing?"

"Of course. You can be a nerd about anything. My roommate in college was a mushroom nerd. She would pull over on the side of the road if she saw a decaying log she thought looked promising."

"Ooh, I have a fun mushroom mind teaser."

Her brows scrunch. "What does that mean?"

"Get this." I shift, walking backward, able to watch Luna's face as I talk. "People eat dead mushrooms, and mushrooms eat dead people." I mime a bomb going off near my temples. "Just blew your mind, right?"

"Oh, no." Luna's eyes are wide as she shakes her head. "You're a dorky dad too. And you don't even have kids."

"Never too early to start with dad jokes." I settle back into her pace beside her. "Do you want me to keep the dorkiness on the DL or something?" The idea has me shoving my hands in my pockets so she doesn't see the anxious way I crack my knuckles. The pops still sound through the material, just muffled.

Working as a salesperson, I know how to adjust the way I portray myself to make the people around me comfortable. I can play the blandly normal non-dork with a little code-switching, but I'd hoped Luna wouldn't mind. Shutting down key parts of a personality isn't the best way to build a relationship.

"Dork it up. Whatever. It's the music nerd I'm worried about." Luna stops then, grabbing my forearm. "Have you heard of Violet Bluefield?"

"Oh, yeah! Her voice is gorgeous. And the way she plays the banjo could make the snobbiest classical fan fall in love with the instrument."

Luna squeezes her eyes shut as if in pain. I shut up.

When she blinks them open again, I'm distracted by how warm the dark brown of her irises are. I want to sink into my wife's gaze. My body leans toward her until I have the presence of mind to stop myself. Luckily, there's a decent distance I would have to cross to get to her.

"Violet Bluefield is my client."

I work to remember what we were just talking about. Then the facts all resurface.

"Really? That's dope! I'm sorry, I didn't realize I married a woman rubbing shoulders with A-listers. You need me to be your arm candy on the red carpet? I'm happy to hold your purse. But only if it matches my tie. We'll need to color coordinate."

Luna glares, but her lips curl in a reluctant smile.

Success.

"You're ridiculous. And no, I don't walk red carpets." The amusement in her expression fades away, and I get a grip on my natural tendency to joke when I sense she has something important to tell me.

"I've worked hard to develop good relationships with my clients. In my business, it's all about reputation. Most of the people who hire me learn about my services through word of mouth. If I get a bad mark against my name, I'm done."

Making sure she knows I'm serious, I keep my voice steady, focus on her. "I'd never want to mess your work up, Luna."

She stares deeper into my eyes. "I get that. But this is more than just not insulting people." Luna steps closer, lowering her voice. "One common reason these women hire me is because they've had a bad interaction with a fan. They're in the public eye, and people stop respecting boundaries. They have to fight for personal space. I can't bring someone around them who threatens that. Do you understand?"

After traveling with my mom, I probably have a better idea than most.

"Of course. I swear I will be respectful to anyone you introduce me to, famous or not." I raise my palm as if swearing in court. "And I will take special consideration with your clients. I promise."

An air of tension eases from Luna's whole being, and that's when I realize she's held tight to a bundle of stress since we left her house.

"Good." She releases her grip on my arm and keeps walking. "And I'm not saying you have to pretend like you don't know who Violet is or that you can't compliment her music. I just wanted to make sure you didn't treat her like she was a pretty toy to be touched."

"Don't worry." My hands find a home deep in my pockets. "I will keep my hands to myself."

Besides, Violet Bluefield isn't the woman I want to caress.

We walk another ten minutes before reaching the shop, but the day is cool, and strolling quietly at Luna's side is peaceful. My mind relaxes into the moment, not bothering with anxious thoughts or worries. I finally understand the appeal of meditation.

A collection of Gibsons sits in the window of C & M Guitars. If my guess is right, there's one from each decade, spanning back to the 1960s. Alejandro, the bass player in my mother's band and the man who taught me everything I know about guitars, would love this place. Hell, I bet he's been here before.

Luna steps inside, and when I follow, I lose myself in the sights. The space is all kinds of warm wood. The floor we stand on and the instruments set out for customers to browse through. Without considering my bank account, I start making a mental list of all the pieces I'd love to take home with me.

I'm no expert musician, but I can appreciate a beautiful piece when I see one.

With impressive effort, I stifle my curious fingers, following Luna, who heads toward the back counter. Three people stand together, two of them conversing over a banjo while the third person, a tall, broad-shouldered man with hard eyes that seem to see everything, tracks my partner and I as we move closer.

"Violet. Hi!" Luna calls out when we're still ten feet away.

The woman gives a little start, but then she turns to us with a sheepish grin.

"Hey ya, Luna. Guess I need to practice my observation skills. Didn't even realize y'all were in the building."

"It takes practice." My wife's voice has a soothing note I heard her use at the animal shelter when praising a nervous dog. "Remember to listen for more than just voices. And practice counting people in the room regularly."

Violet nods, and I watch her gaze bounce around to the other customers, marking the number of people present.

That's when I fully recognize her. I'd been wondering if Luna maybe saw someone else she knew and we were talking to them while waiting for the country music star. But I realize I know this woman's face from billboards and album covers and awards shows.

The recognition took me a minute because of her hair.

Violet Bluefield has curly, moss-green hair that shines bright under stadium lights and gives her an otherworldly appearance.

The woman in front of me has straight, ordinary brown locks flowing out from underneath a baseball hat. I wonder which one is the wig. Luckily, I have enough sense not to embarrass Luna by asking the question aloud.

"Eight people in the shop, including us five. I'll keep practicing," Violet says. Then her attention lights on me. "Now you I don't know."

Luna sets a hand on my bicep, a claiming gesture. "Charlie, this is Violet Bluefield. Vi, this is Charlie. My... husband."

At Violet's brows raise, it's clear I'm not the only one who heard that hesitation before the title.

The corner of Luna's mouth ticks up. "We just got married. Last week. Still getting used to calling him that."

The country star gasps, then opens her arms wide. "That's amazing! Can I hug you? You can say no. Manuel says no ninety-nine percent of the time."

Luna steps forward into Violet's arms and lets the singer hug the breath out of her. When they separate, the woman's green eyes alight on me.

"Same offer, Charlie. Hug. Yes or no?" She's got her arms open again, and never one to turn down physical affection, I accept.

"Good to meet you," I say as she wraps a firm set of arms around my ribs. I gently return the embrace, fully aware of the burning attention on me. But when I step back and glance over at Luna, she seems mildly happy. That's when I realize the heat comes from the man who clocked the both of us the second we entered the store.

This guy doesn't need any advice from Luna. He's gotten his training elsewhere.

"I can't believe you snuck yourself a husband without me knowing. And no wedding invite! You're lucky I don't hold petty grudges." Violet's eyes bounce between the two of us.

"Courthouse wedding," Luna explains.

"Hmm. Fine. But I'm gonna get you a huge obnoxious present. Fair warning." The musician turns to her companions, giving the staring man a knock on the arm with her knuckles as if he's a wooden door. "This is Manuel, my new bodyguard. He's got a stick way up his ass, but I love that about him. Plus, he hates country music. Aren't we a pair?" She grins up at her security. "Will you give my friends a big ol' howdy?" When Violet talks to Manuel, her accent magically grows thicker.

The man gives us both a curt nod. No hug from him.

Luna nods back, appearing satisfied with the stony man. I'm tempted to grin wide and hold my hand out for a fist bump. But that might cause the guy to short circuit. So I just nod too.

And wonder about the one percent of times he's accepted a hug from Violet.

The singer turns to the final member of our group, who's stayed on the periphery until now, her attention on an instrument laid out on the counter. "And this goddess of guitars and other stringed instruments is Cassandra, owner of the shop and repair extraordinaire. I'm not lying, am I?"

Cassandra glances up, removing a set of glasses before acknowledging Violet.

"I can re-fret it. But with these classics, I charge more. And they take longer."

"Oh, that's fine. I'm not touring until the summer. But I'd love to take my Daddy's banjo with me. Never had her on the road before."

The shop owner nods. "I'll finish long before that. Let me get my work form, we'll talk the repair details and have you sign off, then you'll be good."

Violet turns big eyes to Luna. "Do you mind waiting a bit? This is why I had you meet me here. Wasn't sure how long this would take."

Luna shrugs. Her neutral stance about spending more time in the shop reveals my wife doesn't fully appreciate the treasure trove of music we're standing in.

Leaning down, I place my hand on her back and my lips closer to her ear. "You mind if I browse around?" I ask.

Luna blinks in surprise. "You want to buy something?"

I shrug. "More like window shop. Spent a lot of time with my Mom's band."

Confusion twists her brows before they shoot up her forehead. "I can't believe I forgot." She mimes banging her forehead against my chest. "You didn't need my talk about how to act, did you?"

Her embarrassment makes Luna irresistibly cute, and I give into the urge to press a kiss against her forehead.

"A reminder never hurts." I step back. "Now I saw a 1961 Jazzmaster I'd give both my kidneys for. You can find me jamming over there." I gesture toward the front of the shop.

Already I can feel the strings under my fingers. The relief and joy of playing something beautiful. Hopefully, that'll take some of the edge off the fact that I can't strum pleasurable noises out of Luna like I've been longing to since we first met.

Chapter Nineteen

LUNA

"He's pretty good." Violet walks with me down an aisle of guitars toward Charlie, Manuel following a few steps behind.

My fake husband sits on a stool, his body curled around an old electric guitar. That's my extent of knowledge when it comes to identifying these instruments. I'm not musical in the slightest.

Love listening to the stuff, but I couldn't even master the recorder in elementary school.

"I'll take your word for it," I say. Whatever Charlie is strumming sounds pleasant, but I couldn't have said if the song was the easiest thing to learn or a master-level arrangement. Before we reach him, his long fingers stop their talented dance as he converses with a young guy in torn jeans hovering next to his stool.

"...and you see here, this has had a beautiful restoration. I mean, look." Charlie holds up the guitar at eye level for both him and the stranger he's talking to. "A lot of Jazzmasters have a neck angle problem. People try to correct them with a shim, but then that causes bowing in the neck. This one has a nice straight line. And the frets are all perfectly level. Just gorgeous."

"Man. I never knew," the guy says, eyes flitting between the instrument and Charlie, tinged in awe.

"Yeah. Each of these has its own quirks and history. Are you interested in a classic?"

"Totally. I'm all about vintage. Are you buying that one?" The young guy has the look of a hipster. People often use the moniker with disdain, but I'm a fan. Where hipsters congregate, there's usually excellent beer and tasty food trucks. Plus, they're bringing back an interest in nutritious, unprocessed ingredients, which helps with my business.

"Oh, no. I wish. Not in the budget right now. Besides, I have three beauties at home I haven't touched in ages. Can't make a good argument to buy more until I get back in the playing habit." Charlie sets the guitar back on the display stand. "But whoever adds this one to their collection is a lucky SOB. They'll have some envious glares when they bring it out onstage." My fake husband runs one more loving gaze over the instrument, then lifts his head and finds us all watching him. "Hey! Sorry, are you ready to go? Didn't mean to hold you up."

"Don't apologize!" Violet waves a hand. "Love to hear a man compliment beautiful craftsmanship."

Out of the corner of my eye, I catch the almost imperceptible tightening of Manuel's mouth. I wonder if Violet was aiming a well-aimed dig at the guy, or if he just doesn't like it when his client goes around complimenting men.

Interesting. If we weren't in a business relationship, I might try asking her about it.

Violet and I have very different personalities, but I still enjoy whenever we have sessions together. There's an ease between us that doesn't happen often with my clients.

Maybe that's her habit of saying outrageous things.

Or maybe I'm just starved for companionship. I'd be lying if I said having Charlie around my house is horrible. I shouldn't get used to him. Then I might come to depend on him, and that's a whole bucket of issues I'd have to deal with when we peace out in a year.

"You don't have to leave," I offer to Charlie. "We're just going food shopping. You should stay here. Play with all the toys."

"Instruments," Violet corrects with a playful prod to my side.

I smirk her way before meeting Charlie's eyes again. Or at least attempt to. He's currently gazing around the place as if already imagining his hands on every guitar in the shop.

Lucky guitars.

Shut up, horny brain.

"You don't mind?"

"Nope. I'll text you when we're done and come back to pick you up then."

Fifteen minutes later, Violet, Manuel, and I enter an organic grocery store. I don't demand my clients eat organic food. As a dietitian I try to work with realistic expectations, and if they don't want to go to the more expensive grocery store, that's their choice. But Violet let me know she's all organic. To the hipster market we go.

"You really think with the right diet I could be as strong as you?" The country singer glances at my biceps. I get a sudden flush of pleasure. With my shorter stature, people rarely notice my strength.

Not until they see me go a few rounds in the gym or get into a brawl.

Not that I brawl often.

Hearing the observation from Violet threatens to inflate my ego.

"Diet and the right exercise. Yes. No doubt in my mind."

"Well then." The A-lister makes sure her hat and wig are in place, then grabs a cart. "Lead the way. Pour all the magic food in my cart. Please and thank you."

Her supplicant tone has me smirking. No way are we going that route. People can buy all the healthy food they want, but if they don't eat a bite, then it doesn't matter.

"You point out the things you would normally buy. We'll work from there."

Over the next half hour, we talk through Violet's eating habits. There are some items I switch out for healthier versions with similar tastes. Food that I encourage her to consume more of for the benefit to her muscles, and items I suggest as occasional treats rather than staples of her diet.

Somewhere along the line, Violet starts treating the experience like a game, picking random items and asking me yes, no, or switch.

Then I test her.

All the while Manuel is our silent shadow.

"Oh, goodness. I know these are a no already, but my lord. Just look at them." She picks up a large plastic-wrapped package of some name-brand cupcakes. The things are basically handfuls of sugar begging to rot out the teeth of innocent children. And country music singers.

Still, this isn't about denying her things.

"Like I said. Make them a special snack." I step past her and point to a similar package. "Here. These are wrapped individually. You're more likely to only eat one rather than binging."

"Makes sense." Violet sets down her handful and reaches for the alternative.

Then she groans. "Goodness gracious. They've got chocolate and butterscotch." She scoops them up and faces Manuel, as if they've been shopping together today. "Which one?"

"Neither," he deadpans.

"Oh, I see how it is. Trying to impress the dietitian." Violet sets the butterscotch cakes back on the shelf and tosses the chocolate in the cart. "Manuel, why don't you be a dear and walk down the other aisle? You can meet us at the end. I just want to gossip with Luna without you hovering."

The bodyguard doesn't glance at her, gaze scanning the store. "No."

Violet keeps a positive expression on her face even as I watch a muscle in her jaw tick. "And why not?"

"My job is to protect you. I need to see you to protect you."

"But I'm with Luna. My self-defense expert." Flipping her fake brown hair over her shoulder, she affects a stage whisper. "She's got a gun, you know?" Violet gives him an exaggerated wink.

I can hear the strain of him trying not to roll his eyes. "I know."

Good. Any decent security should be able to clock a holster, despite the weapon hiding under my jacket.

"Well then, I think she's perfectly capable of protecting me for one aisle. Besides, it's the feminine product aisle. I'm sure you don't want to be there for that. You know, uterus, fallopian tubes, ovaries, periods. So gross."

His stony face doesn't change as he speaks. "I don't care how heavy your flow is."

Good thing I'm not expected to remain stoic, because that has me snorting.

Violet gasps, then glares in her best attempt at fierceness. "You know nothing about my menstruation, Manuel!"

Again, I give the guy credit for not cracking.

My client turns back to me. "Are you still in the ooey-gooey honeymoon phase where you can't be separated from your man for more than a few minutes?"

"I don't think I was ever in that phase." I do my best to affect the same emotionless tone Manuel used, but Violet merely shakes her head at me.

"Well, that's a bummer. You should work on that. Still, yay for me! Because I want you to come over tomorrow night. Just to hang out. As friends."

My mind stutters over the request. "What?"

"I swear this isn't because I don't want to pay you for your expertise. If we end up talking about nutrition or self-defense, I'll start the clock. But I'm thinking more of a wine and gossip situation. Please? You can say no. I know I'm a little much. That's why Manuel won't hug me."

"I..." Normally I'm quicker than this. But I've never been invited to hang out by a client before. Sure, I've been gifted backstage passes or told my name is on a list at a hot new club. But those were more bonus gifts meant for me to use at my own discretion.

This is friendship.

And that's a strange sensation.

Still, if I've learned one thing about Violet, it's that she's one hundred percent sincere. Almost to a fault. Which means, this invite is real.

"Yes. I...yes, I would like that."

"Ooh, I want to hug you again. But I won't." She marches into the aisle, tossing some tampon boxes into the cart. "Now to the wine! I can have that, right? If you tell me no, I'm going to be such a bitch."

"In moderation," I answer in a daze.

"That's not in her vocabulary," I swear I hear Manuel mutter as he passes by me, following his bubbly employer.

Chapter Twenty

LUNA

"How does someone become a self-defense dietitian?" Charlie's question comes with genuine curiosity in his voice, so I don't immediately put my shields up. When I've stated my job title in the past, people have looked at me like I declared I wanted to be mayor of the moon.

Self-defense dietitian isn't that weird of a word combination.

Okay, maybe it is, but people could still give me the benefit of the doubt.

"I went to college for nutrition. Here in Nashville. I got a full academic ride. Applied for every scholarship I could find and landed a few." I spent all my days after school at the public library using the computers to find the funds to get out of my parents' house. When I got the congratulations letters I cried in my car, the only safe place I had at the time.

"Still had to pay for food and my apartment. I got a few jobs. One was the graveyard shift at a 24-hour gym."

Charlie winces on my behalf, but I shrug, taking a slow sip of my mint chocolate milkshake. After picking him up from the guitar shop, I decided to treat my fake husband to one of my favorite desserts in the city and walk him around downtown. Now we meander along the sidewalks, dodging tourists and listening to the country music spilling out from the different bars. The sun is high and hot, and I tilt my face up to soak in a few more rays as I continue laying out the map of my past.

"Working nights wasn't bad. I slept in the evenings after I got out of class and before my shift started. I did all my classwork at the desk because there wasn't much to fill the time. When I finished my assignments, I needed something else to keep awake, so I grabbed a few pieces of equipment—just weights and stuff—and worked out at the desk. Couldn't use any of the machines while I was on shift because it would've meant abandoning my post."

The life I grew up in made me tough, but not necessarily physically strong. The amount of money Bill and Vivian Lamont left for their kids' food was a lot less than they spent on the latest TV or knock-off designer bag. When I had my own money, access to a gym, and finally some actual knowledge about nutrition, I watched my body get stronger each day.

I'll never be huge, but I'm hardier now.

"Working out got you interested in self-defense?" Charlie glances down at me as we wait at a crosswalk.

"Not exactly. There were security cameras set up around the gym, and my boss saw the video of me doing my desk workouts. Instead of getting mad, he was impressed. He asked if I'd be willing to do an instructional video for them to put on the website."

"Nice." Charlie toasts me with his milkshake before taking a long pull from the straw. He opted for strawberry, and I wonder if kissing him would taste like the pink drink.

Stop imagining kissing your fake husband.

I shake my head and return to the story. "Yeah. I felt awkward at first. I'm not the bubbly, motivational type. But Treyvon—the gym owner—told me to go through reps just like I was explaining the steps to him. No need to cheerlead. He posted the recording, and people liked it. We guess because I showed a full-blown workout they could do at their desk. Most desk workouts are more about getting people to stand up and get their blood flowing again. Mine involved building muscle. Getting stronger."

Charlie nods as I speak. "Okay. Some of the dots are connecting now. What happened next?"

"Treyvon was a retired vet. He was on a team that would be sent in to rescue hostages. Really intense stuff." Was one of the reasons I never minded working for him. He wasn't just a random guy who decided to get ripped one day and open a gym the next. Not that there's something wrong with that. Only I'm not about to hand out my respect to a person just because they've piled muscle onto their frame. That's no true strength in my book.

But Treyvon went through some shit and came out on the other side. And he didn't brag about it.

"He had an idea for a side business. One that taught people how to escape kidnapping situations on their own." I'd been in awe of the concept when he mapped everything out for me. And intimidated. And wildly excited because I wanted to learn every tip and trick he had.

"His goal was to get some A-list clientele, but he knew there was a chance he wouldn't be taken seriously seeing as how it was a new business." Which baffled me, because who wouldn't take Treyvon, the war-hardened vet, seriously? "After my desk workout video did well, he had the idea to make a whole series of videos where we'd demonstrate self-defense techniques and escape maneuvers. He's a big guy—I'm talking taller than you, three times the muscle. While I might be strong, I'm still a short woman. So we teamed up, with me showing how anyone can learn the moves. We made a whole series and got an online following. That built a buzz, which bled into a few pieces on us in local papers and a couple of visits to local morning shows. Once that happened, the business got clients. When I graduated, Treyvon offered me a full-time job." I pause to take another sip of my treat before continuing. "It was a great opportunity, but I'd spent all this time on my degree. Even after I graduated, I went on to become a certified dietitian, and I hated that I wasn't doing anything with that knowledge."

After passing a brick building, we come upon a small park, and we both turn into it without a word.

"What'd you do?" Charlie tosses his empty cup in a trash can before refocusing on me.

"An anxious client gave me an idea. She was nervous from the start, which was understandable. Treyvon simulated realistic kidnapping scenarios, and those are terrifying even if you know they're fake. But we were still going over removing handcuffs when she just broke down sobbing in the middle of the room." I chuckle thinking back on the day and all of our stunned faces. We weren't a group equipped to deal with tears. "Then she said 'I can't do this. Not in a weekend. Not in a month. I don't know how to become this person.'" I'm able to repeat the words perfectly because they were the ones to put me on a new path. They're burned in my brain. "That's when it clicked."

"What?" Charlie asks in a hushed voice, and I'm proud of the way I've captivated him.

"She was right. Survival is a lifestyle, and we were trying to cram the new mentality into a handful of days." I make a sweeping motion with my hand, imagining all the skills we taught those people seeping out from between my fingers just like it would leak from their minds with disuse. "Treyvon's simulation was great for showing people what a real kidnapping would be like. But if someone wanted to know how to get out of one, they'd need more training. You don't learn how to drive a car by doing it once and then never again until you're in an emergency. That's how you wreck."

"You broke off from Treyvon's company?" Even as Charlie asks, he gestures to a bench, and we settle onto the seat side by side.

"More like I became another branch. I gave that woman my number and told her to call me with days and times she'd like to go over the skills. That we'd practice until they were as easy as getting dressed in the morning. And when we reached that point, she'd come back for the simulation. She was my first client, and she directed some of her friends to me." I turn to fully face Charlie, hearing the passion in my own voice as I discuss this topic that I've built my career on. "Part of escaping is strength, and part of building enduring muscle is your diet, so my skill sets all naturally grew together until I became the Self-Defense Dietitian. Now I train my clients for weeks or months, sometimes years, and part of that training is to go through Treyvon's different simulations multiple times. He never minded me breaking off since I'm still the main person funneling him business."

Charlie taps his knuckles against the old wood of the bench as he seems to get lost in whatever thoughts fill his head. "You work with all famous musicians?"

"They're my main clientele because a lot of my business is from word of mouth and that first woman I took on was a country singer. But I also work with some actresses, a handful of businesswomen, and even two politicians." As I mentally tick through my past customers, I sip my treat.

"I think you're amazing." Charlie's statement has me sucking up too much milkshake in shock. I swallow hard and fight off a brain freeze.

"You what?" The question comes on a scoff, but my fake husband just smiles, the tension in my spine disappearing with his natural ease automatically relaxing me.

"I think you're amazing," he repeats. "You've got this impressive skill set, and I just want to get on a megaphone and shout to the world 'My wife is a badass!'" Charlie cups a hand around his mouth, miming the megaphone. "Do you ever work with us average folk?"

"I host a self-defense class at the gym where I used to work. Once a month. Anyone is welcome to come, but I mainly get women." I stare toward the sky, not sure I can handle the intensity of Charlie's gaze on me. "And last year we updated all the videos."

There's the lightest sensation on my cheek, and I glance over to find Charlie's eyes on my face.

"I need to watch every single one of those."

I snort. "Want to practice all the moves too?"

His eyes grow hot with his slowly unfurling grin. "You can tie me up any day."

Chapter Twenty-One

LUNA

I half expect Manuel to open the door when I arrive at Violet's loft apartment. But the stoic security guard is nowhere in sight when the country singer flings open the heavy, metal door to her home.

"Oh, good. I was worried you were going to back out on me." Violet smiles wide, stepping back to wave me inside.

"This is nice," I offer, gesturing around her place. The loft is smaller than I thought it would be. Not that it's small. The place has ceilings high enough for two floors, and my guess is the square footage is the same amount as in my whole house. But from what I can see, this main room is all there is other than an open door that leads off to a bathroom.

I spy Violet's bed arranged against a brick wall on the far side of the space.

"I like an open floor plan," the singer explains, striding over to the kitchen area, her bare feet padding lightly across the hardwood floor.

I guess this apartment makes sense when I connect it to Violet's personality rather than what I expect her net worth is. Open, airy, honest. And then there's the array of instruments hanging on the spaces of wall between each tall window.

The complete exposure makes it even clearer that Manuel isn't around, unless he's hunkered down in the clawfoot tub.

"No security shadow today?" I follow her to the butcher-block kitchen island and see a neatly arranged selection of finger foods. A lot of them we bought together on the grocery store run.

"Nope. Figured my self-defense coach wasn't someone I needed to worry about." Her warm, welcoming expression falters. "Shit. Was that wrong? Should I be on guard here too?"

"No." I hold up my hands, trying to show there's nothing she needs to worry about from me. "I don't want to train you to distrust everyone in your life." Even though that's kind of par for the course with me. "You'll become paranoid if you live like that."

Violet's tension drains away, relief suffusing her face. "Okay. Yeah. He lives just across the hall though. If I need him."

"Really?"

Violet nods as she pulls open her fridge. "My brother bought the apartment. He's the one who hired Manuel. Do you want something to drink?" She rattles off a list of beverages, and because I'm trying to get comfortable in this whole Violet-is-my-friend thing, I accept a beer.

That earns me a beaming expression. "If you're drinking a beer, then that means I can! Hell yeah!"

My mouth creeps up in a smile when she passes a cold bottle to me. But what she said just before the drink offer sticks in my mind.

"Your brother really bought a place for your security guard in your building?"

Violet takes a deep draw of her drink before answering. "He's overprotective. Not without cause. But I already told you about that."

She had. When Violet and I first met, she described an incident with a delusional fan that almost ended in her losing her life.

"I guess I'm not surprised by what he did. More that your brother is the one doing it."

Shit. Put a woman in front of me who's offering to be my friend, and I suddenly start picking at inner scabs that should be left alone.

Violet hops up on a padded stool and then pats the one beside her. Hesitantly, I join.

"You got some brother problems too?"

I shrug, then take a long pull from my beer. The fizz and subtle hint of alcohol put me at ease, and more truth leaks out of me.

"Yeah, but not like you. I guess I'm always the one trying to be the protector."

Violet smirks. "That doesn't surprise me."

I snort. "Right? But they're not like you. I mean, something happened to you. You had no control over it. But my brothers...hell, for a while there I felt like they wanted to fuck up their lives. Like that was their goal. And I tried to keep it from happening, but everything went south anyway."

When I found out Dash and Leo got caught in a hot car, that they were in jail and waiting for trial, something in my chest crumpled. I'd failed them, and I couldn't help.

Now they're out, and Dash has cleaned up his life.

But I'm back to trying to save Leo.

"Well, I can't say I know what that feels like, since I've only ever been the kid sister. But—" Violet taps the neck of her bottle to mine. "—even when my brother goes overboard with his protective shit, I can never get too mad. 'Cause I get that he's doing it all because he loves me. Which is why I may give Manuel a hard time, but I don't try to duck him or anything. Which I bet I could do now that I'm taking your lessons." She winks at me, and we share a laugh. "Anyway, I'm just saying, if your brothers are any kind of smart, they realize what you do for them and appreciate your love."

Suddenly, my cheeks grow very warm. No one has ever complimented me on my loving ability before. Normally I get called a bitch, and I embrace that moniker.

"Maybe," I mutter before sipping my beer.

"And now you have Charlie!" She holds her beer up as if in a toast. "He seems like a capable guy. You're not protecting him too, are you?"

My mouth pops open, then slowly closes as I consider her words.

In the beginning, I thought I would be. Providing him a place to live and paying him part of my inheritance. Being his sugar momma. But this past week together, I haven't felt like his caretaker. Maybe we've fashioned together a different kind of relationship.

"He's more like my partner," I admit.

Violet reaches out to squeeze my shoulder. "That's great. That sounds like exactly what you need. And after a few drinks, I'm going to ask you for all the dirty details, but right now I need to show you the real reason I asked you to come."

There's a twisting in my stomach. This is where Violet asks me about security measures for her apartment or to rate the foods in her pantry based on their nutritional values. Things I'm not opposed to doing, but I'd hoped this interaction could deviate from my professional life.

Violet hops off her stool and jogs over to a giant TV. Woven baskets sit on the bottom of the TV stand, and she pulls one out, removing crinkly, folded mats that when unrolled reveal huge arrows pointing in different directions.

"Have you ever played Dance Dance Revolution?"

"I—what?"

"DDR. I tried playing by myself, but it's no fun that way. And Manuel said I could double his salary and he still wouldn't step on—these are his words—that electronic monstrosity." She gives me the biggest puppy dog eyes I've ever seen. And Dash can lay them on thick when he wants. "Will you play with me?"

Suddenly, I start laughing. I don't know where the sound comes from, but hell, does the bubbling joy of it feel good. I let the sound roll through me, then I throw back my beer and wipe away the dribble from the side of my mouth.

"You better not be a sore loser," I taunt.

Her returning grin has a hint of evil I've never seen on her sweet face. "Cocky much? You might be able to take me down in the gym, but this is DDR." Violet arranges the mats in front of the entertainment center. "Get ready to get your ass kicked."

Chapter Twenty-Two

LUNA

"We're just going to tell them we're married." I try to say the statement with utter surety as I meet Charlie's eyes where he sits in the passenger seat.

"Whatever you want to do," he says. Supportive, as always. "I'll follow your lead."

Guess this is happening. I climb out of the car.

Dash and Paige's home is a cute little thing. Not a house I ever imagined my brother living in, but to be honest, I never thought he'd live a domestic life. I just worried about him living, period.

Now he's married, got a house and a dog and a full-time job he loves. Working on cars, true. But not like Uncle Mike. Dash is legit. Manager of an auto shop. Maybe a strange job for a guy who used to steal cars.

Or maybe the most natural thing in the world.

"Hi!" Paige opens the door before we knock, waving us inside. "Dash and the dogs are out back. Food is in the living room. I made plenty."

My sister-in-law gives Charlie a one-armed hug around his waist, then leads us through the warmly decorated living space until we reach the sliding glass doors. When we step outside, I watch as my younger brother plays tug-o-war with two pit bulls simultaneously. From the way they whip their strong heads back and forth, trying to wrench the ropes away from him, I know my brother will have sore shoulders tonight.

My eyes go to the round gray dog, and I'm hit with a punch of rightness to see Pig so happy, her body and tail wiggling in joy as she plays.

"Dash! Luna and Charlie are here!" Paige calls out as we linger on the porch.

Dash lets the ropes drop, then scoops up a tennis ball and sends it flying. As the dogs sprint after the new distraction, my brother makes his escape, jogging over to us.

"Hey." He wraps me in a hug, and I smell motor oil on his clothes. I wonder if that scent is ingrained in his skin now. "Want to say hi to Pig?"

"Definitely." I follow him, crouching low when the chunky puppy lumbers up to me. "Hey, girl." I scratch her just under the chin, and she snuffles my shirt. "Miss me?"

I take her doggy grin as a yes.

Charlie and I decided us taking a trip to New Orleans to pick up Pig made more sense than asking Paige to transport her. This way, we can also share the awkward news of our nuptials.

"Time to go inside and eat," Paige calls out. I give Pig a final pat, toss a squeaky toy across the yard, then follow everyone inside.

There are plenty of places to sit, but I gravitate toward the loveseat where Charlie settled, dropping onto the cushion beside him. When I turn my head, I find him staring down at me, and I offer him a tight smile. This next bit is about to get awkward. Might as well eat before we drop our bomb. I dig into the finger foods Paige arranged on the coffee table.

For a stretch, Dash and Paige talk me through the steps I'll take for Pig's adoption, but none of that is complicated, and soon the conversation turns to Charlie and me. Here together.

"Your job doesn't mind you taking another trip so soon after our wedding?" Paige fiddles with a tortilla chip as she stares at her friend. "I've been wanting to visit Luna in Nashville too. But Dash and I have to earn some more PTO."

Charlie flicks his eyes to me, and I see the message in them.

Time to start easing into the big news.

"The thing is, I quit my job." There's a strained note under his normally easy manner.

"What?" Paige yelps.

"Yeah." Charlie has the grace to appear chagrined as he meets his best friend's eyes. "It was kind of a spur-of-the-moment thing. And I guess I wanted to tell you when I had a better idea of my next step."

My fake husband glances at me again, and we both know his next step is going to be the real shocker of the evening.

"That's ridiculous. I called you when Martin screwed me over, I had no job, and I was drowning my sorrows by watching a continuous stream of baking shows at my parents' house. You do not need to have your life together to tell me what's going on in it." Paige points my way with a dramatic flourish. "And you told Luna!"

"Well, that's the thing." Charlie props his elbows on his knees. "Luna offered me a place to stay."

Roommates is one way to present our new arrangement.

A bout of surprised silence blankets Paige and Dash as the couple glances between us. Then my sister-in-law grins wide, her entire demeanor flipping like a switch.

"You're living together! That's fantastic." Paige turns her attention to me. "Dash thought you would bite Charlie's head off. But I knew you would be friends."

"Why's that?" I can't help doubting her assumption.

"Because Charlie is friends with everyone. Strangers on the street. The person he sits next to on a plane. The lady behind him in the grocery line."

"I still could have bitten his head off," I point out.

"Maybe." Paige doesn't seem convinced. "But you're loyal. And you love me now, and you know Charlie is one of my only friends. I knew you'd try, which means he'd win you over."

Another silence falls over the room as Charlie grins at me, and I process my sister-in-law's odd way of speaking. Paige does that. Just offers bald honesty.

And damn, is she perceptive.

Originally, I didn't get off to a great start with my sister-in-law. Mainly because I only learned about Paige when she and Dash were dealing with a rough part of their relationship.

But since then, the woman has gotten as close to me as I'll let people get, and I realize she's right. When I first met Charlie, I knew how important he was to Paige, which is one of the reasons I was a nicer version of myself than I tend to be around strangers.

Still, I bet she didn't predict what happened between her best friend and me.

"About that whole friendship thing." I sit up straighter and shove away any hesitation, the way I do with most things in life. "Charlie and I got married."

While Paige's eyes grow wide, Dash's narrow. Both of them showing disbelief in their own ways. Before the pair can start with their interrogation, I keep talking. I lay out my meeting with Uncle Mike, the dollar amount, and how this is the quickest way to get it and get Leo free of the criminal situation.

"Plus, Wai Po was right. I hate the idea of our dad getting the money. That'll be a nice bonus," I finish.

At some point during my explanation, Dash buries his face in his hands.

Paige, however, stares directly at Charlie, the two of them having a silent discussion with a connection only years of friendship can create. I turn my attention to my fake husband, wondering if I'll be able to translate just from his face.

I can't. And for some reason, I get hit with a spike of jealousy.

But that's ridiculous. Charlie and Paige have been friends since they were kids, and I've barely known the guy for a few months. Of course, the two of them have an understanding of each other that borders on telepathy.

Suddenly, Charlie grins wide, the sudden exposure of his teeth stealing my breath. The man has a smile that can stop a heart. Or restart it.

"Okay. Felicitations." Paige raises her glass of water, joy coloring her expression. "How can we help?"

"What?" Dash drags his hands from his face, glaring at the three of us, but mainly at me. "You can't be serious. This is ridiculous."

"Clowns are ridiculous. This plan is full of potential." Paige pats Dash's knee, but the gesture is lost on him as he continues to scowl at me.

"We need to talk. Outside." My brother shoves up from the couch and storms out the back door.

"Luna—" I wave off Paige's concern and press on Charlie's shoulder as I get up, both for balance and to keep him in his seat.

"I'll deal with him. We'll be back."

As I move to step around Charlie, his knees sticking out as a barrier, there's a pressure on my hand. I glance down to see he's grabbed it. He gives a light, comforting squeeze before letting go.

"Good luck."

"Thanks." And funnily enough, that small display of support eases tension in my spine.

At least, until I get outside and face an enraged little brother. Well, younger brother to be more accurate, since Dash is a good foot taller than me.

Damn him and his genes.

"This is a joke," he growls. "Please tell me this is a joke."

"It's not. Deal with it."

"Deal with it?" Dash paces along the edge of the back porch as the two dogs in the backyard watch him. They must have worn each other out because both have sprawled out in the grass, panting heavily, without showing any indication of getting up to say hello.

That's probably better.

"I can't believe you're doing this! I thought you were smarter than this." My brother says this like I'm the irresponsible one in the family.

My calm demeanor chips away at his accusatory tone.

"This wasn't some drunk Vegas wedding. Charlie and I talked it out, and he agreed to help. I don't know why your boxers are in such a twist."

Dash throws his hands up. "Maybe because my sister got married to a stranger in a futile attempt to save our delinquent brother who doesn't want to be saved!"

"Get your head out of your ass," I hiss back. "Charlie isn't some stranger. He's your wife's best friend. And you're naive if you think Leo doesn't want out as bad as you did. But Uncle Mike has him in a chokehold. He's in deeper than you ever were." I stare Dash down, but he just laughs without humor.

"That's a fantasy."

"It's not. I talked to him. Leo asked Mike about leaving, and the asshole demanded twohundred fifty thousand. The same number the old man told me when I went to argue Leo's case. Is that how much you had to pay, Dash? Six fucking figures?"

I can tell my brother is clenching his teeth from the way his jaw muscle pops out.

"No," he eventually admits. Then he points a finger at me. "That doesn't mean you should do all this. Give up the money that Wai Po left you."

"Listen to yourself! All this—" I wave back toward his house where Charlie sits. "—is the only way I get that money. Otherwise, it goes to our shitty father. Bill Lamont getting that money would be the opposite of karma, and you know it."

"Great. Dad won't get the cash, but the criminal organization he works for will. Have you thought about that? How you're handing them all that fucking money to fund all their illegal shit?"

"So what?" The question burst from my lungs in a shout as I battle against the defensive anger in my chest. Hell, I'm tired of this argument that I've already had a hundred times with myself.

"What do you mean so what? You're financing criminals!"

"Don't you get it, Dash?" I step forward, shoving a finger in his chest as if that'll get my words to pierce his thick skull and drive home my point. "I. Don't. Care." I jab with each syllable. "I'm selfish! I don't care about the random people Uncle Mike fucks over. I care about my brothers. You and Leo. I want the two of you to be safe, and fuck the rest of the world!"

My holler echoes across his backyard, probably traveling the entire length of the neighborhood.

When the reverberations of it dwindle, another shout pierces the night from a few houses down.

"Fuck you too!"

Dash and I blink at each other, his shock no doubt matching my own.

Then suddenly we're laughing.

All the tension of the situation melts out of us, the anger rising and falling that easily. Because at the core of every shouted word was the massive amount that we care about each other.

And included in that is Leo.

When our hysteria fades away, the night is eerily quiet. Just the sound of crickets and Pig snuffling in the grass in the corner of the yard.

With a deep sigh, I brace myself for the argument to start up again. "Charlie and I are married. We will be for the next year, and then I'm going to get Leo out of the business. I just—" My throat tightens, and I clear it before pressing on. "I need you to not give me shit about this."

Dash stares at Pumpkin where she snores on the ground in the middle of the yard. He takes his time answering.

"Fine." He rubs the back of his neck. "Fine."

A weight lifts that I didn't realize was dragging me down, and I give into the urge to raise my arms in a shoulder-cracking stretch. Charlie and I made the drive to New Orleans in a day, but it wasn't exactly short, and now my muscles complain with little aches and pinpricks I try to work out.

"You like Charlie?" Dash asks.

That question has me dropping my arms and glancing at my brother suspiciously.

"I trust him to follow through on this, if that's what you mean."

"You two..." He lets the sentence drift off, turning the mystery ending into a question.

"We get along. I think at the end of the year we'll be good friends."

"Friends," he repeats, without inflection.

"Yes," I say, steel in my voice. "Friends. We're just friends."

Chapter Twenty-Three

CHARLIE

"You like Luna." Paige barely waits for the door to shut behind the siblings before she gets straight to the sensitive, secret center. "This is not the normal path of a relationship. Just in case you got confused. The marriage usually comes later."

I grin. "Oh damn. Knew I got something mixed up. Well, guess I'm in it now."

Paige snickers. "Let me get you a beer. I don't know how long that's going to go on for." She waves at the back door where we can hear muffled tense voices.

Paige returns a minute later, carrying a Hefeweizen. I appreciate the wheat beer. One thing I miss about Germany is the beer selection. They know how to brew a delicious wheat over there. Beer might as well be a religion for them.

As I pop the top off the bottle and pour the amber liquid into a glass, Luna and Dash's voices rise to a volume that carries through the back door.

"How's Nashville?" Paige asks, attempting to start a conversation in opposition to the hollering.

"Like what I've seen so far. Luna took me—"

"I care about you and Leo, and the rest of the world can go fuck themselves!" My wife's shout sounds as clear as if she were in the room with us.

Paige and I stare at each other, eyes wide. Then my friend leans forward to squeeze my hand. "I'm sure she cares about you too."

"And you," I add.

"She just wanted a nice dramatic effect for her words."

We nod in agreement, both seeming to have grasped at least a basic understanding of Luna's personality.

Her loyalty.

Abandoning her attempt at small talk, Paige reverts to her original subject. "You like her. What are you going to do about it?"

I shrug and offer a playful smirk. "Marry her?"

Paige just stares at me, waiting for my defense technique to wither and die under her scrutiny.

I sigh. "I'm not sure. But I've got more than a year to figure it out, right?"

"I guess." Paige's lack of confidence has a sharp panic stabbing inside my chest.

"Well, what do you suggest?"

My best friend chews on her lower lip before answering. "Seems like you need to woo your wife."

That's a nice thought, if I could actually make it work.

"Okay. And how exactly do I do that?"

Paige turns her bewildered gaze to me. "I don't know. Why would I know?"

"Maybe because she's your sister-in-law, and you're also a woman?"

Paige fiddles with the end of her ponytail. "We haven't spent too much time together. Not enough for me to know how to attract her at least." She gives me a helpless shrug. "Dash likes when I cook for him. Maybe try that? It could be a family trait. Maybe all the Lamonts are constantly hungry."

"But Luna is a nutritionist. And she makes all her own meals." And makes a lot of mine too. Better than anything I could ever hope to make.

My friend piles cheese on a cracker as she thinks. "Maybe make her snacks then. Or cook on a night she seems busy and it would help her out."

"That could work." We've only been living together a couple of weeks, and her schedule seems to shift based on which clients she's working with. I could probably find a time to take control of the kitchen.

"But there has to be other things. Wooing things that are specific to Luna. You need to keep an eye out for them. What does she like? What does she do for fun?" Paige sits up straight, a triumphant smile curving her mouth. "Give her those things or fill her time with that, and then you'll be an expert wooer."

"I can do that." I think.

Paige gives my knee a friendly squeeze. "You got this. I believe in you." She reaches for her beer, her sip leaving a thin line of foam on her top lip.

Objectively, the sight is adorable. There were plenty of times over the years I tried to convince myself that Paige was the one for me. But that changing our relationship into something romantic never felt right. Then she met Dash, and I knew it would have been a mistake. Paige never looks at me the way she looks at him. And I'm betting I never look at her that way either.

Pretty sure I've stared like a lovesick puppy at Luna more than once.

"I'll ask Dash. He might know the quickest way to her heart."

"I don't think Dash is the best source for wooing his sister," I mutter.

"Why not? He's the person she's closest to in the world, far as I can tell."

"But they're sibling-close."

Paige collapses back onto the couch. "I guess. Being an only child sucks. I don't know what brothers and sisters talk about."

"I guess what we talk about?"

She shakes her head. "But we talk about relationships. You could give a guy some good pointers on how to woo me."

I shrug, not so sure about that. Though it shames me to admit, I was judgmental of Dash when he first came into my friend's life.

Paige had just gotten out of a bad relationship, and I thought she needed to hook up with some random dudes. Not go all gooey-eyed after one with an aloof personality and a criminal record. Seemed to me like she was setting herself up to get hurt.

Couldn't have been more wrong.

Dash is a stand-up guy.

But that still doesn't mean I'm going to approach him for advice about romantically pursuing his sister.

The back door opens, and two dogs charge in, tongues lolling and tails wagging. The Lamont siblings follow the hounds. Both brother and sister have flushed faces and rueful expressions.

"Did you work it all out?" Paige asks.

"Sort of." Dash turns his attention to me, and I suddenly worry he overheard me and is going to start doling out brotherly advice. But no. "You don't have to do this, Charlie. Seriously."

Luna rolls her eyes behind his back.

Does he really think she forced me into this? I guess she could have, but no threats were needed for me to attach myself to Luna Lamont.

"I'm happy to help. And it's not like I'm getting nothing out of the deal." I get to spend an entire year around this captivating woman. "I have a living place, rent-free."

Dash snorts and rubs a hand over his face. "Okay. Fine. You're adults and all that."

"Exactly," Luna adds, probably just to piss her brother off, and by his renewed scowl, it works.

"Right," Paige agrees. "What Charlie and Luna do in their marriage bed is their business."

Luna balks. "What? No! We're just partners. That's all."

"Oh, yes. Duh. You said that already. Guess I forgot. Who wants to order pizza?"

Paige pulls her phone out of her back pocket, presumably to call up the food menu. She may seem unaware of the way she shocked the room, but my guess is my awkward friend knew exactly what she was doing.

Planting a few thoughts. Letting the seeds grow.

Acting as the wing woman to help me woo my wife.

Chapter Twenty-Four

CHARLIE

Sugar melts on my tongue, and I try not to groan at the delicious, familiar flavor.

What would a visit to New Orleans be without indulging in a box of pralines? As the sweetness of the treat fills my mouth, I chew the nutty pecans and wonder if I'll be able to keep from eating the rest before I meet up with Luna.

I'm so involved in the food experience that I almost miss that I'm being watched.

Across the way a guy leans back against a brick building, arms crossed over his chest, stare pointed at me. He's either terrible at being incognito or not trying hard to remain inconspicuous.

What surprises me, more than the fact that the stranger is focused on me, is the guy's face.

It's familiar.

I don't think I've seen him before, but I'd recognize those eyes, that nose, the cheekbones anywhere.

He looks like Luna. A lot like Luna.

Leo.

That's my best guess, unless my wife is hiding more relatives around the city. This has to be her twin brother. And the guy seems fascinated with me.

Did she get in touch with him? I know Luna planned to keep the inheritance payoff to herself for a stretch, but maybe she called her brother and told him she was in town. Or that we were.

As I tuck my wallet into my pocket, I ponder my next move.

I could keep on about my day and let Leo follow me until he gets bored.

Or I could introduce myself.

I've never been good at ignoring obvious things or acting like people don't exist. When I step out on the sidewalk, I look both ways before jogging across the street.

"Hi. Leo, right?" I stop a few feet away, not sure how this exchange will go.

Luna's brother keeps on a passive, mildly interested face, but from the way his eyes narrow, I can guess he didn't expect to be approached. Or for me to know his name.

"Who's asking?"

His defensiveness might put someone else off, but I've never minded being the one to lead a conversation. Maybe that's the salesperson in me.

"I'm Charlie Keller. Saw you watching me from across the street." No reason to dance around the truth. "Figured I'd come say hi."

Leo laughs with a sharp, humorless bark. "Really? Thought you'd show me how big a man you are?"

"I—" That has me rocking back on my heels. Then I recall what I know about Luna's past. The Lamont siblings haven't had an easy time of it as far as I can tell.

Bet this guy is never too far from a fight.

"Yeah. You caught me, Charlie Keller. What the fuck are you gonna do about it?" He says my name with a dark twist. Like he knows something about me, and I try to remember if I have any skeletons in my closet that I should worry about.

There was that time I rolled through a stop sign because I was late for a meeting. But Leo can't know about that.

"Did you need to talk to me about something?" I ask.

Leo shoves off the wall, stepping closer as if he means to intimidate me. Unfortunate for him, I've got a handful of inches on him, so he can't loom over me. Still, I'm completely confident that Leo could beat the shit out of me if he gets the urge. I've never been much of a fighter. Luna could also kick my ass with ease. Paige too.

Better not start making that list because it'd go on for a while.

"I saw you with Luna," Leo hisses. "Looking pretty cozy."

When would he have seen us? Maybe he was watching Dash's house. Or there have been those couple of times we've been around town together. Not sure what Leo means by cozy though. It's not like we're making out in public or anything.

No matter how much I wish we were.

While I'd prefer to have some kind of good relationship with Leo, I'm not going to let him pull this "Keep away from my sister or get a fist in the face" crap. Luna is a grown woman, fully capable of making her own decisions.

"What's wrong with Luna and me getting cozy?"

Suddenly, I'm worried this is a race thing. I know that Luna and Leo and Dash's mom is Taiwanese-American and their dad is white. But being mixed race doesn't mean Leo can't still hold my darker skin against me.

He bares his teeth, growling his next words. "My sister isn't some side piece."

I rock back on my heels. "What?"

Leo sneers down at my hands, and I follow his focus to pick up on what's captured his attention.

My wedding ring.

And that's when I know Luna has told her brother absolutely nothing about what's going on.

I'm not sure how I feel about that.

Luna is going through all this effort to save Leo, and he doesn't even know. He should, shouldn't he? The guy is going to need to know there will be a massive change in his life a year from now. Maybe he could start preparing for it.

Or maybe Luna already has the timing figured out, and she's holding out so as not to give Leo false hope.

False hope about me.

Because I'm the one point this whole plan hinges on. I could leave her at any moment and send the house of cards tumbling down.

Luna trusts me enough to marry me, but not enough that she'll tell her brother about the arrangement.

Maybe that should make me angry. But I'm just sad.

And determined.

A lot of people have let Luna down in the past, but I will not be one of them. I have the sudden urge to prove that to her, here and now.

But she's not here, only Leo. Still, I can make a claim.

"I'm sorry. I don't think I introduced myself properly." I hold my hand out for him to shake if he's willing. "I'm Charlie Keller. Luna's husband."

His new brother-in-law, I realize.

This man and I are tied together. Same with Dash. Whether they're thrilled by the new addition or not, I'm their brother now.

From the shocked expression on Leo's face, I think the guy needs some time to come to terms with the fact.

"We haven't been married long," I assure him. "Only a few weeks."

Leo blinks, and I catch a flash of emotion just before he shuts down his features.

Hurt.

Shit, I wasn't trying to ruin the guy's day.

"You're fucking with me," he deadpans.

"I'm not, but I understand if you don't believe me. It was a courthouse thing. Just us and a couple of witnesses. Still, go ahead and ask Luna. She'll back me up." And maybe hearing that I told her brother about us will help dispel some of her remaining concern.

Leo paces a few steps away from me, ruffling his hair with angry hands. He even moves like his sister, and the déjà vu throws me.

Leo whirls to face me. "This doesn't make sense. Luna is a loner. Always has been. She's not the marrying type." He stalks toward me. "There's a reason. If you're telling the truth, then there's a reason she got married." Perceptive guy. "Do you have something on her?"

Maybe I should be offended. Instead, I decide Leo's reaction is a good sign. Obviously, he still cares about his sister in some capacity. Maybe this guy can be redeemed after all.

As long as he doesn't turn out to be anything like his asshole father.

I hold my hands up, placating. "Your sister isn't the type of woman to give into threats, and I think you know that." I drop my hands then reach into my box, carefully selecting a praline. With what I hope is a calming expression, I offer the sweet to my new brother-in-law. His stare flits between me and the dessert a few times before he reluctantly takes the gift.

This is how Luna and her brothers are. Wary of acts of kindness. Which leads me to believe they grew up expecting the world to deal them blows. Both metaphorically and literally.

"I married Luna because she's fierce and funny, and I want to be around her all the time." Truth. "And she married me for her own reasons. If you want to hear them, talk to her. I doubt you'd believe me about them anyway."

Leo gives a snort of agreement around his full mouth. After he swallows, the guy hits me with another guarded look. "You said a courthouse wedding? Not many people?"

"We didn't invite anyone. Not Dash and Paige. Not even my parents." I don't mention his parents because we both know their daughter wouldn't welcome them near any special occasion in her life.

Leo nods, and I watch as some of the hostility fades from his face. Maybe Leo wants to be more involved in his siblings' lives than he's willing to admit.

"You busy right now?" This is a risk, but my end goal is to earn a spot in their family. Never too early to start. "I'm on my way to meet Luna for a drink. You can hear this all from her."

Leo shoves his hands into his pockets and stares toward the street. "Nah. Can't. Have work tonight."

Working after five on a weekend? I'm about to ask.

But then I realize what kind of work he means. The exact reason Luna and I got married. To free Leo of his obligation to keep up with whatever dark deeds his uncle demands.

"Too bad. We're leaving tomorrow morning, but you should think about taking time off to visit us in Nashville."

Leo studies me again as if my existence confuses him.

"And you should call your sister," I add. "So you know I'm not serving you a plate of bullshit."

Leo blinks, then his careless smirk falls back into place.

"Whatever." He turns and strides away, giving off the air that he could give fuck all what's happening around him.

But I know. I saw those few glimpses, but they were enough.

Leo Lamont cares about his sister.

Chapter Twenty-Five

CHARLIE

When leaving the bathroom for the middle of the night pee, I never expected to run into my wife. Literally.

"Oof." Luna's puff of surprised breath presses against my bare chest, and I shiver at the intimacy of the heat. She shifts back, her movements controlled now despite the unplanned collision.

"Sorry," I whisper, shifting out of the way to clear a path to the bathroom.

But Luna doesn't step through the doorway, and in the soft glow of the nightlight illuminating the hallway, I realize that she's dressed as if to go out. Boots, jeans, long-sleeved shirt.

All black.

"Are you going somewhere?"

"Go back to bed, Charlie." From Luna's stern tone I know that's exactly what I won't be doing. If I'm remembering my bleary glance at the clock correctly, it's just about 3 a.m. Not the time to be going out and doing anything, even in a lively city like New Orleans. Especially because we plan to leave first thing in the morning.

"Where are you going?" I shift my body to the side just as she tries to slide past me.

"I have an errand to run."

"What errand happens at three in the morning?"

My sneaky wife huffs out a sigh. "An unsavory one. Now let me by. I'll see you in a few hours. At breakfast."

"Ah. No. Nope." I place my fists on my hips, taking up even more room in the narrow space.

"Are you trying to stop me?" From the low, threatening octave her voice sits in, I realize I have no chance of holding her back. And Luna knows it.

"Three a.m. errands require backup." Unless this is a booty call and she's about to head over to someone's house for a quick bang. Then my backup would be all kinds of awkward.

We agreed. Single for a year.

And Luna is nothing if not loyal.

It's time that I display the same amount of loyalty to my new wife. If she'll let me.

Luna keeps her voice a low growl. "No way."

"Yes way." I deliver the very mature retort with a confident grin. "Say hello to your new sidekick. Every superhero needs someone to carry their tool belt."

Luna snorts. "I'm not a hero, and by definition a tool belt is wearable. Therefore, no need to have a second body to carry it."

"Then I'll keep an eye on your invisible jet for you." I lean down, doing my best to give her some puppy dog eyes my mom always crumbles for. "Let me come. For my sake."

Luna glares up at me, grinding her teeth. After a second, she offers a curt nod.

"Great." I grin and step back toward my room. "I need to change." And put in my contacts so I can see more than a few feet in front of me. "I'll be two minutes."

"Fine," she mutters, moving toward the front door.

"Oh, and Luna?" When I have her attention, I affect my most innocent smile. "If you forget to wait for me, I'll just wake up Dash and see if he can help me find you."

My lovely wife flips me off. Somehow, from her the gesture seems like an exasperated form of affection.

I hope the threat of me getting her brother involved will be enough to keep Luna from leaving without me, but just in case, I hurry through getting dressed, pulling on black sweatpants and a black T-shirt. It's not the type of outfit I'd normally wear out after dark. As a Black man over six-foot, people are always looking for more reasons to label me as dangerous, and dark clothing apparently fits the bill. Still, I get the sense that Luna is going for incognito. For her, I'll deal with the risk.

Luna sits in her car, engine running. I slide into the passenger seat, and she waits for me to buckle in before slowly driving away from her brother's house, only picking up speed when we're out of hearing distance.

"You going to tell me what this errand is all about?" I ask after five minutes of silent driving.

Luna taps her thumb against the steering wheel, lips twisted. I don't push. My wife is a push-back kind of woman. I wait.

"I don't trust my uncle," Luna says, long enough later that I figured she wasn't going to answer.

"Your Uncle Mike? The one Leo works for?" The guy who runs an illegal chop shop. Color me surprised that he's not the most genuine person in the world.

She nods. "He talks big about honor among thieves and always keeping his word. And I think he mostly sticks to that."

"But?"

"But his business is everything to him. Business is good right now. But I don't know how much I can count on his word if he's suddenly hit. He might decide to close ranks. Go back to just family. He might threaten Leo and Dash to get them to come work for him again."

Asshole. The situation seems inescapable. An ominous low tone that never fades away.

"That's fucked up. Even after you pay him everything?"

Luna's mouth tightens. "I can't risk it."

Unease whispers up my spine as we drive down a street with a lot of industrial buildings.

"What are we doing tonight?"

Luna pulls up to a curb next to an old, abandoned building and throws the car in park.

"You're watching the car. I'm getting some insurance."

. . .

LUNA

"Insurance?" Charlie stares at me. Into me. As if he can coax my entire plan out with enough prolonged eye contact.

He might be the only one who could.

"That's what I said." I turn off the car engine and the lights, letting my eyes adjust to the darkness outside my windshield. My nerves tingle with anticipation. This task calls for skills I haven't used in a very long time.

As I set my hand on the handle, there's a pressure on my shoulder. When I glance back at Charlie, I find his frown in the dark.

I wish I'd gotten out of the house without him noticing.

"Please explain to me what you're about to do." His voice goes deep with a raspy plea. "I'm kinda freaking out over here."

An explanation requires precious minutes, but if I'm right, I have a good bit of time to pull this off.

And I can't risk Charlie trying to follow me.

Like most successful marriages require, I err on the side of honesty.

"On the other side of this—" I gesture to the dark warehouse. "—is the building my uncle's chop shop is in. One of them at least. He may have expanded in the last decade."

If anything, the worried wrinkles around Charlie's frown deepen. "Why are we here? What exactly are you going to do?"

"I'm going to sneak in, get pictures of the VIN numbers of his latest haul, look around for any other incriminating information I can find, then get the hell out before anyone realizes I paid a visit."

Charlie gapes at me, and I try not to sigh in impatience.

"Look. It's not a walk in the park, but I've got this."

"Guards," he croaks out. "There's got to be guards."

"No doubt," I agree. "But they'll be guarding the ground floor. The entrances. No one should be on the roof."

"I don't get it."

Maybe I should've typed this all out in an agenda. Probably would have helped calm my panicked salesman down. "Here's the deal. I'm going up that fire escape." I point out the rusty set of stairs I spotted on my last drive-by of the area. "I'll get to the top of this building, cross over to my uncle's, go in the roof access, and work my way down from the top."

Charlie stares out the windshield as if in a daze, but his mind must still be processing information because he's asking the questions I worked through days ago when I came up with this plan.

"Roof doors lock. You can't just walk in."

"I know how to pick a lock. Unless he's installed some high-tech fingerprint scanner, I won't have a problem." Needing to be done with this conversation, I grab Charlie's wrist, capturing his eyes with mine. My sight has adjusted enough that I can make out his dilated pupils.

"This isn't something I came up with an hour ago. I've thought this through. If there are any unexpected risks that come up, I'll abort. But I need to do this, and I need to go now." I tighten my hold. "Trust me, Charlie. Stay here, and trust that I know what I'm doing."

He swallows hard. Then nods. "How long?"

"What?"

"How long will this take you? If you don't come back when you say you will, I'm calling 9-1-1."

His threat should annoy me, but instead there's an odd warmth that suffuses my chest at the concern lingering in his gaze. "Give me two hours before you start to worry." I plan to be done in one, but no need for him to get trigger-happy if I'm gone longer.

He nods and sits back in his seat. "Be careful. Come back to me."

I'm out of the car before I can analyze the way Charlie said that last line. The quiet of the night presses against me, the air thick with humidity. I'd be more comfortable in shorts and a T-shirt, but I need to blend into the shadows as much as possible. I even have a ski mask tucked in my fanny pack.

Yes, I'm breaking into an illegal chop shop wearing a fanny pack. It's convenient. Deal with it.

To get to the fire escape, I have to scramble on top of a dumpster and jump to catch the bottom rung. Luckily, chin-ups are a regular part of my workout routine, and I only struggle a little to pull myself up the ladder.

Things get easier when I reach the first small landing, the ascent turning into stairs for the next five stories. The rusty metal squeaks under my weight. I step carefully to lessen the volume of my passage.

Maybe Charlie would have felt more at ease if he'd known I snuck out here the first night we got to town to scope things out. I know that this is a huge risk. That my discovery could put the entire deal with Uncle Mike at risk.

When I committed to doing this, I knew I had to do it right.

That's how I know the jump between the buildings is six feet. A leap that may seem daunting but is completely doable.

I crouch on the ledge, scanning the opposite rooftop for movement. Just like I expected, the expanse is empty. Before taking this next step, I slip on my ski mask. With a great heave, I launch myself across the narrow gap, tucking my body to roll over the rough surface of the roof in a less-than-graceful landing. If I'd put too much focus on landing feet first, I would've shortened my range and put myself in danger of missing my mark.

I stay on the ground, listening closely for the pound of footsteps in case my jump alerted someone to my presence.

Five full breaths, and nothing.

Good.

Like I'd hoped, the lock on the roof door is a simple key one. From my fanny pack, I pull out a set of slim metal picks. I could probably get the thing open with a bobby pin, but that's a last-ditch effort kind of tool. Going into a pick job, might as well bring the best equipment.

I get the door open in less than a minute. Not my fastest time, but I'm only racing against the two-hour mark.

My adrenaline creeps up as I enter the building. The stairwell is dark, giving me the sensation of being trapped. I'd rather have more space. Freedom to choose to run if the need calls for it.

Pushing the claustrophobic fear aside, I take quick yet quiet steps down the stairs. When I reach the second floor, I'm faced with a decision. Mike's office or the garage first?

I have no idea what kind of information Mike keeps here. If any. Although I'm less likely to run into someone in the offices, I go down one more floor.

There are slim windows in the stairwell doors, and I peer through the one on the first floor. I don't see anyone, and when I crack the door open with careful hands, I don't hear anyone walking around either. However, I spy a blueish glow and hear muffled voices from below the doorway down on the opposite end of the hall. The doorway I walked through all those weeks ago when I came to ask about Leo.

Must be where the night guard is, and it sounds like he's watching TV to pass these late—or early—hours.

If I'm lucky, the guy will be fully passed out in there.

Now it's just a game of Russian roulette with these other doors. Based on where the garage opening is on the outside of the building, I know I need to check to my right. That leaves me with three options.

The first turns out to be a janitorial closet. The second is a small, not very clean bathroom.

Third door's the charm.

Moving as delicately as I can, I turn the knob and find myself in an office with large glass windows that look out over a garage area dimly lit by an overhead lamp in the corner.

Crouching low, I enter the office and shut the door behind me. Don't need the guard coming into the hall for a bathroom break and seeing anything out of order.

I crawl across the floor to the entrance of the garage, pressing myself to the wall just inside the open doorway. After listening for a full minute, I can confidently say there is no one in the large room unless they're trying to be as stealthy as I am.

Remaining low, I enter the space. There are eight cars in all states of disassembly. From what I know, Mike's guys work fast. I wouldn't be surprised if they break these down and have them gone by the end of the week.

Better to move hot product than hold on to it.

From my fanny pack, I pull out a small flashlight and my phone. After roughly fifteen minutes, I've found the VIN numbers on each car and snapped a picture. By the time I'm done, I'm sweaty and covered in dust from crawling under the low carriages.

Knowing Charlie's anxiety must increase by the minute, I send the photos to him with a brief message.

Almost done Dont txt back

I scuttle like a crab across the garage and back to the office where I entered. Pressing my ear to the door, I don't hear any footsteps, so I slip back out to the hallway. Just as I pass the door to the bathroom, I hear a toilet flush.

My body wants to freeze in panic. Bright fluorescent lights illuminate the hallway. Nowhere for me to hide. But I learned long ago how to ignore my panicked responses. With three long, almost-leaping steps, I reach the door to the stairwell, pull it open, slip inside, and let the thing swing almost all the way shut. I keep my hand braced on the cold metal, cushioning the door a centimeter away from the latch, avoiding even that small noise that could give away my presence. Through the slim opening, I listen to the bathroom door open—the guy didn't bother to wash his hands, gross—and booted footsteps. The tread is slow, moving away from me.

Only when I hear the latch of a second door closing do I slowly guide the stairwell door shut.

On a long, low exhale, I ease away some of the tension.

But I'm not done yet.

Climbing to the second floor, I enter the office space. All the lights are off, the floor empty and eerily quiet. Not even the hum of AC.

On soft feet, I cross to my uncle's office. He left the door locked. I crouch down and pull my picks out again, getting into the room easier than the roof entrance.

Unfortunately, the place seems to be empty. No stray papers lying around. No file labeled "Criminal Business Plan."

In a cabinet, I find a combination safe. I try a few different number sequences on a wild hope, but nothing comes from it. If I used my impressive thigh muscles, I might be able to lift it, but no way could I jump across the gap between roofs. Besides, I don't want my uncle to know anyone was here. Stealing his safe is an obvious tell. Wanting to do something with this, I snap a picture of the safe. Proof that it exists. Not much, but I'll take anything at this point, not sure if the VIN numbers will be a genuine threat if I ever need to play this hand.

When I leave the office, I leave everything the way I found it, including the locked door.

As I retrace my steps, I move with as much caution as I did entering the building. Would be the perfect fuck-up to get through all this only to get caught at the last second. On the roof, I lock that door as well and make my way to the roof's edge. Finally, I slip off my ski mask, the night air cool on my exposed skin.

I suck in a deep breath, experiencing a glow of triumph that's quickly doused by the reminder of why I had to do this—and how like my father's family I am at this moment.

Just another Lamont breaking the law.

But no time to wallow about that. Charlie's waiting for me.

I jump.

Chapter Twenty-Six

CHARLIE

The text should help calm my nerves.

It doesn't. All I can see is Luna lying vulnerable under a car, and some shadowy hulking figure grabbing her ankles and dragging her out, and then...

Hell, I can't even imagine what kind of retaliation her uncle would level against her.

For the first time since our wedding day, I feel like a true poseur.

Obviously, I must be a fake husband. Someone in a true marriage would never let their partner do something this dangerous alone.

But when Luna asked me to trust her, how could I not?

So I sit here, fingers digging into my knees to keep from texting her back, constantly asking for proof that she's alright.

She told me not to text.

"Fuck," I groan, tugging at my shirt collar. The thing is choking me. I can't breathe.

A knock on the window has me jumping in my seat and letting out a high-pitched yelp.

But then there she is, her beautiful face smiling at me through the window. I scramble out of the car and don't bother questioning the instinct to gather her into my arms.

"Damn it, Luna," I mutter, burying my face in her hair to breathe in that tart citrus scent of her shampoo.

"You worried?" There's a teasing note in her voice, but Luna wraps her arms around my middle, giving me a tight squeeze. The strength in her arms reassures me she's okay. Standing here unhurt.

"You scared the shit out of me." This is the part where I should let her go. But I can't. We stand by her car, arms wrapped around each other. "Did you find everything you needed?"

Her shoulders lift and fall. "Those VINs are pretty much it."

"Can you use them?"

When she tilts her head back, I allow enough space for us to meet eyes. "I could turn them over to the cops, tell them where I got them. Would it get my uncle out of Leo's life?" She sighs heavily, her disappointment in the sinking of her body. "Not likely. They're a decent threat if I'm desperate because the info in the wrong hands would fuck things up for Mike for a while. But then he'd have a vendetta. Like I said, this is just an insurance plan."

Letting my hands resettle on her shoulders, I give Luna a thorough examination. There's a tightness to her muscles.

My wife deserves to relax, but I'm not sure yet how to provide her the space to do so.

"But the money should work, right?"

Luna steps out of my hold, heading to the driver's side of the car. "It worked for Dash. It's my best bet."

I slide into the vehicle as she starts the engine. Once we're far enough from the warehouses that I can't see them in the side mirror, I give in to my curiosity.

"How'd you learn to break into a building?"

Shit. That sounded judgmental.

"I never worked for my uncle, if that's what you're asking." Her voice cuts the space between us.

So much for giving her space to relax.

"No. No, I swear I'm not judging you. I'm just...impressed, I guess. Even though you scared the hell out of me, I'm still awed. You're like a badass cat burglar. If I wanted something from inside a building and found out the door was locked, I'd count myself down and out. But that didn't stop you. I'm curious."

Luna shifts in her seat, green light tracing over her skin as we pass through an intersection.

"I taught myself how to pick locks when I was younger. I had a few reasons to learn." From the tick of the muscle in her jaw, my guess is none of them were pleasant. "One was revenge."

My heart stutters at that. "Did someone hurt you?"

Luna glances over at me, a hard smile in place that makes the night a few degrees colder. "People have been trying to hurt me my whole life."

Her words dig into my stomach like a sickness. I want to tell her I would never.

But I get the sense the promise wouldn't mean much.

"So..." I flex my fingers to keep from cracking my knuckles. "How does wanting revenge lead to picking locks?"

Her thumbnail digs into the fake leather covering the steering wheel as she answers. "There was this girl in middle school. She was always coming at me. Not fighting me, which even scrawny as I was, I could've taken her." Luna lets out a sharp exhale. "She would just talk at me. Whisper behind my back. Say things to my face."

"What kind of things?" I don't know why I ask. I'm perfectly aware of the shitty things kids will do to break someone down.

"There were the classic insults about being poor and dirty and ugly. And hell, she must've Googled all the slurs she could. Never ran out of material."

Now I'm the one who wants revenge. Against a teenager.

"I learned early on if you take people's shit, they never stop shoveling it on you. So I told her off one day. A teacher overheard me yelling, and I got detention. And I knew—I *knew*—they'd heard at least some of the crap she'd said to me." If eyes could burn, Luna's would've scorched holes in her windshield. "Next day she started in on me again. We both realized none of the adults were going to help me. If I wanted her to stop, I'd have to do it myself."

"You beat her up?" I guess.

Luna snorts. "Wanted to. But no. I was not going to get in trouble because of her again. I figured out a different way. You know those cheap locks you'd get in school for your locker?"

"Yeah."

"I was messing with mine one day, and I realized it's easy to figure out their combinations. If you get the feel for it, you can tell when the tumbler clicks." Luna gets an evil grin. "I had an idea. Every day I stayed after school, and I went to her locker. I figured out the code, and then I changed it. For two weeks straight, she had to get the custodian to cut the lock off, until eventually the principal said if she couldn't remember her combination, then she couldn't have a lock."

"Okay." I hedge the word. I think that probably annoyed the girl but doesn't sound like too intense of a revenge.

Luna isn't done. "With her locker open like that, it was free game. I'd leave things in it. Tuck an open bottle of milk in the back corner of the top shelf. She didn't notice until it went rancid. Same with the thin slices of cheese I'd slip between the pages of her textbook. One of those turned into a pretty big mold bloom. Dairy products are surprisingly handy."

I huff out a shocked laugh. "Clever."

Luna nods, smirking as she drives us through the early morning. "Didn't stop there. Because she didn't stop either. She knew something weird was going on with her locker, but not who was doing it or why. I wanted to make her pay." Luna's triumph dims, and I catch a hint of pain in her voice. "But more than anything, I wanted her to stop."

"Of course, you did." I keep my tone soft. "What did you do?"

"Well, after enough smelly items ended up in her locker, there was always someone watching. Teachers, one of her friends, other students who were curious to find out who it was. Even after school, people hung around to see." Luna turns the wheel, and I realize we've made it back to Paige and Dash's house. "So I went at night. I'd found a video online about picking locks, and I tried it on a side door at the school. Worked like a charm. Then I took a permanent marker and wrote every shitty thing I ever heard her say on the inside of her locker. Space filled up fast. I wrote on the outside of the locker too. Then I dumped a can of cat food inside. Next day came around and my art display was the talk of the school."

"You didn't get in trouble? When they knew it was you?"

"That's the thing. They didn't know. Because I'm not the only person she said fucked-up shit to. I wrote all of her hate down. Could've been any of us. All of us. She didn't know."

"Wow." I let my head fall back on the headrest, impressed and intimidated by my wife's evil genius mind.

"Plus, I left open cans of cat food in all of her friends' lockers as a warning. None of them wanted to go through the stinky locker torment. She had zero backup."

"That's...impressive."

Luna laughs, but there's no humor in the noise. "Yep. That's the kind of woman I am. Guess I should've told you before we got hitched. Bet you're glad for that end date now, huh?"

"Luna—"

"But that's the thing about bullies. It's not only that they hit you or say mean things." Luna turns a defensive glare on me. "It's the fact that they steal your sense of safety. Maybe they'll go an hour without bothering you. Or maybe a day. Or a week. But you don't have their fucked-up schedule. You're just braced every second you're anywhere near them, waiting for what torture will come next."

Her strong hands fist, and I want to reach across this small yet gaping distance between us.

"They tried taking my safety away. So I took theirs away. They never knew what I would do or when. They were never completely sure it was me either. Not enough to prove it. But they eventually figured out if they left me and mine alone, the chaos in their life stopped."

"Luna, I'm not judging you." I speak quickly and firmly. And I do reach for her, pressing my palm against her thigh in what I hope she sees as a reassuring touch. "I'm wishing I was in that school with you so you didn't have to fight back on your own. Hell, I would've carried the can opener for you. Helped you put the milk on the top shelf so you didn't need a stepladder."

She glares at me then, but this time the expression attempts to cover a curl of her lips. "I reached just fine."

In the dim car, I grin at her. My fierce wife who's had to fight her whole life.

Luna amazes me, and I long to do more than convince her I don't judge her vengeful actions.

I'm desperate to prove I'm worthy to be in her presence.

And if I'm lucky, in her heart.

Chapter Twenty-Seven

CHARLIE

"Why won't she stop crying?" Luna stumbles into my room, bleary-eyed, with an anxious pit bull trotting at her heels.

We arrived back in Nashville late, having stayed longer at brunch with Paige and Dash than we'd planned. Plus, the return trip required more stops to give Pig bathroom breaks. When we got home after dark, we took the time to walk our new dog around Luna's yard and into each room of the house, showing her all the dog beds and toys I stocked up on.

The two of us headed to bed maybe an hour ago. But Pig doesn't seem to have gotten the sleep memo.

"Maybe she misses Pumpkin?" I offer as I reach for my glasses on the bedside table. Once I slip the frames on, everything loses its blurry edge and I can meet Luna's eyes.

She blinks at me, more awake than I first thought.

"You wear glasses?"

"I wear contacts." I sit up straighter in my bed, hoping the bulky frames don't make me look too dorky. "But I take them out when I sleep. Glasses are just so I don't trip over anything when I'm walking from the bathroom to my bed." If I even bother to put them on. Sometimes it's more work to find the frames in the middle of the night than it is to stumble through the dark house. Not like I can see much in the dark anyway.

"Hmm." She tilts her head, studying me, but gets distracted by Pig hopping up on the mattress and curling into a seemingly content ball beside my feet.

"Okay," Luna uses a hushed tone, her whole demeanor cautious. "She's quiet. She's happy. I'm just going to back out slowly." The woman takes careful steps backward out of my room. She gets just out of eyeline when Pig pops her massive head up and starts a new round of pitiful whimpering.

With a defeated huff, Luna stalks back into the room. Then she keeps on coming, climbing onto my bed and settling on the other side of her dog. My fake wife swipes the remote off the table beside her and flips on the TV mounted on the wall across from the foot of the bed.

"Let's watch something. Maybe she'll fall asleep and I can sneak out. Sound good?"

"Works for me." I try my best to keep my tone casual, even as I'm a bundle of nerves and excitement on the inside.

Luna is in the bed with me. Well, me and Pig.

The dog thumps her stubby tail in a couple of happy wags, then burrows her head into the soft covers.

"What do you want to watch?" Luna asks, flipping through the thousands of options on a single streaming service.

"Something with no plot." No doubt this brief wakefulness will wear off in a few minutes.

"Reality TV it is." Luna ends up choosing a show about tattoo mistakes and cover-ups. With the entertainment selected, she settles back against the pillows, her hand coming to rest on Pig's head, giving the pup affectionate scratches.

My mind imagines what it would be like to have Luna's strong fingers on me, digging into my skin, massaging my muscles. Maybe leaving scratch marks as she gasps out my name.

Back up. Not going to go there.

Not when she's right next to me anyway.

As the vaguely interesting show keeps playing, I find myself sinking deeper into the bed, leaning toward Pig. Luna and I almost cradle her with our bodies, and the position soothes the dog until she's sleeping, her eyes shut as little puppy snores eke out.

Turning my head to Luna, I expect to see her eyes on me with a silent message that she plans on sneaking out. But I find that Luna has drifted off as thoroughly as her dog, the two of them now passed out in my bed.

My chest tightens. But the sensation doesn't hurt. More like the pressure pulls against the inside of my rib cage, encouraging me to do something. To revel in this perfect picture of domesticity.

But what can I do other than memorize every detail of this moment? The sound of the show not fully drowning out the gentle puffs of breath from Luna and her hound. The smell of the fabric softener she uses that scents the sheets. The warmth of two bodies close but not touching mine.

More than anything I ache to cross the space between us. Reach out an arm to tuck a stray strand of hair behind Luna's ear, then brush my thumb against her sharp cheekbone.

Eventually, I slide my glasses off and set them aside, allowing this dream of mine to blur. To remove a small ounce of the need to beg for this marriage, this home, this perfect place for me, to be real.

Chapter Twenty-Eight

LUNA

My husband is wearing gray sweatpants and looking way too good in them. I try to blame the scent of the braising beef for the drool collecting in my mouth. But that would be a lie.

I should buy Charlie some ill-fitting overalls and add to our marriage rules that he's required to wear the baggy denim whenever he's in my presence.

At least I have a task that keeps my eyes busy.

"I want to help." His voice comes in a low, coaxing rumble.

Why can't he speak in a high-pitched, needy whine? That would be easier to dismiss.

Still, I don't give in.

"You're doing enough just by staying married to me. Don't men dream of cracking open a beer, zoning out in front of a TV, and having dinner made for them?"

I keep my focus on the cutting board as I chop cilantro and talk to Charlie. Just because I have a degree in nutrition does not mean I'm suddenly a master chef. My dicing skills are slow going. When I find a recipe to try, I normally have to double the prep time to get an accurate idea of how long to plan for.

"If that's the kind of men you know, you need to up the caliber of people you spend time with."

Done slicing the tiny, fragrant leaves, I set down my knife and meet Charlie's stare. He stands on the opposite side of the kitchen island, leaning toward me with a pleading expression on his face. Pig wears an almost identical pout, but her focus rests entirely on the stovetop where all the delicious meaty smells waft from.

I'm not giving into either guilt trip.

"I'm serious, Charlie. I've got dinner. Just chill out and let me be your sugar momma."

He grimaces. "Okay, that was funny the first time you said it, but can we erase that term from all future conversations? It's weirding me out."

"Yeah. I heard it too. No more sugar momma." Carefully, I scoop the cilantro off my board and dump the green leaves in a bowl beside my dough. "Still, I've been living on my own for over a decade. I've never needed more hands in the kitchen. Just because I have a husband doesn't mean I'm suddenly helpless."

Charlie absently cracks his knuckles—a sign of agitation I'm beginning to recognize—before tucking his hands in the pockets of those teasingly tempting gray sweatpants.

"I didn't say you *need* help. I'm saying I want to help. I hate being useless."

"I told you—"

"Yeah. The marriage. Sure. But in a day-to-day situation. I need to do more."

"You walk Pig."

At the sound of the word, my pup's ear twitches. But apparently beef is a higher priority than going outside.

"This doesn't have to be a tally-keeping thing. No points to keep track of. Fake or not, we're husband and wife. Can't we just be partners for this next year? Like..." Charlie strolls over to the table, and he's already picking up the little piece of paper before I realize what he's doing. "This is the recipe you're making, right? If I swear I know you can slice cucumbers, can I please cover that task?"

My arms fling out before my body freezes in panic, my heart beating at a frantic rhythm. When Charlie turns and notices my pose, his brow dips with concern.

"Luna? What's wrong."

"Put down the recipe." I hiss the command, animosity stinging through my voice.

Pig whines, and Charlie flinches as if I've slapped him. He gently sets the paper back where he found it. When the handwritten recipe settles on the table surface, I can breathe again.

"Sorry," he mumbles, staring at his feet. "I'll go hang out in my room." As he shuffles away, I realize I'm the biggest ass.

Did I just kick a happy puppy? Because it sure feels like it.

My dog stares at me with wide eyes full of innocent worry that only hurts my heart more.

"Charlie!" My call stops him before he can disappear. He waits, his back to me. But maybe that's better. I don't open up to people, and right now I need to show a little vulnerability to explain my temporary freak out. "The recipe. It's my grandmother's. She wrote it down herself." I have to clear tightness from my throat before I keep going. "I only have six."

Charlie faces me, the hurt gone as easy as it arrived. "Six recipes?"

I nod. "I visited her six times since I found her. We made a new dish each time, and she wrote what we did as we did it. She said the recipes were in her hands, and she only remembered them when she cooked them."

Charlie retraces his steps, approaching me as if I'm a rattlesnake and my tail is buzzing in warning. He has a right to be wary. I sunk my fangs into him only a second ago.

"I'm protective of them." The paper is plenty sturdy, not like she wrote the steps down on tissue paper, but I can't help worrying that they'll disintegrate under the wrong touch and I'll lose this last bit of her. Of my history.

"I'm sorry. I promise not to touch them again."

If I were someone who people-pleased, I'd apologize further and claim I overreacted. Instead, I simply say, "I'd appreciate that."

Charlie leans a shoulder against the wall, looking more handsome than should be allowed as he studies me. "Making the recipe yourself also means a lot to you?"

Perceptive man.

I hunch over my cutting board, focused on slicing the scallions as thin as Wai Po showed me. "I want the recipes to be in my hands too."

He nods, quiet for a moment longer, then pushes off the wall and strolls down the hall, disappearing into his room.

For someone who's been completely happy living on their own, I'm surprised at the clench of regret in my chest at his departure. Almost like I wish he'd stay here with me to keep me company.

Well then, maybe you should've let him help instead of snapping, a snide voice whispers in the back of my brain.

But before I can lay into myself further, Charlie reappears.

This time with a guitar.

"Do you mind if I mess around with this?" he asks, warm eyes meeting mine.

"Go for it."

Charlie settles at the kitchen table, and while I carefully work through Wai Po's recipe for scallion pancake beef rolls, he tunes his instrument.

Then my husband fills our house with music.

He plays covers. Acoustic versions of some pop, some rock, some R&B. Later, Charlie drifts into a familiar country tune, and I grin when I recognize his choice.

"That's Violet's," I point out, as if he doesn't already know.

Charlie raises his head, fingers still strumming as his cheerful smile entrances me. "Guess I'm not too rusty then. If you can tell what I'm playing."

"You're good."

He shrugs. "I'm average."

"Seriously?" I pretend to glare at him. "Do you think I would marry someone who is average?"

His mouth widens to a grin, showing off his gorgeous white choppers that lately have me thinking what it would be like if he bit me. Not too hard. Just a gentle press of his teeth on my—

Nope! Not having those thoughts about my husband.

"Okay," Charlie says, jerking me out of my accidental lust spiral. "I'm above average. How's that?"

"Better." I turn back to my food prep, blaming my growing hunger on the errant thoughts about biting. "Do you have rock star dreams? Long to travel the world like your mom?"

"Nah." The song shifts to a blues number I think I've heard Regina Keller perform on the radio. "Had enough of the transient lifestyle when I was a kid. Think I'd rather stay in one place for a while. At least long enough to call it home."

Is that what New Orleans is for him? Home?

"Well, there are lots of music venues in this town. You could get a gig if you wanted."

Out of the corner of my eye, I watch him shake his head.

"I'd rather play for fun when the urge takes me. Don't need to perform for anyone else."

"This show isn't for me? Stab me through the heart, why don't you?"

Charlie whips his head up, but he must catch the humor in my eyes because he smirks.

"You're right. I play for myself, and I play for my wife. The only opinions that matter."

"Pig's too."

"Of course." He smiles down at the pit bull. She finally accepts that the meat isn't her treat, trotting over to settle by his feet.

They make a picture. Man and beast. Relaxed and adorable.

And damn, if the man gets any hotter, I can forget the stove and just cook the entire dinner on his bare chest.

Don't tempt me.

Chapter Twenty-Nine

LUNA

What a surprise that my father shows up when I'm handling shit.

The terraced planters I built for myself at the beginning of the previous fall have sat empty for months. But now they're full of a fragrant mulch, just waiting for seeds.

I'm about to grab the small handwritten labels I made, mentally mapping out my rows of future herbs and veggies, when I hear the squeak of the gate hinges.

I turn, expecting to see Charlie.

Instead, the man on my property is the last one I'd ever give permission to be here.

"Hey, baby girl." My father wears a falsely affectionate smile.

The nickname and the lie on his face boil anger in my gut. This man is a walking, talking danger, encroaching upon my territory. I should sprint to my house and throw the dead bolt, getting walls between us.

That's what I tell my clients.

Run.

Run to train. Run on your property. Run in daylight. Run on the treadmill to get your strength up, then run through your house to get comfortable with the sensation.

And then, when you have even the slightest worry that someone intends to harm you, run.

Don't worry about being wrong.

Don't worry about looking ridiculous.

Just run.

But I don't run.

Because I let my rage override common sense and hold me in front of this man as he grins like the victor in an arena.

If this comes to a fight, things won't turn out the way he thinks.

"Get out."

Some people might have asked what do you want? Or why are you here?

But I don't care about those answers. All I care about is if he's going to leave on his own or if I need to make him.

"That's no way to greet your daddy."

Like I ever called him that.

Dad at first.

Asshole behind his back since I was ten.

Piece of shit to his face since I was eighteen.

"Get. Out." I speak the words slowly but with every ounce of hatred I hold for him.

He's in my yard, at my house. This is my safe space, and he showed up here like our lives cross over in the way of normal families. We're not normal. I moved states away so I'd never have to see his face again. I kept this address to myself, but it's probably public record.

Knew I should've changed my name when I finally left their house. Maybe I should reconsider becoming Luna Keller. Maybe Charlie could share his parents with me for the next year, letting me live in a brief, happy fantasy land filled with parental support.

"I'm not leaving until we have a chat. A family discussion." Bill Lamont leans back against one of my planters, and the wood creaks under his weight.

"That's not a bench," I hiss.

Mistake.

His eyes drop to the planter I spent a week carefully constructing.

Then he glances back at me with a spark of triumph in his milky-blue eyes.

Almost thirty years old, and I still haven't mastered the art of handling my father. The best thing to do is remain calm and dismissive. But the man even breathing air in my vicinity pisses me off, which means I accidentally reveal weaknesses. Like the fact that I care about my planters.

When I was younger, my dad would use Leo and Dash against me, knowing I would do anything to keep my brothers from hurting.

"Sorry, baby girl. I'll leave these be, and we can have our little talk."

"We have nothing to talk about."

"Sure we do. But maybe you forgot because you didn't mention it last you came to visit." His gaze sharpens, trying to cut through me.

Disquiet trickles down my spine. Instead of asking the question he wants me to, I keep my mouth shut. Bill Lamont is too much of a showman not to get around to the big reveal even without my prompting.

After waiting long enough, he laughs, as if I'm a silly child. "I got the most interesting letter. About an inheritance. My inheritance."

Fuck. Fuck fuck fuck.

His smile turns as hard as his stare. "You should've told me about that, baby girl. I know you knew."

Calm and dismissive. "So what?"

"So..." He steps closer. "I know you'd rather chew your leg off before tying yourself down to some man. Just thought I'd stop by and make sure you weren't planning something stupid."

Good thing I have on gardening gloves or else he'd know I have zero intention of letting him get his grubby hands on Wai Po's money.

The safest thing to do would be to disengage from this situation. To stroke my father's ego, drop my eyes, let him gloat until he gets bored, then wait for him to leave. He's a quarry I'm familiar with, and I know exactly what leads to violent reactions.

But with Bill Lamont, my logic always seems to evaporate.

All that's left is a rage that demands I hurt him.

"You're pathetic." I leave my hands loose at my sides, ready to bring them up for defense. "Can't make your own money, can you? Need an old lady's cash just to survive?"

His condescending smile morphs into a snarl. "Shut your mouth."

"Why? So you don't have to hear about how you're a waste of oxygen? An embarrassing use of space?"

"You ungrateful bitch. If it weren't for me, you wouldn't even exist." The man who never earned the title *father* looms over me. "And I know you're the reason I've been getting those calls!"

I keep all signs of triumph off my face, even as I savor an evil cackle in my mind. Glad to hear the number Leo gave me wasn't a dud.

There are a few personal ads out in the world now describing how Bill's looking for a connection. Specifically, he's looking for people to call him using a baby voice and commenting how tiny his junk is. Available 24/7.

Anyone who insults my sister-in-law deserves to be taken down several hundred pegs.

"Get off of my property now."

"I put a roof over your head for years," he spits while grabbing for my arm. I shove his hand away and step hard on his insole, grounding down with my heel until he yelps and stumbles back a limping step.

"That's assault!"

"Oh, yeah? Go ahead. Call the cops on me." I paste a wild grin on my face, knowing the expression is eerie as hell from the way he shuffles farther away. "The second you dial those numbers I'll be on the phone to Uncle Mike telling him how you're getting cozy with the law." I lean close, making sure he's listening to the hatred in my voice. "Besides, I've got years of you smacking me around to pay back. We're not even close to even. Not when I never called the police on you, no matter how many bruises I went to bed with."

"You ungrateful, crazy—"

"Hey!" The single word, barked out from the door to the house, adds another layer of tension to this situation.

Damn it, I yell in my head as Charlie steps through the sliding glass door and approaches us. Why couldn't he have taken Pig on a longer walk? Out loud, I say, "I'll be inside in a minute."

Take the hint.

But Charlie only strides up beside me, worry creasing deep lines in his face as he flicks his eyes between my father and me. At least Charlie left Pig inside. I can hear her whimpering and don't know what she'd do around the toxic presence of my father.

"Who's this—" Bill Lamont ends his question with a disgusting slur he says with ease from a lifetime of use.

My mind blanks for a moment, shame and rage a drowning mixture that engulfs me at the sound of the offensive word my father calls Charlie. Next thing I know, my dad's backing away, hands raised, sneer twisting his mouth, and triumph in his eyes.

That's when I realize I'm trapped, wrapped in a strong set of arms that hold me back from clawing my father's eyes out.

"Let me go," I snarl.

"That's what he wants," Charlie whispers in my ear.

"Let go before I make you."

My fake husband doesn't respond, but he also doesn't loosen his arms.

"You let your friend fight all your battles for you?" My dad taunts me even as he keeps his distance.

Before I can warn Charlie to keep his mouth shut, he's already talking.

"I'm not her friend. I'm her husband."

The mocking superiority drains from my father's face.

Fucking hell.

I should've run.

Chapter Thirty

CHARLIE

When Luna mutters a string of curses under her breath, I know I've messed up.

"You fucking bitch." The older white man's face turns an ugly blotchy red.

The insult shouldn't surprise me after the word he just threw my way. But I find myself angrier on Luna's behalf than on my own.

Still, I'm not a fighter. Never prone to getting into physical altercations. And yet I burn to punch this guy in the face, even if I break my hand in the attempt because I don't know the right way to throw a punch.

Now Luna could probably tear the man limb from limb, but she didn't seem bent on a brawl until he insulted me. No way am I letting her put herself in danger on my behalf.

The red-faced stranger looks ready to implode.

"You want that money for yourself! You called me greedy? Like father, like daughter, huh?"

"I'm nothing like you!" Luna pushes against my hold. But she doesn't break free, and I'm ninety-nine percent sure she could if she wanted to. If she didn't mind hurting me in the process.

The man who must be Bill Lamont steps toward us, and I stare in disgust at the person who should love and support the woman in my arms unconditionally. Instead, he insults and threatens her. I can barely comprehend the horror of it.

I need this man as far away from my wife as I can manage.

Sirens sound in the distance, sparking an idea.

"I called the cops before I came out here," I say, meeting his bloodshot gaze.

Mr. Lamont flinches back, wild eyes flicking toward the front of the house where we all hear the faint sound of the emergency response. His feet turn the way of his stare, and he makes a retreat.

Just when I think we're free of him, Luna's father snaps out a quick kick at his daughter's raised garden. The wood splinters under his heavy boot, letting fresh soil spill onto the ground.

"This isn't over!" he bellows, picking up his pace as the sirens get louder. The gate clangs shut behind him, and a second later we hear the roar of an engine.

I drop my hold.

"Did you actually call the cops?" Luna asks, voice strained.

"No. I lied. Worked though." Without her in my arms, I fight an empty sensation, cracking my knuckles as a distraction. "So, that was your dad?" I can see why she'd never want that man to have the money.

"Damn it!" Luna stomps across the yard away from me, then stops to glare down at the ground, her arms crossed and entire body tense.

"Luna?" My voice borders on cautious. Is she wishing I had called the authorities? We can still give them a report. Maybe get a restraining order.

"You shouldn't have told him!" She shouts the words at the sky, but I know they're aimed at me.

"Told him what?"

"That we're married." Luna drops her hands to her sides, fingers clenched in fists in her dirty gardening gloves. I wonder if she wants to hit something. Like me.

"I'm sorry. I didn't think we were keeping it secret." A defensive note creeps into my voice.

"He knows." Luna whirls to glare at me. Eyes hard. "He knows about the inheritance, and now he knows I'm going after it."

"Ah." Shit. From what I just saw of the guy, Luna's father does not lose with grace.

"Yeah. *Ah.*" She paces again, getting her rage out through her feet. "He's going to do something. I don't know what. Hell, he probably doesn't know what yet. But he wants that money, and I'm standing in his way."

My chagrin curdles into a sick, angry mess in my gut.

Seriously? The guy will do something to his own daughter? With a loving set of parents like mine, the idea is hard to fathom.

But I trust Luna's worry. She knows the man better than I do.

"Luna, I'm sorry." This time the apology doesn't come with any caveats. I wish I could have helped her without revealing our relationship.

She sighs, some of the anger leaching from her expression, but her shoulders stay tense. I follow the direction of her stare to the destruction. The planter Luna's spent the morning working on has a splintered side with thick, brown soil spilling from the fracture.

In my life, I've rarely applied the word "hate" to anything.

But I hate Bill Lamont.

Luna heads toward the house. Her abandonment of her project sends a spike of panic through me. Is she walking away from it forever?

"I'll help you fix it!" I hurry over to the planter, glancing around the yard to see if there's anything we can use to patch the breach.

"Charlie." Luna's voice is tired. "I'll deal with it tomorrow. I just can't right now."

When I turn, she's on her little back porch, peeling off her gardening gloves. As she slips the fabric from her left hand, I catch a glint from her wedding band. Our partner rings.

That's what I need right now. To be her partner. To be here for her.

I walk toward her with careful steps.

"Can I hug you?"

Luna hesitates, and I sink down to sit on the porch step beside her, not wanting to loom.

My wait ends in shock as she slides into my lap, straddling my hips and wrapping her arms tight around my neck.

I meant to comfort her. But this is different. More.

I twine my arms around her waist, pulling my wife close to my body. My cheek cradles against her breasts, which she doesn't seem to mind. Luna rests her chin on the top of my head and lets out a shuddering sigh. With her in my arms like this, I sense the slight tremor in her body.

I wonder if she shakes from fear, adrenaline, anger, or all three.

"He might try to hurt you," she mutters.

Don't worry about me, I consider telling her. But selfishly, I keep my mouth shut. Because the thought of her concern warms me.

A high-pitched whine sounds from behind me, and Luna lets out a reluctant chuckle.

"Our dog wants in on the hug," Luna mutters, and I think I hear the hint of a smile in her voice.

Our dog. Like Pig is a bridge between the two of us. I glance over my shoulder and spot the puppy's over-excited face at the door. I think her blocky head is cute, but I know the world often sees her as something fierce. Something intimidating.

But she's as harmless as I am. If Bill Lamont decides to fuck with me, I'll probably end up in worse shape than Luna would. She's the tough one in this marriage. Her strength awes me, but I don't want to be a burden.

"Ever think about getting a restraining order against your dad?"

Luna shifts back, and I allow my arms to slacken, no matter how much I ache to keep holding her against me.

"Those don't do a lot." She grimaces. "I've had clients who tried them and still ran into trouble with stalkers. It's a piece of paper that a determined person won't take seriously." Luna brushes some dirt off her jeans with brusque movements. "More likely it'd piss him off and make my uncle jumpy." She meets my eyes, face hardening into a mask. "The Lamonts don't have a good history with law enforcement."

"What's our next step?"

Luna rises from my lap, and the void of her hits harder than a moment ago.

"Not sure." She grabs the handle of the sliding door. "But don't worry. I'll figure it out."

Even Pig's energetic spring into the backyard can't distract from the unspoken words.

I'll figure it out on my own.

Chapter Thirty-One

LUNA

My dad's unexpected visit leaves an invisible tension hanging over our household. Every time I leave for work, there's a nagging voice in the back of my brain telling me I need to check in on Charlie. That if I'm not here, something bad will happen to him.

The same voice shouts at me when I'm at the house and he goes out.

Charlie often takes Pig with him on errands. Guess Nashville is a pretty dog friendly town because he always seems to find stores that allow our pit bull inside as long as she stays on a leash. And ultimate dog dad that he is, Charlie loves the constant bonding.

Pig's heart is going to break when this marriage ends.

I'm torn about them going out together. On the one hand my dad hates dogs, so she might help in that arena. On the other hand Charlie is a tall Black man and Pig is a pit bull. The world doesn't look kindly on them separately, and together I can imagine the ignorant, hostile interactions that could happen at any moment.

No matter how I look at the situation, I worry.

This is why I don't let people into my life. Dash and Leo give me enough stress.

Even though I know my persistent anxiety would only make my father happy, I can't seem to eradicate the worry. The apprehension seeps into every inch of my body, and I find myself jogging from my car to my front door, eager to check that my little—temporary—family is safe and secure.

A week later when I arrive home from work, a savory scent drifts to me when I enter my house. I pull in a deeper breath.

"Charlie?" Following my nose, I find him in the kitchen, bent over the stove.

He straightens and offers a sheepish smile. Pig trots up to me, wagging her tail wildly as I scratch behind her ears.

"Hey." Charlie continues to stir a large pot. "How was work?"

The question is so domestic I'm immediately on guard.

"Fine." I drag the word out. "What's this?"

Because he's not just making dinner. There are fresh flowers in a vase on the table, and my fake husband wears a white button-down shirt and a pair of dove-gray slacks that hug his ass so well there should be a monument built in honor of the curves.

Not something I should notice about my fake husband, I remind myself for roughly the thousandth time.

"Come here." Charlie steps around the island, picking up a beer on the way and pressing the cool glass into my hand as he guides me to the kitchen table. On the wooden surface is a stack of wrapped gifts.

"My birthday isn't until May."

"Ah. But this isn't for your birthday." Charlie kneels on one knee beside my chair. If we weren't already married, I'd be concerned he was about to propose. "Happy one-month anniversary."

"Charlie," I groan as realization hits. "Seriously? We're fake married! You can't get me gifts for a fake anniversary."

"Too late!" He grins.

"Well then, return them." I shove the packages away like the ungrateful bitch I am.

But Charlie only shrugs, his smile not wavering in the slightest. "Can't. They're personalized."

I mutter a curse as he straightens and returns to the kitchen, likely to finish making whatever delicious creation I smell. For a full minute I sit pouting and sipping my beer. Charlie doesn't prod or get mad or insist I open the gifts.

He just keeps cooking.

Eventually, curiosity overwhelms my good sense, and I pull the first wrapped rectangle toward me. There's a certain pleasure in tearing off the paper. Until all I find is an empty frame. Picking it up, I check the back, then the front again.

But nope, nothing to see.

"It's empty," I announce.

Charlie makes a noncommittal noise in his throat.

I move on to the next one.

And the next.

And the next.

And so on until I've opened six empty frames.

Well, this is a certain kind of bullshit. And when I realize I'm disappointed, I have to admit I let myself get excited about a surprise that shouldn't even be happening.

"Here." Charlie sets another wrapped rectangle down in front of me.

I use all of my willpower not to glare up at him. "You forgot one of the very important empty frames?"

Charlie barks out a laugh but doesn't answer, choosing to set the table instead.

My bar resting very low, I tear off the gold paper.

The string of empty frames ends when I stare down at a small, thin hardback book.

At the sight of the cover, I suck in a sharp breath, every muscle in my body tightening. "Where'd you get this?"

"Dash." Charlie's voice has lost its teasing edge, all sincerity now.

The image is of me, not exactly smiling, but I know I'm happy no matter what my face says. Because beside me is my Wai Po. Dash took this photo on our second visit when the three of us went to the botanical gardens. Behind us is a colorful meadow I never would've thought to find in Delaware.

If I look at the picture much longer, I'm not sure what I'll do. Since there's a risk of tears, I flip the cover open.

Only to be slammed with another heart-aching memento.

One of my grandmother's recipes.

"I'm sorry. I broke my promise. I touched them. But I swear I wore gloves, and I only took each one out for long enough to scan them and then put them back. They're all safe and accounted for."

"You made a recipe book?"

"I thought you could use this when you're cooking. That way you don't have to worry about getting food on the originals. Or if you'd rather stick with the originals, you can have this as a backup."

"The frames?"

"I thought if you like the book, then maybe you'd frame the originals. That way they're safe, but you can see them without worrying."

Six frames. For six recipes.

"You don't have to say anything." Charlie circulates between the stovetop and the table with jerky movements, not meeting my eyes as he does. "I know it's a weird gift."

"It is not weird." My voice sounds stiff. Overly formal. Because if I let what I'm feeling out, I'll start crying, and I hate crying. "It's a good gift. A really good gift."

My fake husband offers me one of his wildly handsome smiles, and I barely restrain myself from breaking the marriage rules and jumping him.

Charlie will make someone—not me—a very happy partner one day. I try not to dwell on how that causes a throbbing ache right in the center of my chest.

"So, food." His voice grows gruff, and I watch his cheeks darken with a blush. "Hopefully, this doesn't put me on a nutritionist hit list, but I made us mac and cheese." Charlie opens up the oven, releasing a delicious herb scent. With oven-mitt-covered hands, he slides a skillet out and places the heavy pan on the stovetop. "There's also green beans and a salad, so dinner is not entirely melted dairy."

Damn him. He's coming at me from all directions with his thoughtful gift and savory food. If the stuff tastes good, I don't know if I'll be able to keep my hands to myself.

"Another beer? Or wine?" My fake husband moves around the kitchen with such purpose no one could ever deny that he belongs there. Unfortunately, his competence has my thighs clenching.

"Wine." I choke out the word, the only one I can manage in the face of this domesticity.

Charlie does everything for the dinner. Setting the table, serving the food, making sure I have a glass of wine and the bottle at hand. I can't fathom why he's gone through all this effort. On a good day, I'm a mildly tolerable fake wife. But he's acting like I've done something worthy of this care.

And I don't get it.

"Just sit down," I command when he jumps out of his chair again to move the salt and pepper closer. "You're making me dizzy. I don't need anything else."

Except maybe a casket, because when I bite into Charlie's mac and cheese, I'm sure I've died and found paradise.

"Oh, fuck yes," I groan, my mouth full. I'm torn between chewing faster versus letting this first bite linger for days.

"You like it?" Charlie leans partway across the table, his eyes fixated on my mouth in a way that has me suddenly self-conscious about how I chew. Then I immediately get over that insecurity because who has time to judge themselves when there is more of this ambrosia to consume?

"So good," I mumble through another mouthful. For the next few minutes, all I focus on is consumption. I can't bear to glance Charlie's way again and find him staring at me with that same intensity.

Or worse, ignoring me in pursuit of his own delicious meal.

Something is wrong in my brain. At some point a couple of wires got crossed, and now I'm too focused on how Charlie interacts with me. As if he's integral to my well-being.

Which he is not.

"I made dessert too." Charlie's declaration pulls me out of my thoughts and forces my eyes up from my plate.

The sheepish expression on his face softens all the hard points inside me. The ones demanding I protect myself.

"You did?" I glance around. "Where is this mystery dessert?"

"Things didn't go exactly to plan." His eyes shift away.

Consider my curiosity piqued. I stand from the table, peering around the kitchen, wanting a glimpse of this food that has Charlie off-kilter. "What do you mean by not going to plan?" I stroll toward the island, but only see the remnants of the dinner. Nothing sweet. "Is it edible?"

"Yes. The baking part didn't go wrong."

I face him. "But something did go wrong? What is it? What are you hiding?"

Charlie pulls his napkin off his lap before standing and striding into the kitchen. "No need to go hunting for it, I'll show you."

Even though he says he will, my fake husband hesitates, fists on his hips. While he works out whatever silent debate he's got going on, I boost myself up to sit on the clean part of the counter. This puts me closer to his height. Gives me the sense we're on equal footing.

"Come on." I reach out my leg, poking his thigh with my toe.

"It's embarrassing." Still, he's smiling again.

"Do you not remember the first day we met? Or how about the one after that? You, Charlie Keller, are a pro at embarrassing yourself in front of me." I tilt forward, lowering my voice as if we're sharing a secret. "And it only makes me like you more."

Maybe I shouldn't have revealed that, but when he gives me such a joyful grin, it's hard to regret my honesty. Something about Charlie turns me playful. He naturally surpasses my bitchy armor without effort.

He lets out a defeated sigh. "Okay. But I need to preface this by saying I tried, but I won't be offended if you laugh."

"Alright," I say, dragging the word out.

Charlie opens the fridge, retrieving a platter. The serving dish holds something resembling a cake, and I wonder what would have me laughing about that.

Then he stands in front of me, and I choke on air.

"What is that?" I don't know whether to lean close for a better look or run away screaming.

Charlie offers a defeated smile. "I tried to make it look like Pig. The plan was sound, but something went wrong during the execution."

I'll say. The thing before me is a strange splotchy mixer of vanilla and chocolate icing, with unbalanced eyes and a gaping mouth that looks more like a demon trying to swallow souls than my friendly animal companion.

"It's," I snort, "hideous." More laughter spills out of me, filling the kitchen and easing all the tension from my shoulders.

How can he do this? Put me at ease without even trying?

Part of it has to be the vulnerability. Charlie never puts up shields between us, while that's all I ever seem to do.

Because it's all I've ever known.

He sets the monster cake down and grabs a plate. Next thing I know, he's handing me a fork and holding up a section of the offending dessert.

"Let me know if I at least got the taste right."

I guess this is my punishment for laughing. Now I have to be the cake guinea pig. Mastering my self-control, I don't let even the slightest cringe appear when Charlie offers me a forkful. *He's feeding me*, I think, just as the chocolate hits my tongue.

Before, I'd thought I'd hoped for too much. That there was no way something could both be that ugly yet also taste delicious.

But Charlie managed it.

"What do you think?" my fake husband asks.

"Good." I lick my lips. "Really good. I'll take my piece." When I hold out my hands, he passes the plate over. Then he cuts himself one, pleasure creeping over his face as he chews his first bite.

Proving to himself I wasn't lying.

"How'd I do?" Charlie accepts my empty plate, setting them both in the sink.

"Like I said, the cake is tasty."

"Thank you, but I meant with the anniversary. Was this too much? I figured since we're only going to have a year's worth, better make it count. And have them more often."

"You're going to do this every month?" The skepticism coats my voice, but I guess the guy has a lot of time on his hands to plan things if he wants.

Charlie steps closer to me. "Probably. How else will my cake game improve? Speaking of, you have some icing, just here." He taps a long finger to his bottom lip.

I try to wipe the same spot on my own face, but he shakes his head. "Here. I'll get it."

And as if we're a real couple and he's done this hundreds of times before, Charlie cups my cheek in his warm palm and carefully swipes his thumb over my sensitive lip.

And a tension inside me snaps.

Chapter Thirty-Two

LUNA

The caring look in Charlie's eyes paired with the swipe of his finger does it. That simple touch has me forgetting the final rule of our marriage. The one that I wrote down because my subconscious knew that at some point Charlie would touch me in exactly the right way, and I wouldn't be able to stop myself from kissing him.

The question is, why did I think a single line handwritten on a piece of paper would stop me from claiming what I crave?

I fist my hands around the straps of the apron he's still wearing, barely keeping myself from jerking him down to my mouth.

"Kiss me. Now," I demand.

Charlie's brows shoot up. "Luna..."

If I was a different woman, the hesitation in his voice would cow me. I'd read the pause as disinterest. Pity. But I know Charlie now. How he cares. How he smooths over conflict, concerned about how others will view a messy result.

Crossing this line will cause a mess.

But with his plush lips so close, I can't concentrate on the future. All that exists is surviving the present, and the only way I'll survive is if I get to taste him.

I scoot to the edge of the counter, then spread my thighs wide.

"This is your last chance," I warn.

I'm lying. I don't give up easily.

But as I guessed, the ultimatum spurns him to action. Charlie surges forward, cupping my cheeks with his warm palms. Despite the heat in his eyes, the man stays gentle as he lowers his mouth to mine.

A groan of impatience tears from me, and when I reach for his face I'm not gentle. I grip the back of his neck and hold him in place, demanding what I want. Sucking on that sinful lip, pressing my tongue against his in a dirty promise. Charlie moans, the hot rush of the noise breathing into me. His hands drop to my body, fingers digging into my waist to pull me forward.

Against an impressive erection.

I can't help rocking against the hard length, my mind wandering down a tangent about whether my husband has ever gripped himself to thoughts of me. The way I've massaged my clit to thoughts of him.

"Charlie." I never knew I had this breathy voice in me, but there's no stopping needy edge when he pulls away.

Charlie's hands drag to the tops of my thighs, long fingers puckering the skin when he digs his grip in. As if he needs to hold on to me for balance. Glad to know I'm not the only one off-kilter right now.

Then he kneels. Straight down, knees hitting the wood of the kitchen floor with a soft thud. My husband stays in front of me. Beneath me. Leaning forward, Charlie presses a kiss first to one knee and then the other, as if he's not bothered in the slightest by the rough skin and calluses I earned from many brawls and sandbags. He worships my skin with his hot mouth as if I'm the smoothest silk, untouched by the sharp world.

Those worshipful acts have me relaxing back on my palms, allowing him to continue his sensual moves. Letting him slide my athletic shorts and sensible black underwear off.

People have gone down on me before. This isn't the first time someone has been eye level with my vulva. But Charlie treats the moment with so much reverence that I can't help thinking this time is different than all the others.

He stares.

No, he gazes at this intimate part of me while his fingers slowly drag up the inside of my legs, leaving goosebumps in their wake. Every inch of me shivers. Part trepidation, part anticipation.

Then his lips follow the trail his fingers mapped, lips and tongue dragging over my already sensitive flesh. When his teasing breath brushes against my pussy, my hips rock with repressed need. It takes a good portion of my mental strength to keep from grabbing the back of his head and dragging him the last few inches to my core.

But I'm not sure if he's ready to get smothered by my arousal.

Charlie has the audacity to hold my eyes as his thick, pink tongue extends and slowly licks up my intimate lips.

"Oh fuck," I mutter, digging my nails into the marble countertop, ready to smash through the stone to get at the man.

My husband.

That word, the ownership in it, pushes my pulse to a faster pace.

This man is between my legs pleasuring me, and that's my ring on his finger.

He's mine.

In this moment, nothing between us feels fake.

"Luna," he groans my name against my folds, upper lip brushing my clit. I jerk at the streak of pleasure, and my hands release their death grip only to cradle his head as he devours me.

Charlie growls an animal sound, licking deeper as he slings my legs over his shoulders. When his grip comes to my ass, I gasp at the possession he takes. Almost as if this act is just as much for him as it is for me. As if I'm the most delicious taste he's ever sampled and he'll bite the hand of anyone attempting to take away his feast.

Sweet, laid-back Charlie goes feral, consuming me. Demanding I experience an arousal so fierce the edges of my vision blur, and my toes curl so hard I'm worried they may cramp.

When every muscle tightens inside me, on the edge of pain, Charlie wraps his lips around my clit and sucks.

I choke out a scream of his name, the sound angry on my lips, my muscles snapping free, as if all my bones broke and their marrow was pure pleasure that pours into every nerve in my body.

And as the erotic mind fog clears, I'm left with one thought.

How dare he do this to me?

. . .

CHARLIE

Luna meticulously wipes all emotion from her face.

This is one of those life-changing moments. Where one wrong step might send everything I've wanted careening over a cliff's edge to land in a fiery wreckage on impact with the rocky ground.

This could be when Luna calls everything off. Us living together, the inheritance, and most importantly, our marriage.

If I'd let myself think, I would have realized this was too fast. Damn it, I have an entire year to build up to physical intimacy, but I couldn't last a month.

Still, I won't let what we could have go without a fight. And as long as I approach this battle correctly, I might have a chance.

One thing I've learned about Luna is she's a gladiator. Send her into the ring and she'll win. Hands down. Every time.

That's why this moment doesn't need a battle. I need to retreat.

But not with my tail between my legs.

With my wife on the counter, thighs still spread, her pussy lips on display, wet from her arousal and my tongue, I long to stay on my knees in supplication.

Instead, I stand, lean forward, and press a kiss to her forehead, trying to convey how much she means to me in that simple gesture.

"I'm going to walk Pig," I murmur against her flushed skin. When I meet her eyes, I'm satisfied to see some of the stoicism crack with her confused blink. In her befuddled state, I'm able to dive in and steal a quick kiss from her lips. "Don't you dare touch those dishes." Then I force myself to back away, dropping my hands to my crotch to cover the tent in my pants. Good thing it's dark outside. No neighbors have to see me walking around sporting major wood.

"Come on, little piggy," I call to the sleeping pit bull. Pig lifts her head, then gives an undignified groan as she heaves herself out of her dog bed. When the two of us head toward the hallway, I glance behind me and spy Luna still on the counter, watching my departure with her mouth open wide in shock.

The sight is adorable. I fight the urge to sprint over and ply her with more kisses. But that would leave me vulnerable to her knee-jerk argument reaction.

Luna needs space to process what we just did. Pig gives a full-body wiggle as I slip her harness on. After I close the door and head out to the sidewalk, I tuck my still-hard dick into my waistband just in case I run into someone.

Space gives Luna time to think, but it's also the same freedom for me. Time to replay, over and over, what just happened. Hell, I can still taste her arousal on my tongue. Hear her growl my name. Feel the scrape of her nails against my scalp.

This is not helping my dick soften at all.

Pig demands we stop as she intently sniffs a collection of bushes.

There's another reason I left, blatantly avoiding a fight with Luna. Keeping the erotic memory free of any shadows. For both of us.

Without me there to start an argument with, hopefully Luna sees we don't need to have one. That life can be this easy. We can fuck on the kitchen counter, then I'll take the dog out and do the dishes. Simple as that. Life doesn't have to be complicated. It can be shockingly easy.

We can be easy together.

I know I shouldn't get ahead of myself, that I should accept what happened as a happy reality and not let my brain imagine more. But I can't help playing the fantasy out of me returning home, cleaning up the dishes, then walking into my bedroom to find her naked under the covers waiting for me.

Now that I know what her pussy looks like, tastes like, I long to learn the sensation of her tightening around my shaft. To be inside her when the next orgasm hits.

I would empty out my savings account just to hear her moan my name.

"She's not going to be in my bed," I mutter to myself, needing to say the words aloud to try to force them through the lust-fogged part of my brain. Pig throws me a curious glance, then pulls to get us moving faster.

I'm eager to get back to Luna but also worried about what I'll find there.

Probably nothing. Luna will likely shut herself up in her bedroom, playing ghost with me for however long she can keep that up for.

Despair digs claws into my gut at the thought, but I'm not the type to badger a woman who doesn't want to be around me.

Even if that woman is my wife.

Chapter Thirty-Three

LUNA

He left.

Just strolled out the front door. With my dog.

And now I'm alone in the kitchen, all wound up for a fight with no sparring partner.

Should I shout into the air? Shadow box with my fear that this careful arrangement is ruined?

That I ruined it?

But this isn't on me. It can't be.

Charlie never should have made me this ridiculous dinner. He shouldn't have gotten me gifts that show how much he cares.

He's a fake husband. When he acted like a real one, he fooled me. My body tricked me into thinking the touching, kissing, licking was all okay. That this was all part of the deal.

But it is specifically not part of the deal because fucking my husband will ruin everything.

"Damn it," I mutter. I'm torn between waiting here to have it out with Charlie and retreating to my bedroom where I can pretend like this never happened and nothing changed. That nothing will change for at least another year.

But as I avoid looking at the area of the counter I just orgasmed on, my eyes adhere to the stack of dirty dishes in the sink. Remnants of the delicious dinner Charlie made for me. Some corner of my mind that wishes the world was fair informs me I can't leave the mess for him to handle on his own.

With clenched teeth, I pull on a set of rubber gloves and open the dishwasher.

The appliance is full and I'm hand washing the remaining items when the sound of the front door opening tenses my muscles. Heavy footsteps approach the kitchen, stopping somewhere near the doorway. I'd have to turn around to find his exact location, but I decide to stick to the ignore-him tactic for the moment.

There's a part of me that wants to yell, but I don't know what words would even come out at this point.

I flinch as a tall body steps up beside me. Charlie slides a dish towel off the hook and picks up a large pot I just set in the drainer.

He's helping. Of course, he is.

"I've got this," I gripe, needing him and all his delicious smilingness to find another room to be in so he's not here, looming over me.

"I don't mind." The sound of his voice starts up a new throbbing between my legs, which I ignore.

I continue through the task, moving robotically. Hating every silent second. The lack of noise is a weight bearing down on how big of a mistake I just let happen.

Encouraged to happen.

Maybe Charlie just went along because he felt he had to.

Ugh. The idea curdles my stomach.

Likely now my fake husband is trying to figure out the best way to let me know this agreement is over. To break this crushing tension, I decide to give him an opening. An easy door to step out of my life so we can end this awkward night sooner than later.

"If you want out, I get it." With a more forceful push than necessary, I shut off the sink. Luckily, I don't break the faucet with my heavy-handed moves.

"Want out? Of what?"

"Of our fake marriage. Hell, I didn't even bother to tell you I don't have any STIs! What we just did, it crossed a line. Broke the rules we set out."

Charlie doesn't look at me. Doesn't respond for a long time as he places a dried glass into the cupboard. *Why does shelving drinking glasses require so much of his concentration? Couldn't he just say thanks and then we can be done?* Tomorrow I'll get up early to help him pack. And then I'll go in the backyard, dig into my garden with a vengeance, and try to figure out some other way to save Leo from his thoughtless life decisions.

"I don't want out." His words fill the kitchen, unyielding in their certainty. "If anything, I want more in."

"More in? What does that mean?"

Charlie turns his back to the counter, leaning against the granite and gripping it on either side of his hips. His searching gaze meets mine.

"I don't like the idea of not being married to you. Ever."

"What?" My volume increases tenfold, and I wait for him to laugh at his ridiculous joke.

Charlie blinks down at his feet. "I like you, Luna. What we did here, that wasn't just a spur-of-the-moment attraction thing. I've wanted to do that for a while."

Needing to hold on to something, I grip the counter opposite him.

"A while? How long is a while?"

Charlie meets my eyes, his mouth held in a serious line. "The boat."

"The..." The boat. The first time we met.

Oh hell.

"You cannot be serious!" I pace away from him, digging my fingers into the roots of my hair. "You agreed to a fake marriage even though you have some silly crush on me?"

"Doesn't seem silly to me." Charlie cracks his knuckles before shoving his hands in his pockets.

I wish I had a punching bag in front of me to pummel.

"You lied to me!" I throw at him, not sure why there's such a sharp pain in my chest.

My deceitful husband pushes off the counter, crossing to me with serious eyes. "You asked me if I wanted to marry you. I did, so I said yes. I never lied."

"You misled me!"

"I didn't share all of my feelings with you, but I've followed all of your rules."

"Not tonight you didn't."

He stares at me hard. "I'm not the one who broke first."

"Fuck you!"

Charlie's face goes blank. A completely closed off expression I've never seen him wear before. "It's late. Let's talk about this tomorrow morning." He maneuvers around me, heading toward his bedroom.

"What about couples never going to bed angry?" I yell at his back.

My husband pauses, but he doesn't turn around. "I don't think that's a good rule. Emotions are always more manageable when the sun is out." He lets out a short whistle, and Pig scrambles up from her dog bed to follow him.

Once again, I'm left alone in the kitchen. Only this time I'm reeling for an entirely different reason.

What's a woman supposed to do when her fake husband admits he has real feelings?

Chapter Thirty-Four

CHARLIE

As I lie in bed, I strain to hear any kind of movement through the wall. Some hint that Luna is getting ready for bed. That she didn't leave the house as soon as I was out of sight.

Eventually, I catch the rush of water hitting tile. Her shower turning on. The relief is short-lived when I think about why she's washing off so late at night.

Getting rid of my touch. The remnants of what we did earlier.

Fuck, just the memory of her is enough to get me hard. I glare down at the bulge in my shorts, wanting to remind my dick that we're not going to get any attention for a long time.

I'm not sure what drove me to confess my true feelings. Just, after what we did today, moving backward seemed impossible. How could I go from my head in between her thighs back to pretending our entire relationship is fake?

My mind doesn't work like that.

Pig shifts on her side of the bed, then lets out a big sleepy sigh.

At least the dog doesn't hate me.

The shower shuts off, and images of Luna soaking wet fill my mind.

Damn it. This infatuation is going to get much worse.

She moaned my name.

And now she's freaking out. Which I understand. I really do. This agreement we have is all in pursuit of setting her brother free. A selfless act. And no doubt Luna's worried I'll start demanding more from her now in order to continue the ruse.

The thought that I'd try to manipulate Luna has me wanting to gag.

That's not how you treat people you care about.

Tomorrow, I'll figure out how to tell her even though I'd like things to change, they don't have to. That I'm here for her in whatever capacity she needs.

I just can't tonight.

I'm about to roll over and try to force myself to sleep when my bedroom door opens, and I jerk to attention when Luna pokes her head in. With quick fingers I slide my glasses on, wanting to see her face rather than a blur of features. The expression she wears isn't any more welcoming than before, but she doesn't hiss at me to leave her home.

"I want my dog," she says.

Of course. She's here for Pig, not me. Silently, I say farewell to the pup's innocent, comforting presence.

"Not holding her hostage." I give the pit bull an encouraging push toward Luna. The dog stays relaxed, a dead weight in the middle of my mattress.

Luna steps farther into the room. "Pig. Come. Come here, Pig."

The dog cracks an eyelid. But then she just snuggles her head deeper into my comforter.

"Pig. Come." Luna's voice has shifted from asking to demanding.

But Pig doesn't seem to care.

"She can sleep here tonight," I offer.

So can you, I almost add.

No doubt that second statement would receive the same scowl my first comment gets.

"Pig likes sleeping with me," Luna declares.

And normally, she's not wrong. But tonight, Pig seems hell-bent on staying in my bed, going full boneless when Luna tries tugging at her collar.

"Fine!" Luna gives up and stomps out of the room.

There's no victory in this. Only more tension between us.

But then a moment later, Luna's back, carrying a blanket. "I'm sleeping with my dog," she announces.

As if I'll fight her on the idea of us sharing a bed.

The mattress dips as she climbs onto the other side, attention focused on her pillow and blanket rather than me. Once Luna is prone, she tosses an arm around Pig, the big spoon to her dog's little.

The sight causes an ache in my heart even after I place my glasses on the bedside table and shut off the lamp.

I crave for this pair to be my family. *Luna, Charlie, and Pig.*

Sounds perfect to me. I bet I could get Pig on my side as easily as she spills over into my space on the bed now.

All we need is our stubborn woman.

But I won't force her.

I'm just about to bring that up despite what I said earlier. Only Luna speaks first.

"What did you mean when you said emotions are more manageable when the sun is out?"

The memory of when I first heard those words has me smiling.

I was maybe nine, and I walked in on my parents arguing. They weren't yelling. My parents never yelled at each other. But their words were tense, and frowns marred both of their faces. Upon my arrival, my mom announced she needed some time. She pressed a kiss on the top of my head, then left the room.

I was terrified. I ran up to my father, grabbing his shirt on the verge of tears, begging to know if Mom was leaving us. The angry expression on his face disappeared instantly at that question, and he leaned down to scoop me into his arms, hugging me tight to his broad chest. I was approaching the age where I scorned getting snuggled like a baby, but that night I gripped him back just as tight.

And he told me no. That Mom was just going to bed. That sleep gives people time to sift through their emotions. That kind words come easier at the start of the day than at the end of it, and they would finish their talk in the morning when it would be easier to be kind to each other.

Then he sat me at the table and scooped us some generous portions of ice cream. The next morning, I came downstairs to find them kissing in the kitchen.

And I never forgot that lesson.

"Just something my dad likes to say. That it's okay to go to bed angry. People shouldn't argue when they're tired or hungry because that just makes everything worse. And that sunshine puts people in a better mood. If you still want to yell at me tomorrow after breakfast..." I trail off, because I'd rather not give out permission to be screamed at.

"I don't want to yell at you," Luna says. "That's what my parents do."

"I don't want to yell at you either."

Luna snorts. "Can you yell, Charlie Keller?"

In the darkness, I grin up at the ceiling, hope alighting in my chest at her teasing tone.

"Oh, yeah. Definitely. I can scream like a banshee. Just put me in front of a good band and I'll yell my head off."

There's a scoff from her side of the bed. "That's fan girl screaming."

"Excuse me, that's fan *person* screaming, and I am accomplished at it."

She emits a soft chuckle that warms my whole being. "People would hate us if we went to a concert together."

"Why's that?"

The bed jiggles as Luna shifts around, then there's a doggy groan and Pig stretches her legs further into my space, not caring in the least that her paws are digging into my side.

Bed hog.

"Because I would take full advantage of you there."

I almost swallow my tongue, but Luna keeps talking.

"When you're only a few inches above five foot, trying to see the stage is a bitch. I'd insist you boost me onto your shoulders so I could get a better seat. Which would turn us into a giant two-person monster with you doing whatever obnoxious screaming you do. The ultimate concert menace."

A weird laugh groan spills out of me at her description. I can imagine what a ridiculous sight we'd make. But fuck, I can also fantasize about exactly what it'd be like to have Luna's strong thighs cradling my head.

Like earlier tonight.

We spend the next hour exchanging concert stories, our tales punctuated with yawns until eventually we both pass out.

And neither of us ends up going to bed mad.

But the next morning, my bed is empty of both dog and wife.

Chapter Thirty-Five

LUNA

"Can I just say, your husband is adorable." Violet grins at me over her zip-tied hands.

"Less chatting, more breaking free." I sit cross-legged next to her, eyes on my stopwatch. I intentionally do not look at the brown bag lunch Charlie packed me that sits on the bench across the room. Definitely not noticing how he used a heart instead of an "a" when he wrote my name on it. "The point is to get faster, not more casual about this."

"Yeah, yeah," Violet mutters under her breath as she slips off her bracelet that's actually a cord made of extremely strong fiber. She toes off her shoe, loops the cord around her big toe, grabs the other end with her teeth, and proceeds to saw through her binding. A moment later the plastic snaps.

"Ta da!" Violet returns her deceptively useful jewelry to her wrist.

"Good. Next time you're going to do it blindfolded."

She puffs out a sigh as if exasperated with my lessons. I know her pouting is all an act, rising from the dramatic part of her personality. Violet is the one who hired me. Our phone call from a few months back sits clear in my memory.

"My brother has a security guard living up my ass." I'd heard the annoyance in every bitten word. "And not in a sexy way. He thinks this guy is some cyborg superman who will defend me from all evil. But I won't put all my eggs in his terminator basket. I need to be able to save myself."

Said security guard lingers along the wall, leaning back against the cement like he's the most important support beam in the place. Manuel's face is a blank mask, scanning the private gym I've booked for our session as if he expects gang members to jump out of every nook any second.

Not that I fault him for his level of alert. Better to be overly watchful than slacking off in his line of business.

Still, I don't miss the way his attention inevitably comes back to Violet, tracing over her form.

Is he checking after her well-being with that full-body scan? Or could that be a spark of longing?

Even as I try stifling my curiosity, I wonder if Manuel volunteered for this position. I guess unrequited love could be an added motivator to keeping your charge safe.

If anyone threatened Charlie, I'd dig their still-beating heart from their chest.

Not that I love the man or anything.

Shaking off an uncomfortable zing of energy, I stand and move over to my bag, pulling out a bandana.

"Kinky." Violet grins as I cover her eyes and knot the fabric behind her head, careful not to tangle her sea-foam curls in the knot. "Do you and Charlie use this in the bedroom?"

Would I trust him to blindfold me?

Stop thinking about sex with your fake husband!

I blame Violet.

"You know," I say, "I think you're ready for hands behind your back too."

She lets out a squeak of affront as I move to reband her hands. She starts testing the bonds the second I let go.

But her task still doesn't detract her prying questions.

"So am I you or Charlie right now? Who's the dom?"

Giving into an evil urge, I glance over at Manuel, who is resolutely not watching his trussed-up client.

"Hey, Manuel!" I wave him over. "Let's make this closer to the real deal. Why don't you give our favorite singer a turn around the room? Maybe a few spins?"

The guy presses his lips together, but I'm almost certain I see a twitch at the corner of his mouth. He moves toward us in ground-eating strides, then scoops Violet off the ground to sling her in a fireman's carry over his shoulder. She squawks an inelegant sound I'm sure she'd never allow out of her mouth onstage.

Manuel glances at me, one brow curved in question.

"Just a few circuits. An abrupt turn or two. Something she'd deal with if a kidnapper was moving her."

At that, any minuscule glimmer of humor ices out of his face.

I think if any person were to damage a single molecule of Violet Bluefield's body, Manuel would take the incident personally and begin a lifelong vendetta. She's the puppy to his John Wick.

Not a bad person to have on your side.

"You're both cruel!" Violet yelps as her bodyguard power walks around the room with her. He zigzags at random points and makes multiple 360-degree turns.

"Clock starts as soon as your ass hits the ground!" I walk as I talk, so she doesn't have a bearing on her place in the room.

When Manuel finishes giving her a good shaking, he sets her down. Though the man committed to his attempts to disorient her, he sets Violet on the thick mat as if she were made of glass. He takes two steps back, then stops, crossing his arms as he looms over her.

"I can tell you're there," Violet accuses. "I wouldn't try to get my bindings off in front of the kidnapper, right, Luna?"

"Good instincts." I smile across the way at my pupil even though she can't see me. I nod at Manuel, and he stalks toward the exit, opening the door and then shutting it with a bang without stepping through. That's when I start the timer, and one of country music's biggest stars begins writhing around on the ground like a worm at a rave hyped up on ecstasy.

As Violet works to get loose, my mind flips back to her casually suggestive questions. And from there it's a short leap to my kitchen and sitting on that countertop.

I may have had the high ground, but Charlie dominated me. The way he coaxed my pleasure to the surface as if he understood every secret my body has ever tried to hide. My nipples tighten at the memory, and I cross my arms over my chest so the points pressing against my sports bra don't show.

My attention gets pulled back to Violet when her restraints snap. She tears off her blindfold with a whoop of triumph. My thumb presses to stop the timer, but I give her my sternest look.

"Sorry." My friend ducks her head. "Next time I will celebrate my victory quietly."

I nod and show her the time, and she grins wide. "I bet I can beat that."

And if Violet weren't rubbing her wrists like the reddened skin pained her, then I might go another round. But these lessons are meant to keep her from getting hurt, not cause injury.

"Next session we'll go again. For now, I think we need to revisit rule number one."

Violet groans. Manuel tilts his head side to side, loosening the muscles in his neck as he moves to stand near the door, hand on the handle.

I don't let the country singer's—admittedly adorable—pout sway me. "When you sense danger, what is the first rule?" I use my coldest instructor's tone.

She rolls to her feet and heads toward the exit.

"Run."

Chapter Thirty-Six

CHARLIE

For the past three nights, Pig has crawled into my bed, eventually followed by my wife.

The sleeping arrangement always stays platonic, with the snoring dog between us. Nothing like what happened in the kitchen. The first morning after, I told Luna nothing had to change about our arrangement. I expect nothing more than what we originally agreed to.

She'd given a firm nod, told me that sounded good, then accepted the bag lunch I packed her and left for work.

Since then, things have been...odd.

Almost like hooking up in the kitchen opened Luna up to more physical closeness. But nothing sexual. I don't know where I stand, but I'm just glad we're not over.

And that we're sharing a bed.

Luna left the covers a few minutes ago, and I can hear her beginning of the day routine down the hall in her bathroom. Palming my morning wood, I wait 'til I hear her shower running before climbing out of bed and ducking into the guest bathroom.

Thoughts of my wife fill my head when I grip myself in the shower. The gasps she made and the rake of her nails against my skull. By the time I'm out and drying myself off, the slam of the front door lets me know she's gone. I wasn't intentionally dodging her. Luna's schedule changes daily based on her clients, which means I haven't been able to plan to be in the kitchen with her when she's making breakfast. Some days it happens, other days Pig and I have the house to ourselves.

To avoid thoughts about the uncertainty of my relationship with my wife, I try to focus on my life plan. But just like every other day this month, time passes, and I still have no solution.

Pig is no help. The dog trots beside me now, tongue lolling out the side of her wide mouth as she happily pants after her hour of tussling in the dog park. We could have gone straight home afterward. Pig got plenty of exercise. No need to walk along this city sidewalk.

But with nothing to do at the house other than clean, I find myself drawn to a place that calms me.

C & M's Guitar Studio.

With Pig at my side, I have no plans to go in, but the shop has an amazing selection on display in their front window. I spend a good ten minutes running my eyes over the Gibsons while Pig sits patiently at my feet.

"That's a well-behaved dog." The observation comes from my right in a vaguely familiar voice. I meet the stare of Cassandra, the C of C & M.

"Thank you. I'd like to take credit, but she basically came this way."

Cassandra nods, giving the two of us a speculative look. "As long as she stays mellow, you can bring her in. I've got some new stock. More interesting than these."

The woman pulls the front door of the shop open and holds it for me.

"Thanks." I eagerly follow her, leaning down to give Pig a pet because she's a good girl. "I've been meaning to come by dogless, but Pig and I tend to spend the entire day together."

The store owner snorts. "Pig?"

"She came with that too. Fits her though."

We both glance at the dog, with her short legs, slight potbelly, and heavy nose that gives the appearance of a snout.

"I see that."

The three of us maneuver through rows of guitars, dodging the occasional customer on our way. Some people give my dog a strange look, but my girl keeps being her well-behaved self. Constantly proving all the myths about pit bulls wrong.

"Back here." Cassandra holds open a door leading to a well-equipped repair shop. There are a few disassembled instruments on high-top tables. The pieces give my gut an anxious twinge, and I'm glad I'm not the one in charge of putting them back together. Even with as much as I know, I'd never get them all right.

"Here. I found these at an estate sale in Georgia. Aren't they gorgeous?" Cassandra gestures to four guitars propped side by side. I crouch down to get a better look, realizing that she has a collection of Fenders.

"Are these all pre-1960?"

"You got it. They need some work, but man, do they have good bones."

"They're beautiful." I reach out to stroke my thumb across the strings. Not trying to play anything, but just experimenting with the sound.

"You should come by once I've gotten a chance to work on them. Or come by any other time, I don't care. You seem like good people." Cassandra's blunt way of speaking has me smiling to myself.

"Thanks. I'm glad I met you."

She wanders away from me. "Violet does that. Brings people together. She works with your wife, right? Newlyweds. How's that going?"

I glance up at Cassandra from where I'm crouched. She's moved over to one of her work benches and looks to be testing the strength of glue she applied to a neck.

"Things are..." I trail off, realizing I don't want to lie to this woman. Not after she's shown me these beautiful instruments. I get the sense that Cassandra is trying to reach out to me. Maybe make a new friend.

And friends shouldn't lie to each other.

"Honestly, they're a little tense. We're not balanced."

Someone used to repairing delicate instruments would know how important balance is.

"How so?" Cassandra asks.

While I'm on her level, I scratch Pig behind her ears, and her tail raps happily against the ground. There are so many ways Luna and I are off-center. My ever-present crush could be the most prevalent reason. I long for her to a massive degree, while I doubt Luna feels more than an average level of attraction.

But that's digging a little too deep for a new friendship.

I choose another, more relatable answer.

"Luna is the breadwinner. And I'm fine with her making more than me. We both agreed I'd take this year off from work to figure out a new life direction. A new career. But I haven't made much headway. Sometimes I feel like I'm not contributing anything to our relationship."

Luna would argue that me being in the relationship is enough, but it's not for me. Not when she only sees me as the key to some cash. If I'm jobless by the end of the year, would I have the nerve to ask her to consider continuing our marriage?

"You're switching careers?"

"Trying. I worked in fabric sales. Over in Germany. But I got antsy. Fabrics just aren't something I'm passionate about, and that's what I want in my next job."

For someone trying to pursue desire, a marriage of convenience sounds like the most emotionless choice I could make. And yet my fake relationship has more passion than anything else in my life.

Cassandra studies me while I rise to my feet. "Was it just the fabrics part or did you also dislike being a salesperson?"

Luna asked a similar question back when I first admitted my dissatisfaction.

"Actually, the sales part was enjoyable. Getting to know people, figuring out which product would meet their needs, having them leave happy. All that was great. But then I'd get home at night and realize I was just talking about fabric all day. Like, yeah, I found the product they needed, but do they truly care about it? Once they have what works, do they ever give it a second thought?" I shrug. "That slowly sucked any ounce of joy out of it."

Cassandra continues to watch me. "What if you were selling

something people were passionate about? Something they loved and appreciated every day of their life?"

She creates my dream with her words, and it's not a far jump to figure out her destination.

"You mean work here? Sell guitars?"

Cassandra runs her fingers over the body of a Gretsch Rancher, the wood gleaming from whatever treatment she used. "I opened this shop five years ago with my husband. He was good with people. Better than I am." She doesn't look at me as she says that. If she had been, she'd have seen the disagreement on my face. Cassandra has been nothing but kind to me. A little stiff, sure, but still pleasant to be around.

"We had a perfect setup. He ran the front of the shop, and I handled the back end."

The past tense she's using warns me to brace myself.

"He passed last year. Lung cancer." She huffs out a laugh with zero humor. "He quit smoking before we ever met, but the cigarettes still got him in the end."

"I'm sorry," I murmur. As if sensing the woman's sadness, Pig wanders over and snuffles at Cassandra's pant leg. That earns her a pet and a genuine, if sad, smile.

"My point is I wasn't meant to work this place alone."

Her words confuse me because I saw at least two people with C & M staff T-shirts on the sales floor.

"Are you offering me a job here?"

Cassandra glances at me as her fingers continue to scratch Pig's blocky head. "This town is full of people looking for part-time work. They want a discount on guitars and flexible hours so they can make their gigs. And they'll drop this job as soon as someone offers them a little cash and promises of a record deal. Those are the people I offer jobs to. What I need is a partner. Someone looking for a career. Do you think that could be you?"

I open my mouth a few times, fully intending to answer, only to realize I don't have words. Not a great show for a potential salesperson.

Cassandra holds up her hand, maybe sensing the riot of thoughts swirling in my mind.

"This is an idea I just came up with. Right now. How about you think it over, and if you're interested, then send over your resume and some references? If you're not, no harm, no foul. Come into the shop whenever you want. Bring this one with you." Cassandra pats Pig.

I decide to head out before I blurt something that'll have her rescinding the offer.

Could I take it?

What would Luna say to the idea of me staying in Nashville?

Chapter Thirty-Seven

LUNA

I'm just leaving the gym when my cell phone buzzes. After giving a last wave to my second client of the day, an heiress to a hotel fortune, I dig the device out of my bag.

> **Dash**: You need to control your husband.
> I stare down at my brother's cryptic message, at a total loss.
> What could Charlie—the sweetest man alive—have done to piss him off?
> **Luna**: Not following.
> The next text is a picture. Pumpkin appears on my screen sporting a hot dog costume. I snort on a laugh as the next message arrives.
> **Dash**: Charlie sent this. Paige insisted we put it on her.
> **Luna:** Seems like you're pretty lucky to have such a giving brother-in-law.
> **Dash**: She says he got a hamburger costume for Pig.

A slow grin tugs at my lips as I imagine Charlie in a pet supply store shopping for dog outfits. He's taken on the role of dog dad and run with it. I half expect to arrive home to find him giving Pig a pedicure.

I'm in the middle of typing a response when an unfamiliar number flashes on the screen, I almost let it go to voicemail. But then I remember that 302 is a Delaware area code.

"Hello?"

"Ms. Lamont? This is Daniel Carmichael."

Why is Wai Po's lawyer calling me?

"Hi. What can I do for you?"

The man coughs on the other end of the line, and all my muscles—loose and warm from my workout—tighten up quickly.

"I received a concerning call this morning."

"Oh, really?" *Give me one guess who the caller was.*

"Yes. The party expressed concern over your ability to fulfill the stipulations your grandmother set forth in the will."

Unbelievable.

No, scratch that. Totally believable. I should've known my father would have pulled this kind of shit.

"And what, exactly," I bite the words out, "did this party say was the problem?"

He clears his throat. "That you were already married, and therefore any new arrangement would be false, and because you are not living with your legal husband, you aren't fulfilling the requirements."

I bark out a laugh, the sound harsh in my throat.

"I have only married one man, and that is Charlie Keller." I almost add that he is the only man I ever want to marry, but the thought isn't relevant and also shocks the hell out of me. But I push past it. "Did this party provide you any proof of this fake previous marriage he claims I was in?"

Silence. "Not as of yet."

I grit my teeth, wishing fixing things were this simple. But knowing Bill Lamont, they won't be.

"I'm going to assume the person who contacted you is my father, and I would like you to consider what he has to gain if I fuck this up."

There's a sharp cough on the other end of the line, and I can hear the disapproval of my cursing in the noise. Damn it. I need this guy on my side. Or at least neutral.

"You may or may not be aware," I grind out, doing what I can to keep my cool, "that my father has known criminal associates."

"Like your brothers."

Fucking hell, I wish I could punch this stuck-up lawyer straight in his jaw.

"Yes." I keep my voice deadpan because that's the best I can do. "If you receive any kind of documentation that claims I've been married in the past, I would appreciate it if you give me the chance to refute the document because I can assure you it would be a forgery. And I am sure you and your office would hate to find out that you paid out an inheritance to the wrong benefactor if I were to prove the document was invalid at a later date."

There's a stretch of silence on the other end of the line, then a stern response. "As you are the intended benefactor, I of course would give you the opportunity to demonstrate you have adequately fulfilled the terms of the will. No funds will be paid out until all proper channels have been followed."

"Thank you," I manage to say.

After we disconnect the call, I stride with stiff legs to my car and climb into the driver's seat, where I pause to breathe in deeply through my nose and exhale in big gusts out my mouth.

In. Out. In. Out.

Doesn't help.

"Fuck you! You piece of shit greedy dick-nosed scumbag!" My fists pound the steering wheel with each curse and insult.

I only stop when I accidentally set off the car alarm.

Just when I start to get centered in my life, my father has to ruin it. And the ridiculous thing is if Bill Lamont had just been a slightly decent human being, he wouldn't have had to fight me for this money.

Because by every account, he was the one who urged my mother to cut off contact with her parents when they didn't approve of him. Instead of trying to be a better man, someone Wai Po and my grandfather could respect, Bill got their daughter to ghost them.

Not that I'm giving my mother an out, but she's always let my father lead. And if he'd suggested mending bridges, she would have done it.

After my brothers and I were born, my grandparents likely wouldn't have fought against the match.

But no. Neither my mom nor my dad ever reached out to Wai Po. Not in over thirty years.

And now he wants her money?

I'm still a swirling cloud of anger when I walk in my house, but I stifle the turbulent emotions enough to crouch down and give my dog the love and affection she deserves for being the most adorable doggo in the world.

"Sweet piggy puppy," I murmur to her while giving her belly a thorough scratching.

The sound of guitar strings drifts to me from deeper in my house, enticing me toward the soothing noise. I know what I'll find at the end. And that only makes me eager to seek the origin out more.

I find Charlie on the back deck, sitting on the steps that lead to the yard. His body curves over the wooden neck of the guitar. He's not playing a song at the moment. His fingers twist the little nobs I think are used for tuning.

Despite spending a decent amount of time around musicians, I still have little clue how their instruments work.

The random, directionless strums he makes should be annoying. But to me they sound comfortable. Casual. They show me Charlie is relaxed enough here to fiddle with the hobby that makes him happy. He's not rigorously practicing to become some huge music star. He's just having fun.

I need more fun.

I need more Charlie.

"Hey." His voice pulls me out of my head, and I realize I was staring off into the distance while listening to him. "You're home. How was work?"

Anger still thrums in my veins, not as strong as before but enough to have me holding back my words. Worried I'll end up snapping at Charlie though he's done nothing wrong.

Instead of answering, I settle onto the step beside him. Close enough that my leg and hip press against his. That our arms brush.

"Is something wrong?" He keeps his voice careful, his hand releasing from the guitar to cover mine where I've left it resting on my knee.

I shouldn't be doing this. Demanding comfort from him with my body. The man is already doing enough for me. There's nothing in our contract about being my emotional support beam. But I don't move away.

"Not really." Whatever my dad comes up with, I'll prove he's lying. All this means is more frustration and headaches. But the course forward hasn't been derailed.

Pig trots past us, bumbling her way into the yard until she finds a mangled rope toy and drags it over to us. I grab hold of one end, playing tug-o-war until I trick her into loosening her hold. Once I have possession of the toy, I send it flying across the yard, and her stocky legs work overtime to chase after it.

"Let's do takeout tonight and watch one of those K-dramas," Charlie offers, not pushing me on why I'm not okay.

I snort. "One of those K-dramas? You say that like you didn't watch every second of the last episode with me. And I heard you groan when I turned the TV off instead of starting the next one. You're a K-drama fan too. Just admit it."

"Guilty." He strums a dramatic chord. "I can't get over the way they stare intently at each other for five minutes straight." Charlie gazes at me now, making his eyes overly wide until I can't help laughing. "And damn, they know how to make a cliffhanger."

"So true." I sigh. "You can play a little longer. I'm not hungry yet." Besides, watching Pig do a happy roll in the middle of my lawn helps dispel some of my annoyance.

"You don't mind?"

I shake my head. "I like when you play."

I like you, I almost add. But I catch the words before they escape and leave a vulnerable opening in my chest.

This marriage between Charlie and me is changing already. Every time I notice the shift, I try to remind myself this is good. We should get along because that'll make everything easier this next year as we spend our time together.

Charlie plucks a series of strings, and the resulting music has me grinning. One of Violet's songs. I wonder if he already knew her discography or if he learned it after he met her.

I make a mental note to myself to invite her over. We are friends after all.

Then Charlie starts singing, his voice low and deep and so smooth I imagine a knife spreading peanut butter. He lends a different perspective to the country pop song about a lost love, and soon all thoughts of my father are forgotten.

All I can focus on is the ache in my chest. And how I'm terrified of the gaping wound I'll be left with a year from now when Charlie leaves.

When I'm the one with a lost love.

Chapter Thirty-Eight

LUNA

The club is sizable, but the dim lighting and strategically placed tables give the main room an intimate atmosphere.

"There's my dad." Charlie nods to the left of the stage, then places a palm on my lower back to guide me. Even through my shirt, the warmth of his hand burns and has me wanting to melt back into him.

Instead, I press forward.

When we get close to the table, Charlie's dad rises to greet us. Mr. Keller stands at an average height, barely reaching his son's shoulder. He gives me a warm grin in greeting, reaching out to shake my hand.

"Dad, this is Luna."

"Of course. Didn't think I'd recognize my own fake daughter-in-law?" His words are jovial, a twinkle in his eyes telling me he finds our situation more amusing than disconcerting.

I breathe a touch easier.

After our talk about telling our families the truth, I still worried the Kellers would get defensive or protective, thinking I'm taking advantage of their son.

I am, but not maliciously.

It appears I wasted my time worrying, as the older man pulls out my chair with a welcoming flourish. Before Charlie takes his own seat, he gives his dad a firm hug.

The gesture fascinates me. What would it be like to have a relationship with my parents like that? Where family members pass gestures of affection back and forth rather than insults and cutting remarks?

Chances are I'd be a lot friendlier today if those were the type of guardians I'd grown up with.

"Y'all have enough time to order a drink before your mom goes on. She's looking forward to singing here. Says they've got great acoustics." Mr. Keller waves for a passing server.

Charlie glances around the space at his father's words, as if he can discern the truth of them on sight alone. Maybe he can. After living together for just over a month, I've become familiar with Charlie's hidden musical depths. Multiple evenings I've come home to find him strumming his guitar on the back porch with Pig laying rapt at his feet.

After the waiter takes our drink orders, Mr. Keller leans toward me. "I hope you don't mind if I hold off on the get-to-know-you-better portion of the evening until after my love's show. She's gonna want to ask you the same questions as me. No need for you to have to repeat yourself."

"No problem." I glance at Charlie in time to catch the amusement curling at the corner of his mouth.

I'm considering if I should be the one asking questions when the waiter returns with our drinks, and just as I'm taking the first sip, the lights dim everywhere except for the stage.

When Regina Keller steps onto the stage, I discover where Charlie's height came from.

The woman is statuesque, rising high above us all. Soft, kinky curls halo her face and glow in the stage lights. A gold dress hugs her curvaceous figure, and if I didn't know she had a son in his late twenties, I might assume she'd only lived two or three decades herself so far.

"Hello, everyone." Her voice is music even when she speaks. "I'm glad you could join me tonight. I haven't sung in Nashville for many years now, but I know a city that loves music as much as you all would always welcome me back. Let's have a good time tonight."

The audience claps and cheers, then the band behind Charlie's mom starts playing a beat, the instruments coming in at different times, blending seamlessly. Once they've warmed into the rhythm, Regina finally adds her voice to the mix.

And holy mother of musical goddesses, the woman is amazing. Even I, a novice in the world of music, can recognize she has some golden pipes on her.

At one point during the set, when her voice drops low and the words ring of hard times and struggles, my own darkness stirs in recognition. Without thinking. I reach under the table until I find Charlie's hand. With the silent request, he entwines our fingers together, and we stay connected through the rest of her show.

For a full hour, she sings. There are pauses when Regina talks to the audience, connecting with us all by sharing anecdotes from her travels and her thoughts on certain songs. She takes the time to introduce every member of her band, giving them opportunities to solo their instruments. The bass is my favorite, the deep notes reverberating in my chest as if the thick strings caress my heart.

When the show finally draws to a close, the whole audience stands, roaring and stomping, applauding the magic of Regina Keller. The band plays her off the stage, then they continue with unobtrusive background music as conversations at the tables pick up.

A moment later, the star of the show arrives at our table, and I'm so awed by her, I momentarily forget she's Charlie's mom.

"You were amazing, love." Mr. Keller stands, embracing his wife and brushing a kiss over her cheek that apples with a smile. Regina presses her lips to her husband's cheek in return, immediately wiping off the red lipstick smear.

Then her powerful attention turns to Charlie and me.

Few people in the world intimidate me anymore. Mainly because there aren't many whose opinions I care about.

But I care about Regina's.

And she intimidates the hell out of me.

"Hi, Mom." Charlie stands, pulling me with him because our hands are still linked. He gives his mother a one-armed hug. "This is Luna."

When her honeyed eyes meet mine, I stand as straight as I can and wipe my sweaty palm on my pants—thank the universe they're black—before offering a hand to shake.

"Hello, Luna."

My name in her smoky voice becomes something beautiful, and I find myself wishing I knew her well enough to get a hug of my own.

But that's ridiculous. I don't need hugs. I'm tough.

"Nice to meet you, Mrs. Keller," I respond in a polite tone, not at all revealing I'm obsessed with her. Or her son.

"Please, call me Regina." She returns my shake but clasps my hand between both of hers and takes an extra second before releasing me. As if the gesture means more than just a polite greeting.

The four of us settle back in at the table, and Regina sips from a dirty martini her husband ordered for her.

"Now, my dear, sweet, faux daughter-in-law. We got some of the story from our son, but why don't you tell us your version of these hijinks?"

Just as I start to tense up, Regina leans forward, reaching over the table to give my shoulder a reassuring rub. "We're not here to judge. Just to listen."

"We trust Charlie," Mr. Keller adds. "If he agreed to help you, then that must mean you're good people."

"Of course, we knew you were anyway, just from spending time with your brother." Regina raises her glass, toasting Dash as if he's standing beside her.

"Don't give my family a pass for Dash's sake. He's the kind-hearted oddball out." I already feel dishonest enough, no need to add more half-truths to the pile.

"You both are." Charlie drapes his arm along the back of my chair, and with his warmth surrounding me, I find myself easing into the conversation. Still, I shrug off his compliment. Maybe I'm not a bad person, but Dash is the sweet one. I'm a prickly bitch most of the time.

"Okay. My side of the story, huh? Well, Dash and I have a brother..." And I go on to relate most everything. The Lamont family criminal enterprise. Leo's entanglement in it. My uncle's exorbitant price. My Wai Po and her inheritance full of caveats.

And then I start talking about Charlie.

I never meant to. The words simply spill out of me as if I overfilled my brain with Charlie observations and now I finally have a place to empty them. All over his parents.

And the things that come from my mouth are honest and revealing.

How he's done great as my fake husband, never letting me doubt we can last the full year. How we have a good time living together, taking care of Pig. How I enjoy his guitar playing whenever I'm cooking and wish I could be as equally entertaining when it's his turn.

Then my mind brings up how we finished the last meal he made, and my words dry up. I take a hearty swig of my drink, letting the prickle of the ginger beer clear away the nervous dry throat.

Why did I just babble for so long? I never babble.

I think it must be something about Regina's smile. The kind way she looks at me has me wanting to share every inner piece of my soul with her.

But vulnerability is dangerous. That's how people hurt each other.

"You two sound like you're doing well together." Mr. Keller claps a hand on his son's shoulder.

"Temporarily," I point out, trying not to grimace with how much I hate the sound of the word.

There's a lull, Charlie glancing off to the side as if he sees something fascinating at another table. A pain sits just below my breastbone, but when Regina speaks up, her voice distracts me from the ache.

"For a year. Of course. But you tied him down closer to home for now. We're happy to have him nearby."

Charlie offers his mom a smile. "You say that like you plan on sticking around New Orleans for more than a month or two."

The Kellers share a look, then his Mom grins wide.

"I accepted a teaching position at the university."

"Wait, seriously?" Charlie's brows curve up.

She nods. "All the traveling was fine when we were younger, but I'm tired of sleeping in hotel rooms and sitting in airports for hours. Home has been looking better and better these past few years. We think it's time to stand still. At least for a little while."

Charlie's parents are staying put in New Orleans. From the grin on his face, I know this has to delight him. This is what he said he wanted. To find a place to settle, where he can see his family regularly.

I bet at the close of our year together, Charlie won't want to wait before moving down to New Orleans.

Not like anything will be keeping him in Nashville.

I'm the one who just made sure to remind everyone we're temporary.

The lime in my drink must have been bad because there's a sick sensation in the pit of my stomach. Luckily, I'm good at keeping unwanted expressions off my face. I offer a smile to the table.

We spend the next hour hearing gossip from New Orleans and the plans Mrs. Keller has for teaching her future class. And as I sit here with this family overflowing with love for each other, I can't help feeling like I'm playing a role.

Of course, we all already know this is a farce.

It just hurts because some part of me wants this to be real.

"Well, I think I'm done in for the night." Regina half sighs, half yawns. "Honey, would you mind pulling the car up? Wearing heels this tall was a mistake."

The man chuckles as he kisses his wife on the cheek. "Of course." He stands smiling down at his son and me. "I'll see you both at breakfast tomorrow."

"I'll walk out with you, Dad. Grab our car too." Charlie turns to me. "Sound good?"

I want to point out I'm perfectly fine with trekking the block to our car with him, but that would mean leaving his mom alone at the table. No way am I abandoning Regina, even if this makes me feel like I'm giving into the patriarchy.

"Good with me." I raise my still half-full glass before taking a sip.

Charlie grins wide, placing his hand over mine and squeezing briefly before he gets up. Then they're gone, and I'm left with a woman giving me a detective-level gaze full of curiosity. Just as sweat gathers in my pits, she speaks.

"You know, I have eyes on that stage."

The comment throws me, and I try to recover. "Yes?"

She nods. "Most people think I can't see them. And often I can't when the lights are up high. But here, I could see the first few rows. And when I glanced over at your table and watched you sitting next to my son, you know what I saw?"

I brace myself. "What?"

Her soft palm rises to cup my cheek.

"Potential."

Words fail me as I stare into her warm amber eyes.

"Good things don't have to be temporary," she continues. "If you're strong enough, you can hold on to what you want. Figure out a way to make it work."

"I—"

"Charlie is worth it. Isn't he?"

Oh hell. The way she looks at me now is a challenge.

Do I tell her he's not?

Because then I'd be lying to her and myself.

Her lips slowly curl in a triumphant smile. "You're worth it too, you know." She grips my chin and leans in to press a kiss against my forehead. "No one gets to bad-mouth my daughter. And that includes you talking bad about yourself."

Regina sits back, swiping a thumb across the spot her lips just were, likely cleaning off the mark of her burgundy lipstick, and then moves to stand from her chair.

My mind goes back to the moment on the boat when Mr. Herbert had called Dash his son. My heart had swelled for my brother to have found more people to love him for the amazing man he is. And I can't help wondering what it would be like to have the Kellers think of me as their daughter.

The idea is so tempting it's dangerous.

Chapter Thirty-Nine

CHARLIE

Luna sat quietly the whole car ride back to the house. Ever since we left my parents at the entrance of the club, she's faded to some other place in her mind. Not like she's shut the door in my face. More like her attention drew inward.

When we step through the front door, Pig gallops to greet us, her entire body wagging. Luna scratches the pit bull's head, then immediately heads to the back door to let her out. As the sliding glass door clicks shut, I can't stand the distance anymore, rabid with curiosity over her thoughts about the night.

"Hey." I catch Luna's arm as she's about to walk past me. "My parents liked you."

Her smile has a curious edge to it. "I liked them too." Her eyes meet mine, holding me with their intensity. "A lot."

Then the spell breaks as she glances away and continues into the kitchen. After kicking her heels to the side, Luna groans, stretching her toes on the ground. The sound has my blood pumping hot.

But my wife doesn't pay attention to me. She just reaches into the freezer, pulling out a container of mint chocolate chip. After grabbing a spoon, the minx has the audacity to boost herself up onto the counter right in the spot where I ate her out.

"Want some?"

My whole body jerks at her question, and I need a second to realize Luna's tilting the ice cream carton my way and holding out a second spoon I didn't realize she'd grabbed. Not wanting to shatter this domestic spell, I carefully step up beside her and accept the utensil she holds out. Time passes where the two of us simply scoop out spoonfuls of ice cream and savor them in silence.

Luna eventually sets the ice cream down on the counter, closer to me, as if she's had enough. My hand has been scooping robotically. I taper off along with her.

"I don't want to sleep alone tonight," Luna announces to the kitchen.

Since she's been in my bed for the past few nights, I can reason she means something different tonight.

This moment sits heavy in the air. An opening that may never come again.

Luna leaving herself vulnerable to me.

"You don't have to." I step in front of her, placing my hands on her knees.

You never have to again, I silently add, guessing she's only ready for so much honesty.

Her eyes meet mine, and behind the fierceness I spy excitement and anxiety.

"Then take me to bed," she commands.

Yes.

I press her knees wide, stepping between them, sliding my hands under her ass, and boosting her into my arms. Luna helps by wrapping herself around me, but she hinders my progress by placing hot, open-mouthed kisses on my neck, threatening to buckle my knees.

When we reach her room, I collapse onto the bed, letting my wife land on top of me. And there she stays, rubbing her body on mine, drawing her lips up to capture my mouth in a scorching, slow-paced kiss.

This is different than the frantic session in the kitchen, where we moved fast as if to stop each other from backing out. This session still leaves things needing to be said, but not everything. Luna wants me in her bed tonight. The entire night.

And I want to be with her.

I ease into the experience, running my hands along the strong shape of her body, giving small presses on her back and hips to keep her rocking against me. She's captured my hard dick between us, and every time she moves, the pleasure jolts up my spine.

Luna breaks off our kiss, planting her hands on either side of my head to hold herself above me. She stares down with lust-hazy eyes.

"You would let me do anything to you. Wouldn't you?" She rocks her hips against my erection.

"Yes," I moan, ready to follow whatever direction she gives.

"You shouldn't." Her voice drops to a hush. "I'm not good for you. I'm not...good." Luna's sentence cracks on the last word, and her body stills as she turns her head, blinking rapidly.

What?

I sit up so fast she jerks in surprise. But she doesn't retreat.

Can't when I cage her in my arms.

"Good is relative." I cup Luna's face in my hands, making sure she's looking at me. Listening to me. "You're fierce, strong, and loyal. You fight for what's yours." I lean in, pressing a light kiss to her lips before admitting, "I want to be yours."

A groan wrenches from her throat, and I find myself pinned down to the bed. Luna has her hands pressed to my shoulders, hips back to rocking, eyes on fire.

"I want you," she growls, making every muscle in my body clench.

"Luna." I choke on her name when she shoves off me. But the second she's standing, her hands rip off her blouse and then her pants. I don't have time to admire her black underwear before the set is discarded too. Naked, she pulls open the drawer on her bedside table, taking out a foil packet. Next thing I know, her fingers are undoing my belt, unzipping my fly, and dragging out my heated cock.

No time for even a word to leave my lips before she's back over me, sliding the head along her slick folds. I groan at the decadent sensation, every muscle in my body jerking as she rolls the protection down my length. With her muscular thighs clenching, Luna lowers herself onto every throbbing inch of me, and I swear I hear entire symphonies play across my eardrums.

My wife takes me, just like she promised. Luna rides me in a hard, steady rhythm, palming her bare tits, pinching her own nipples, and holding my gaze the entire time.

Somehow I manage not to come in the first five seconds. I think the only thing stopping me is the fear of what'll happen when this all reaches the crescendo. When Luna's pace stutters and her lids flutter, I know she can get to her climax. I'm determined to help, reaching out to spread my hand over her lower belly, then sneaking my finger past her intimate hair, under her hood, to caress her clit.

My woman gives a yelp as her hands fall to my chest, fisting in my shirt. My dick enjoys the tightening pulses of her orgasm, each one drawing me deeper.

Luna finally comes back to the present, panting, chest heaving, a curtain of dark hair cutting her eyes off from mine.

"Hey," I speak gently, reaching forward to brush aside some strands, wanting to make sure she's okay.

I meet a glare.

"You're mine," she pants. Then her hips rock hard, and Luna starts to truly fuck me, steady and demanding. My back bows off the bed, and I have to hold onto her thighs to give myself some grounding in reality.

"You're mine, Charlie Keller."

I groan her name like a desperate prayer, the pleasure too much for my mind to comprehend. There's a live wire connecting my spine and my balls shooting straight electricity down my cock.

She demands my climax, pulling every ounce of sanity from me as her body milks me dry.

Even after the orgasm is technically done, I twitch with aftershocks.

Eventually my mind and heart calm down enough to realize Luna has sprawled her glorious body over my chest, not bothering to separate where we connect.

I struggle for the right thing to say, but then realize she's fast asleep.
Worn herself out.

With me. I grin wide, replaying everything she said in this past hour.
Has my wife finally claimed me?

LUNA

. . .

The first time I wake up is when Charlie climbs out of bed. In a whisper he tells me he's going to let Pig back inside, then come back to bed. I'm asleep before I can discover if he fulfills his promise.

The next time I wake up there's a dog leg digging into my back and a warm man at my side.

Despite being fully awake, there's nothing strong enough to pull me out from under these covers. Charlie still sleeps beside me, his long, lean body sprawled out over his portion of the bed. He's belly down, arms gripping a pillow, his face turned toward me, jaw slack, and emitting faint snores in his sleep.

I can't pinpoint exactly what about last night forced me out of my comfort zone and demanded I do something about my attraction to Charlie. But when we got home and I felt his eyes on me, I couldn't imagine going to separate bedrooms or sleeping in the same room but with our normal dog buffer. I couldn't imagine being married to Charlie for one more day without treating him like my true husband.

I just wanted him. Wanted to pretend this could all be real.

That we could be happy together. That I could fall in love with him.

When I was a kid, I wasn't really a kid. My mother's disinterest in parenting meant the responsibility of caring for myself and Dash—and at times Leo too—fell on my shoulders. I grew up fast, missing out on all the freedom children get to enjoy when they don't have to worry about grown-up things. Where the closest they get is playing house.

I want to play house now. I want to pretend with this man. Believe we're a happy little family with no problems on the horizon.

Can't I have that? Can it be my birthday present to myself? Pretend for this year, we're not in a fake marriage but a real one. Indulge in the fantasy.

And then, at the end of the year, the game will end.

I'll have had my taste of joy and partnership, and I'll use those memories as comforting blankets when he's gone.

And he will leave.

They always do.

"Good morning." Charlie's voice rumbles deep with sleep, pulling my focus back to the bed and his warm eyes.

"Morning." I shift on my pillow, facing him. "I want to amend some of the marriage rules."

A slow smile pulls his mouth wide. "You do?"

"We'd both have to agree."

"Of course."

"The no sleeping together rule."

"You added that in the first place. You want it gone? It's gone."

We both know it was truly gone when he sat me on the kitchen counter and licked me until I was gasping his name.

"Okay. It's gone."

"Good. And what else?"

The one saying this ends at the end of the year, my mind begs. But I don't let the urge take control of my mouth.

"That's it."

He frowns. "You said rules. Plural."

Shit. I did. I scrape my brain for the other items on the list.

But that's the thing. I have trouble remembering what they are.

Because when I'm with Charlie, I don't care about the rules. All I think about is him, how he makes me feel. How I want him to make me feel.

With his hands. And his mouth. And his tongue.

And that perfect dick of his.

The thoughts are too much. I lunge across the mattress, pinning him back against the sheets, bracketing him with my thighs, and stealing possession of his lush lips. Charlie kisses me back just as hard, melding our mouths together.

Pig lets out an unhappy huff at all the jostling and climbs off the bed, throwing us major side-eye as she waddles from the room.

We share a laugh before I recapture his lips. My body aches for him, and I rub myself against his form, searching for every way we can touch. Be together for this short time we have.

Charlie's groan spills out, vibrating through me.

I trace his strong jawline with harsh, hurried kisses. "I'm on birth control, and I want you. Now." I growl into his ear before biting the lobe.

He jerks, and in a surprising move, he turns us until I'm under him. Not a position I normally let partners claim, but his weight on me sets off delicious twisting in my lower belly. His chest against mine has me sinking into the mattress.

"I need you." Charlie hisses the words against my neck as he slides inside me.

I let the pleasure of being with him rise, ignoring his words. I know what it's like to be needed.

But that doesn't mean I'll ever let myself need somebody else.

Chapter Forty

CHARLIE

Luna lets me hold her free hand as she drives. Even better, she was the one to first slip our fingers together once we got on the road.

Pig sits in the back seat, panting with a happy dog grin on her face. And her innocent joy is all from riding in the car with us. She doesn't yet realize we're heading to her favorite place.

That's right. This is a family trip to the dog park.

But on the corner ahead, I spot a familiar building demanding a brief detour.

"Hey. Pull in here. Wanna take a quick trip through the drive-through."

"More caffeine?" She raises a slim brow and shoots me a smirk before pulling into the parking lot of the coffee shop. "Didn't I see you drink a half a pot this morning?"

"You can never have too much coffee." My thumb sneaks along the rough calluses adorning her knuckles.

"As a dietitian, I can tell you with great confidence that yes, in fact, you can. And this officially makes me an enabler." The car rolls to a gentle stop behind a minivan taking its turn at the speaker. While we wait, I tug Luna's hand up toward my mouth, pressing my lips against the thin skin of her wrist. One of the few delicate places on her.

"Charlie." She says my name with censure but doesn't try pulling away.

I trail kisses to her palm, then gently bite the meaty part at the base of her thumb.

"You're impossible." Luna lets me keep her hand as she drifts the car forward as the minivan moves. "Do you think you can hold off long enough to order what you want?"

No matter how much she tries to scold me, I can pick up the breathless note in her voice. Reluctantly, I pause tasting her in order to lean toward the driver's side window.

"What can I get for you today?" the voice crackles out of a speaker.

"One small black coffee with cream, and one puppucino, please."

"Puppucino?" Luna mutters, her hot breath brushing against my ear because of my position.

I tilt my chin to press a quick kiss to her mouth. She gasps in a breath, tempting me to sneak my tongue past her lips. But the worker asks for confirmation of my order. Finished, I settle back in my seat.

Luna glares at me, but there's no heat in her eyes. At least, none from anger.

As Luna pulls the car toward the window, our pittie starts wiggling and whining in excitement.

"Check this out. Can't drive down this stretch of road without getting Pig a puppucino."

When the window opens, I spy a vaguely familiar face.

"It's Pig!" the coffee shop employee crows. The girl peers through Luna's window and spots me. "Charlie! Hey!"

"Hi!" I wave, remembering I saw her last time Pig and I came through here, which was only a couple of days ago.

We're becoming regulars.

"Here's your drinks!" The girl passes Luna a cardboard cup carrier holding a normal-sized coffee and a smaller cup filled to the brim with whipped cream.

"This is a puppucino." To demonstrate, I pick up the smaller cup and hold it tight as Pig attempts to stuff her entire brick-shaped muzzle into the minuscule cup. Her wildly wagging tail practically shakes the car.

"Oh my god." At Luna's exclamation, I shoot her a grin, enjoying the baffled delight in her slack-jawed face. "How often do you get her one?"

I shrug. "Whenever we happen to be driving by."

Which may or may not be multiple times a week.

Luna shakes her head as she pulls us back out onto the road, but I can see the wry curve of her lips. "You're spoiling our dog. I think you treat her better than most people treat their children."

My chest nearly explodes with happiness at the "our dog" comment. Does Luna see Pig that way? As belonging to both of us?

A guy can dream.

A few minutes later, we pull into the parking lot of the dog park. Pig has her head fully out the window, whimpering at the delay to her fun.

"Calm down, piggy puppy." I try soothing our pup by reaching back to scratch her behind, but she only lets out an excited yelp.

"Yeah, yeah." Luna parks the car, and we unload. The moment we're in the fenced enclosure, Pig lumbers off toward a yellow lab, and the two quickly start up a race around the park. Our short-legged hound has no chance, but she tries her best.

"She's going to pass out tonight." Luna makes the observation as she scoops up my hand and pulls me toward a picnic table. And like Pig, I follow along joyfully, ready to be led wherever she wants to go. We sit side by side on the sun-stained wooden bench, and I relax, trying to ignore the eager thrumming in my veins encouraging me to tell Luna how deeply I feel about her.

What's the rush? I reason. We haven't even reached her birthday. I've got more than a year to work up to telling her I fell in love almost immediately.

What if she doesn't want a husband in love with her? The worry resounds in my head like the painful note of an untuned guitar string. In that case, I should tell her how I feel so she can end things with me and find another man to marry before she turns thirty.

Could I survive the split?

A vulnerability scrapes through me, and I snake my arm around Luna's waist, pulling her into my side so I can bury my face in her short hair and smell the mandarin shampoo scent I'll forever associate with happiness.

"I don't know who's more affectionate. You or Pig." Luna laughs through her words, unaware of the worry plaguing my mind.

"Mmm." I lean back enough to meet her hooded eyes. "What's going on at work? Have you only been meeting with Violet?"

Luna drags her short nails up and down my forearm, the light scratch teasing my nerve endings. "No, I have multiple clients. Right now, I'm working with ten different people. Some I meet weekly. Some multiple times a week. Some just every couple of weeks. Depends what type of training they need." Luna's gaze drifts away from mine, her head turning until she finds Pig wrestling with a husky across the way. The fight is playful, so neither of us moves to act as referee. "I also teach a class at Treyvon's gym the last Wednesday and Saturday of every month. Open to anyone."

My fingers press into her side, feeling the hard muscles of her abdomen. My wife is a beast.

"Could I go to one of those classes?"

Luna raises a single sharp eyebrow at me. "You could. But you know we live together, right? Meaning you get my expertise for free."

"Very true. What would you teach me?"

Luna leans back just a touch farther, running her eyes over me in an assessment. My pride wants me to flex the few muscles I have, but I don't bother. Sounds like she runs in a crowd that could tie me in a pretzel.

"I'd approach training you differently than most of my clients. Most people who come to me are smaller women. They need to know how to grapple. Get their way out of a hold of someone larger. But you've got reach." To demonstrate, Luna circles my wrist with her fingers and extends my arm, which goes a good number of inches past the tips of her fingers. "I'm thinking more evasion. But with you being so tall, we also need to lower your center of gravity. An attacker will try to push you over." Luna pokes a playful finger against my stomach, and I puff out a burst of air as if she socked me in the gut.

"But..." I drag the word out, inching closer despite the nonexistent space between us. "What if I want to learn grappling? Maybe roll around on the floor? Get tangled up?"

Luna huffs a laugh as her eyes flare with heat. "We might be able to go over some moves. Tonight. In bed."

Yes. I don't say the word because I'm too busy kissing her, which is prematurely interrupted by a sharp bark. When I break away, breath heavy with desire, I glance over to find our dog staring at us, panting from her own exertions.

"I think she feels ignored," Luna observes in a dry tone.

"We're bad parents," I agree, reluctantly unwrapping myself from Luna's tempting figure. Tonight, she said. We'll be together again tonight.

We both leave the table, taking turns finding toys to throw for Pig until she doesn't want to run anymore.

"Thirsty girl?" I reach for my backpack and pull out a bowl and water bottle I filled this morning. Pig eagerly waits as I struggle to open the screw-on top I twisted on too tight. Just as I'm considering asking Luna to assist with her superior strength, the lid comes loose. In fact, the bottle opens too fast, jerking in my hold, uncovered and slopping a wave of water over the side.

Directly onto Luna.

The two of us stand in shock. Me clutching the half-empty bottle, her staring down at her drenched white shirt.

"Damn it. Luna, I'm sorry." I quickly dump the remaining water into Pig's bowl, then turn back to my wife, wondering if there are towels in her car.

Luna gives me a wry smile. "This is my fault. I knew what I was getting into when I married you."

I try not to cringe at the memories of all the other embarrassing incidents I can't help stumbling into whenever I'm around her. Then my mind blanks when her strong arms wrap around my torso, pressing the damp fabric of her shirt between us until I'm soaked through too.

When I tilt my chin to meet her eyes, there's a mischievous sparkle in her dark stare. "I kind of love how klutzy you are, Charlie Keller."

The word love hangs in the air between us, lingering there. Waiting for me to grab the four letters and let them spill from my mouth.

I love you, Luna Lamont.

Maybe the declaration plays on my face before making its way to my tongue, because in the next second Luna lets go, stepping away and looking at anything but me.

"I think Pig is done for the day." She pats the panting dog before clipping her leash on. All the playfulness has disappeared. This is business Luna.

"Yeah," I agree, managing not to choke on the simple word.

For a brief time, everything was right in the world. Now I follow a few steps behind the little family I'll have to give up in a year.

Because I *will* give them up. If that's what Luna wants. She asked to change some of our marriage rules but not the expiration date.

Funny to know the exact day in the future when my heart will break.

Chapter Forty-One

LUNA

Pig won't stop whining at the back door.

"I just took you on a walk an hour ago! You cannot need to pee again already."

She yaps out a demanding bark and scratches at the glass.

"Fine. Stop it. You'll mess up the door." I stalk up to her and slide the door open, letting the pit bull out into the fenced area, hoping if there's a squirrel taunting her, it gets its little fuzzy ass in gear. Pig may look like a lumbering mess, but she can book it when she wants.

I return to the kitchen and my half-finished grocery list. But I'm interrupted again when the doorbell rings.

A groan leaks from the introverted section of my being. I hate it when people just show up at my house. Not that it happens a lot, but still. I fantasize about being an old-timey aristocrat who has a butler acting as the go-between, sending callers away without me ever having to talk to them.

Still, I have the next best thing.

After my dad's visit, Charlie and I agreed a security system would be a worthwhile investment. Now I have a nifty little doorbell camera to see who's on my front porch and an intercom. I don't even have to open the door if I don't want to.

Studying the screen now, I get an overly round view of a delivery man in uniform.

I press the intercom button. "Hello?"

I watch his head tilt toward the outer speaker.

"Hi. I have an express package requiring a signature for Luna Lamont. Is she at home?"

My friend Camilla is a jewelry designer and texted a couple of days ago she'd be mailing some prototypes for brass knuckle rings she wanted me to test. Because I don't have an office, I occasionally get work items sent to my home.

"Be right there."

This is what I love about Camilla. The few products she usually makes regularly sell out, but instead of sticking with them, she's always experimenting with new designs. That's an artist, I guess. Driven to create. Half the time, after a session with Violet, I see her scribbling away in a notebook. She told me once that lyrics come to her in random moments, and she needs to get them down before they evaporate.

The life of an artist. Work never truly stops.

I unlock the dead bolt and pull the door open.

The delivery guy holds a small box and electronic clipboard against his chest, not making a move to hand them over. The hesitation sets off my internal alarms but not quick enough.

Bill Lamont steps around the corner of my house, gun aimed at my chest.

Make sure your cameras don't have any gaps in their view, I silently instruct myself as my blood runs hot with adrenaline and shame.

This is officially the worst advertisement for my business.

"Inside," my father commands with a wild edge to his voice. "Now."

I back up, assessing the situation as I go, wondering if there's a way I can get to my own weapon. Doubt it. I locked the gun in a safe in the hallway closet. Even if I could get the door open, he'd be on me.

The delivery guy follows us in, closing the door behind him.

"Got a job at the postal service?" I ask my father, and Bill smirks at me.

"Got all kinds of people on the payroll, baby girl."

The bait seems unconcerned about being here. The way he lounges against the wall while my father talks.

A silence descends, and I know Bill's waiting for me to ask him what he's doing in my home threatening me with a gun. But that's a pointless question. He's here for Wai Po's money. Only question is how he plans to get it. Murdering me seems like the most direct route. But if he's caught, then all the money goes bye-bye.

Commit a crime, lose everything.

Even Bill Lamont is smart enough to know the risk. He must have some other play.

"No smart mouth today?"

I shrug.

He sneers. "You're going to keep quiet like this. Come nice and timid, and nothing bad has to happen."

Don't let them take you to a second location. The instruction I tell all my clients plays through my head.

"No. We can talk here," I say.

Bill steps forward, pressing the muzzle of the gun to my forehead. Even I, who trained myself not to give in to fear around this man decades ago, fight off lightheadedness from my proximity to death.

Wild barking snags some of my father's attention, his gaze flicking to the backyard. I can imagine Pig's blocky head at the door, staring in on a scene she doesn't understand.

A spark alights in my father's eyes, causing a sick twisting in my gut.

"If you need some incentive to behave," he mutters, "I can provide it."

I want to spit in his face. This vile man who thinks he has some claim to me, shoving his way into my home and threatening one of the few things I care for. And yes, I love the silly dog I never wanted in the first place. She was Charlie's idea. She should be his soft spot, not mine.

Of course, I now have two vulnerabilities I never planned on.

The idea of my husband coming home to this makes the decision simple. My father may not have any love for me, but he picks up on my weaknesses easily enough. And he uses them.

"Fine," I say. "I'll go with you."

He grins down at me, pupils dilated. "Good girl."

Bill steps back, keeping the gun trained on me. "Where are the keys to your car?"

I wave toward a hook beside the refrigerator.

"Escort her out, Nicky," my father commands with a jerk of his head.

I glare at the lackey, who approaches me without meeting my eyes. My whole body tenses when he circles behind me. I hate having his menacing presence at my back.

"This is a bad idea," I warn them.

"Getting rich is never a bad idea," my father steps close, his greed creeping along my skin, clinging like a sticky film.

Then he nods his head and a second later a sharp pain cracks through my skull and blackness leaks over my eyes.

Chapter Forty-Two

LUNA

I never thought I'd step foot in this room again. Much less be locked up in it. But when I regain consciousness, I know my exact location the moment I open my eyes.

My childhood bedroom.

The place has changed a lot since I lay claim to it. My parents are far from the sentimental type. Not ones to keep mementos of their children once they've left the house. At least not mine. Mom may have built herself a Dash or Leo shrine for all I know. She does care about them in some twisted version of affection I never warranted.

As seen by the complete stripping of any sign of me from this space.

The walls are painted, the bed is gone, and racks of clothing fill the room. Seems this is now a walk-in closet for Vivian Lamont's ever-expanding wardrobe.

All this I absorb from a prone position in the middle of the floor, trying to distract myself from the worry that I was out for the entire trip from Nashville to New Orleans. Either that guy Nicky hit me harder than I've ever gotten knocked around before or Bill dosed me with something while I was already unconscious. I'm guessing the latter. Now, I lay on the ground, hands and feet cocooned in duct tape.

My father, ladies and gentlemen.

Always taking up new, hip hobbies. Like kidnapping.

He's obviously new at it because he made some beginner errors. Like the duct tape. And leaving me alone. Seems Bill Lamont hasn't gotten any smarter over the last decade. He always underestimated me to his detriment. Why mess with tradition?

Just then I hear heavy footsteps coming down the hall.

When I was younger, that sound always set my nerves on edge. My body has the reaction ingrained into its DNA, and no matter if I'm stronger, smarter, and tougher now, my heart rate picks up.

But when my father opens the door, I keep all trace of fear off my face.

I don't let him see anything at all as I play unconscious.

"Fuck this," he mutters. And that's all the warning I get before he grabs the front of my shirt, hauls me up, and slaps me.

Hard.

I may know how to take a hit, but a gasp still escapes at the shock of the sting.

"You awake now?" My father shakes me, and pain collides in shocking ways, ricocheting throughout my skull. The dull throb from the knockout hit melding with this new sting. There's a strong iron taste of blood in my mouth. Seems my tooth caught my lip in the wrong way during his blow.

I shouldn't do it. I know I shouldn't.

But I've never been able to fully stifle knee-jerk, irresponsible urges around my father.

I spit a glob of blood into his face.

Bill drops me, and I land hard on my hip. Stumbling backward, he curses my name and tugs off his shirt to wipe the drool and gore off his cheek.

With him in front of me shirtless, I acknowledge the one department my father hasn't been lazy in is his workout routine. Mid-forties and he's still roped in wiry muscle. If only he'd set up my old bedroom as his weight room. I'd have a lot more to work with once I get time alone to search for weapons.

"You're disgusting," he hisses at me.

"And you're pathetic, jellybean." *Never antagonize your captors*, I often tell my clients. Why can't I listen to my own advice and keep my mouth shut?

Do as I say, not as I do.

"Bill!" My mother's voice gives him pause in the act of kicking my rib cage. We both look to the room's open door.

And there she is. The woman whose face I always wish I could never see in my own. She stares back and forth between us, shock in the sky-high set of her brows. Because even for our family, a tied-up beating isn't normal.

"What did she do?" my mom asks.

Of course. Briefly, I'd let myself hope my mother would be some kind of ally. That she'd let a little bit of selflessness into her heart.

Naive.

I should have known she'd never truly question my father. That the idea of her daughter deserving this treatment only requires a simple explanation before her sign-off.

"She's been keeping secrets from us. Trying to steal from us." My father has the confidence of a man with no conscience.

"What do you mean?" Did I hear a quiver in her voice? Probably at the fear of losing money.

"I mean your mother's money. We're going to get it." His words ring with triumph. The hero saving the day. "Enough to set us up for a long while. As long as your daughter stops lying."

Funny how it's *their* money, but I'm *her* daughter.

My dad retrieves a slip of folded paper from his back pocket, handing it over to his wife.

"It's all there. Luna only gets the cash if she's married by her birthday and stays hitched for a year."

With hesitant hands, my mother takes the papers.

I can't help smirking at the man looming over me. "Do you carry that around like a baby blanket? Does it keep you warm and safe at night?"

This time my father does kick me, and I curse both him and myself.

When am I going to learn to shut up?

"What does this matter?" Vivian glances between the two of us. "Luna isn't married."

"Seems we didn't get an invite to the nuptials. Our little girl found herself a sucker, and she's going to use him to steal the money right from under our noses. Or she was, before I found out."

"You got married?" my mom whispers, sounding genuinely hurt.

Did she expect me to invite her? Under the layer of duct tape, I feel the light pressure of the ring Charlie slipped on my finger. Even if I had the grandest ceremony possible, with thousands of guests on the list, her name wouldn't have been included.

I wonder if she's found out about Dash's wedding. If not, I'm not about to be the one to tell her. She might send her own kick into my aching gut.

"She won't be married for long."

The tone my father uses sets all my internal defense systems on high alert.

"What do you mean?" my mother asks, saving me the trouble.

Answering her but staring at me, my father crouches down next to me on the floor, his grin full of triumph and mockery.

"Because she's not leaving this room until she signs some divorce papers."

I snort, again not taking a moment to determine if that might be a bad move.

But the disrespectful noise doesn't faze my father. He just grips my chin in his rough hand, making sure our eyes lock.

"You think I'm a bad guy? You don't even know." He lowers his voice so my mother won't hear. "I have some nasty friends, baby girl. Men who will slit a throat for a hundred bucks."

He drops me, and I'm too lost in the idea of what he's describing to brace myself.

"There's more than one way to lose a husband. You can be a divorcee." Bill leans in close enough that his hot breath coats my face. "Or you can be a widow."

"Fuck you," I spit at him.

He laughs and stands, moving to throw an arm around my mother's shoulders.

"We'll let you think on it. Shouldn't be hard. All you have to do is stop lying. Tell the court you don't want to be married, and you can go back to your life and we'll get the money your momma always deserved."

He pulls Vivian out of the room with him. Some other girl, with some other mother, may have tried to catch the woman's eye. To silently beg her for help.

But I don't bother.

I'm on my own, just like I've always been.

No. I have Charlie.

Charlie. My husband.

The truth tears through me, undeniable when I'm in pain, ashamed, and fighting off fear. There's no more denying, and I can't remember the reason I tried to in the first place.

He's more than my husband.

He's the man I love.

The man I will do anything—*anything*—to save.

Chapter Forty-Three

CHARLIE

When I hear the frantic barking, I know something is wrong.

The moment I step from the car, Pig's racket hits me, the sounds wild. Feral. Briefly, I worry she's contracted rabies from an infected raccoon or something.

Jogging through the house, I catch sight of the leaping, howling, growling beast trying her best to break down the back door.

"Pig? Calm down." I open the door, and she lunges past me, sprinting around the house, whining all the while. She tears through the rooms as if searching for something.

Or someone.

Why would Luna have left Pig outside?

Her car wasn't in the driveway, so I assumed she went out on an errand. But she's not the forgetful type. Luna is a stickler about having Pig sit in her dog bed and shake for a treat before she leaves the house.

"Luna?" I call out.

No response.

As our dog continues her frantic searching, my heart rate speeds to match Pig's quick, clicking steps. I follow her.

"What is it, sweet girl? Did something happen?" I can't help asking though I know she can't answer.

Pig whines as she continues to sniff. Her attention seems to focus around the kitchen, and I notice a piece of paper sitting on the island.

I pick it up and read the few lines typed across the page, needing a full count of five to register what the sentences say.

This marriage was a mistake. I'm going to go stay with a friend back home. Don't try to follow me. I'll send you divorce papers in a few days.

Panic swamps me. Every insecurity I've had about our relationship and her feelings rising to the surface. I clutch at the center of my chest, sure I'll find a gaping wound where my heart's been torn out.

But as I gasp through the emotional torture, logic slowly overrides my initial reaction.

Luna wouldn't leave like this. The thought sustains me.

Even if this is how Luna feels, she'd never type out a note and leave. She would tell me to my face, glaring all the while. Luna doesn't run from confrontation. She batters her way through.

Which means someone else wrote this note.

And my wife is missing.

I jog to her bedroom, finding one of her duffels is gone with drawers pulled open and clothes strewn about. Someone left in a hurry. But again, I know it wasn't Luna.

"What the fuck happened?" I drag my hands over my scalp, trying to get my mind to focus through the fog of panic.

I sprint to the front door, pausing on the porch and staring out into the road as if there will be a neon arrow pointing in the direction she is.

That's when I remember the security system. I rush back to the panel just off the front hall. Immediately, I know something is wrong with the tech. The display is completely blank when normally there's a subtle glow as it waits for someone to tap the screen to life. When I try, the thing doesn't do anything. I practically wrench it off the wall in my rush to discover what's gone wrong with the overpriced technology that was supposed to protect the woman I love.

The wire leading to the wall is cut.

Fuck.

Definitely foul play.

And that's when I know.

Her father.

The answer is so obvious, I'm tempted to bash my forehead against the wall. Of course, it was Bill Lamont. The man knows where we live. He has every motive in the world to do something to her.

"Fuck," I moan.

A terrifying fact blares in my mind: Luna dead means the money is his.

Could the man kill his own daughter?

Bill Lamont's twisted mind makes no sense to me, but I can't risk hoping he'll be gentle with her. With frantic fingers I dig my phone out of my pocket. My first instinct is to call 9-1-1.

But I hesitate.

From what Luna's told me, the guy is tied up with a lot of criminal activity.

If he hears sirens, what'll he do?

Panic? Shoot at the cops?

I don't want the woman I love caught in the crossfire.

Instead, I call Paige. She picks up on the second ring.

"Hey, Chili Dog."

"I need to talk to Dash. Now."

"I'll get him." My best friend knows when I'm not joking around.

A second later a deeper voice comes over the speaker.

"What's wrong?"

"Luna's gone. I think your father took her. He knows about the inheritance."

Dash doesn't waste time doubting me, curses pouring from him like poison seeping from a wound.

"I didn't call the cops," I say. "Should I? Fuck, I don't know what to do." The one thing I do know is I can't stay in Nashville when Luna is likely in New Orleans.

Pig has been following at my heels whimpering. I grab her leash, hooking it to her collar and snatching up my keys, all while keeping the phone pressed to my ear.

"Bill is a piece of shit, but he's not homicidal." There's rustling on the other side of the phone like Dash is moving around.

"She wouldn't have just gone with him," I point out while ushering Pig into the backseat of my car.

"No," Dash agrees. "He could hurt her. He's done it before."

"Damn it." I pound my fist against the hood of my car.

"Don't panic. We'll figure out where she is. Can you come here?"

"Already on my way." I slide behind the wheel, shoving my keys into the ignition.

I'm not a violent man. But for Luna, I'll tear New Orleans apart.

Chapter Forty-Four

LUNA

The duct tape is easy to get off.

Most people would think the pendant necklace I wear has some kind of sentimental meaning. They wouldn't notice the smaller, sharper edges hidden in the curves of the metal.

All I have to do is bend my arms at some interesting angles to maneuver my hands in front of my body, slip the necklace off, and grip the cord of the jewelry in my teeth as I catch the tape on the sharp edge. A few slices and splitting through the bindings becomes as easy as ripping open a bag of chips. With free hands, the tape around my feet doesn't stand a chance.

I pause to stretch my muscles, shaking out the cramps and aches of lying in an uncomfortable position for too long.

With careful fingers, I probe the back of my head. The area is sore to the touch, but my hands come away clean. That's a plus. I'll still need to visit a hospital when this is all over to check I don't have a concussion.

Walking on light feet, I explore the room that used to be so familiar to me. Unsurprisingly, the door is locked. Not the escape route I want to use anyway. Leaving through the door means I still need to navigate through the house, almost certainly alerting my father to my escape in real time.

Better if I'm able to get out without him knowing.

Crossing to the window, I discover there is still something in this room left over from my childhood.

A row of nail heads have been hammered in a haphazard line into the bottom of the window frame. Holding the window firmly shut.

Despite his ease with laying hands on me now, there was a time when my father rarely used his fists to punish me. That was for the boys, he always said.

Instead, Bill Lamont would lock me in this room for an indeterminate amount of time.

No food. No water. Just endless hours to contemplate how I'd wronged him. There was one time I really pissed him off. I can't remember what I did, but it was enough to have the lock still firmly in place two days after the incident.

That was the day I climbed out the window.

I got down to the street and jogged to the closest gas station, where I used the bathroom before scarfing down two hot dogs and almost a liter of water.

When I climbed back into the bedroom, the door was still locked, but my father came in a few hours later, wearing his aren't-you-happy-to-see-me-now face.

It took a year for him to discover my escape route.

That's when he nailed things shut.

That's when I started having panic attacks at the thought of this room. Most nights, I would end up sleeping on the floor of Leo or Dash's room to avoid coming in here.

And now I'm back, locked up all over again.

The panic still claws against my brain, but I stifle the dread with my survival knowledge.

I can get out of this room.

I'll probably have to break the glass, which will bring my parents running. But as long as I'm prepared to shimmy down the drainpipe faster than it takes my dad to unlock a door, I'll be good.

There's nothing in the room particularly good for breaking windows. I'm in the process of wrapping a few of my mother's shirts around my fist when I hear the yelling through the door. The whole house shakes with the noise.

Footsteps pound the stairs, and I glance between the window and the door. I'd banked on the time it takes them to run up the stairs to give myself precious seconds to clear away shards of broken glass that can cause real injury if I try climbing through them. But if my dad is right outside the door when I break the window, I don't stand a chance of climbing out without his interference.

I drop the shirts and hurry to stand just beside the doorway, sliding a rack of clothes closer to shield me for the brief moment when someone first enters the room.

This may be my only chance to escape.

Let's just hope my father isn't carrying one of his guns. Not much room to dodge a bullet down the narrow staircase.

Even as I tense to run, the people who pounded toward my room don't seem ready to greet me just yet.

"She's my daughter! I can do whatever the hell I want with her."

Uh, no, you fucking cannot.

But then I pause at my father's phrasing.

Is he arguing with someone about this? Is he arguing with my mother? The woman who has never stood up for me in her entire life?

The idea doesn't compute.

Then a deeper voice sounds through the flimsy wood.

"When I say let her the fuck out, I mean it. Now!" Uncle Mike's booming bass rattles the window. I wonder if maybe he'll create my escape route just with his anger.

"You don't get it!" There's a note of whining in my father's voice, as if his big brother is taking away a toy he wants to play with instead of telling him to free his kidnapped daughter. "She's got money. I just need to keep her here until she gives it up. Then we're good. And I'll give you your ten percent like always." My father says this last bit with an air of coaxing. Like he's offering some tasty morsel.

I almost laugh.

"I know about the money, you fuck-up." The doorknob rattles, and I can envision Mike's meaty fist wrapped around it. "She's paying it to me. All of it."

"What?" Panic brings a sharp edge to Bill's words. "No. She'd never agree to that."

"She's paying for Leo!" Mike snarls. "That girl of yours wants both her brothers out of the game, and she'll pay just about anything to make it happen. She's sure as hell got a lot more family loyalty than you've ever shown."

"Mike—"

"Bet you weren't planning on telling me about the cash, you greedy fucking bastard."

"I was." Through the door, I can hear the lie in his voice.

Maybe, going off this conversation, I could hope to put my faith in Uncle Mike. The problem is my father has this persuasive knack that works particularly well on my mother and his brother. Time and again, Bill talks the two out of getting mad at him. He even goes so far as to persuade them to his way of thinking.

His bullshit doesn't work on me. It hasn't since I was six years old. Maybe it's because he never tried too hard until I got older. And by that time, I saw through his flimsy veneer of sincerity.

And no way his persuasion will work now. Not after he threatened Charlie.

But Bill could get my uncle to change his mind. No way am I sticking around, hoping the chop-shop owner will maintain his slippery grip on his honor.

"Open the door," I hear my uncle growl from the other side of the wood.

A long pause, then there's a slip of a key into a heavier lock than I remember. Sounds like even if I'd picked my way out of here, I would have come up against a dead bolt.

Through the hanging dresses, I watch the door open.

"What the hell?"

The first rule is run.

I burst out from behind the clothes, grab my father's shoulder, and whip him around straight into my fist.

Guess I won't tell anyone about how bad I am at following my own rules.

The crunch of his nose is a beautiful sound, but not as lovely as the pained squeak he lets out when I knee him straight in the balls. Shoving him to the floor, I bring my heel down hard on his right hand. The one he used to hold the gun against my head. More bones crack, and my father screams.

Violence pounds through my veins. I want to keep going. Draw more blood. Shatter more bones. Strike terror into his heart whenever he thinks of my name.

But I want to leave this room, this house, even more.

I turn on my uncle, who actually holds his hands up in surrender, despite the foot of height and hundred pounds he has on me.

"If anyone," I pant, riding a surge of adrenaline and ignoring the ache in my ribs, "touches my husband, I will kill this piece of shit." I'm too pissed to think of a childish candy to call him. I let rage flow through me as I smash my heel down on the same hand, the burn of his slap still throbbing along my cheek.

"Bitch," he whimpers.

I crouch down and grab his chin the same way he grabbed mine earlier.

"I am what you made me, snickerdoodle."

Look at that. I did have one in me.

When I stand up and glare at my uncle, there's something like humor in his expression.

"You can keep your money if you come work for me." Uncle Mike smiles. "Could use another enforcer."

"Not going to happen." I straighten my spine further. "You get my inheritance, Leo's out. That still the deal?"

Uncle Mike nods, and I return the gesture before strolling out of the bedroom.

Where I face my mother.

She stares at me, eyes wide with some emotion I can't read. Not that I bother trying. I just brush past her, moving down the stairs with measured steps as a sudden vertigo messes with my balance.

Just as I reach the bottom, the front door breaks down.

Chapter Forty-Five

LUNA

They're here.

My mind can't fully comprehend that my brothers are here. There's only the two of them, and still, I find myself counting them off in my head.

One.

Two.

Leo.

Dash.

One.

Two.

Dash.

Leo.

They're here.

And from the way they encircle me, escorting me out of our childhood home, hands on my shoulders, fingers on the back of my skull, questions pouring out of them, I know they're here for me.

Both of them.

For me.

"Calm down," I gripe, only able to deal with their affection by affecting crabbiness. "I'm fine."

"You have blood on the back of your skull," Dash sees fit to announce to the world.

Oh. Guess it was already dry when I checked.

"Who's here?" Leo growls. He has a Glock in his hand. "Who's involved?"

I meet my twin's eyes and see murder in them.

And because my head and emotions are thoroughly fucked up, the sight warms my chest.

They're here.

That's when the enormity of their actions clicks.

I'd envisioned escaping the house, sprinting to the nearest bus stop, riding until I was far enough from my childhood home that I could figure out my next steps.

There was no scenario where I imagined a rescue crew would come for me. Not one consisting of my brothers.

Because as much as I love them both, neither has ever shown up for me.

Not in decades.

Despite everything I did for them when we were younger, they still chose to work for Uncle Mike. I went to their court hearings when they got arrested in possession of a stolen car. They were both still in prison when I graduated from college. I didn't bother walking at the ceremony.

Who would've come to see me cross the stage?

No one.

When Dash was released from prison, I picked him up at the gate. I helped him set up his new life. And when his heart broke, I drove the eight hours from Nashville to New Orleans to comfort him.

When Leo was freed, I didn't know because he never told me. Just went straight back to the family business.

But I'm still ready to jump through every hoop to get him out.

I show up.

They don't.

Until now.

"Why are you here?" The question comes out as hard and betrayed as their continued abandonment has made my heart.

Both of my brothers look at me, eyes wide, confused.

"Charlie called me," Dash says. "And I called Leo. We thought the two of us could get you out, hopefully without bloodshed." My little brother uses a pointed tone as he stares down at the gun Leo definitely doesn't legally own.

I'm still comprehending the fact that I'm not alone when the creak of a step on the old wood of the front porch announces another arrival.

"Leo? Prince?" My mother comes out the front door, which hangs off one hinge after their forceful entrance. But Vivian shows no sign of noticing as she stands with a hand over her heart, her eyes watering. "Oh, boys. I'm so happy you came by. But things are tense right now. Maybe—"

"Tense? You think?"

My mother's face slackens in shock at the biting tone from an unexpected source.

Leo.

The golden boy.

The beloved son who's now stepping toward her with a smoldering expression of menace.

"Dad took Luna, didn't he?" My twin stares over her shoulder.

"He was upset." Vivian can't seem to decide between a glare and a pout. "But I called your Uncle Mike. Things would've gotten sorted out just fine. If your sister had waited instead of flying off the handle."

I bark out a laugh. "Of course. How silly of me to be a little pissy about getting abducted and threatened. Should've sat like a good little girl duct taped in a locked room."

"What the hell?" Dash wraps an arm around my shoulder.

"Damn it, Mom!" Leo's shouting now. "Why didn't you just let her out?"

"Your father—"

"Is the piece of shit you always chose over us! Fuck that! Fuck this!" Leo turns his back on her and stalks past us to his Mustang, which I didn't realize was sitting halfway up the curb. "I'm done. He comes near Luna or me or Dash, I'll fucking kill him. You tell him that."

Wow. Death threats from two of his kids in one day. Dash should toss one in too just so we can hit the worst-dad-in-the-world trifecta.

"Leo," my mother whimpers his name, readying the waterworks.

Maybe the tears are real, but I have trouble believing any emotion from her other than the mysterious disdain she's always shown me.

He ignores her. "Come on. Let's get the fuck out of here."

Dash guides me to the car. Like I'm fragile or something.

Despite the bump on the back of my head, I'm physically sound.

Emotionally though, I'm working through some shit.

Only when I'm strapped into the passenger seat can I let my mind sift through the roiling contents of my new realizations.

My brothers showed up for me today, and the support—though unnecessary, because I got my own ass out of that disaster—feels great.

The high is temporary though. This one attempted rescue doesn't fix the twisted mess of our past.

But it does help me realize something important.

I never expect Charlie to show up.

And he always does.

He's been there for me more times in these past few months than my family has in thirty years.

Even my grandmother let me down. Not by dying—no way I could blame her for having cancer—but by hiding her decline from me. Not warning me our time was limited.

What I crave more than anything is someone I can rely on. But I can't seem to let myself believe that type of person exists. Or that they would want to be with me.

But Charlie shows up.

Charlie has only ever given his full self to me. And I know if he says he wants to stay, he will. I just worry he'll say he won't. Because no one else has.

Glancing over at my older brother, I consider people's ability to change. Our relationship has never been a fair exchange. I give more than he does.

He showed up for me today, though, which tells me he can do it again. Maybe we'll never be a balanced equation. So be it. I still want to buy his freedom.

But I can't spend an entire year pretending I'm not wildly in love with my husband.

Charlie needs to hear my truth.

The car's momentum slows, and I realize we've pulled into the driveway of a house. A very large house. Bigger than anyone in my family could afford.

"Where are we?" I glance between Leo and Dash.

My younger brother answers.

"The Kellers'."

Chapter Forty-Six

CHARLIE

When I burst into my parents' house, Luna's voice is the first I hear. I follow the lilting notes of her conversation like a hound dog, my actual dog at my heels.

I find her in the kitchen, sitting at the counter, talking to my mother who stands at the sink washing lettuce.

"Everyone thinks a dietitian has to love kale, but I just can't deal with the stuff raw. I'll put it in soups though." My wife rests her chin in her hand, relaxed in my childhood home.

As I pause in the doorway, knees weak at the welcome sight of her, Pig pushes past my legs and charges forward, letting out a pitiful whine as her whole body wags.

Luna faces us and quickly slides off her perch, crouching low to gather the affectionate pit bull in her arms.

"Hi, Pig. I know, I know. I missed you too." Luna gets peppered with doggy kisses and has to provide a reassuring belly rub before I get any of her attention. When she looks up from her crouch, I watch the strength in her normally determined face waiver.

"Luna." I only get her name out before she launches herself up, high enough to hug me around the neck.

As my arms encircle her firm waist, the panicked swirling in my chest finally settles enough for me to suck in a deep breath. The inhale bombards me with the glorious citrus scent of her shampoo, which only calms me further.

"You came." The wording is a statement, but I hear the fragile question in her voice.

"Of course. I'll always come for you." My body begs to squeeze her tighter, but I don't know what injuries she might have sustained. Just the thought has my heart rate going up again. "I'm sorry I wasn't there." Like I could have done anything, but still.

"You're a horrible fake husband," she whispers against my shoulder. The words pierce my gut, but when I move to release her, Luna keeps her hold around my neck. "You're the worst fake husband in the entire world."

If this is what she needs, I'll be her punching bag. I'll take all the hits if it helps ease the pain and anger of her traumatic experience.

"A good fake husband would only be nice enough to tolerate. A good fake husband wouldn't make me fall in love with him."

Her confession rocks through me, and I use my embrace to lift Luna up and set her ass on the counter, meeting her eyes straight on. A part of my brain realizes my mother must have left the kitchen at some point. It's just the two of us. And Pig, of course.

"What did you say?" I cup Luna's face in my hands, shocked to see wetness gathering in the corners of her eyes. The strongest woman I know in tears.

"I didn't want to fall for you," she admits. Her gaze flicks to the dining room where I notice a few more members of our families pretending like they're not eavesdropping. My parents. Her brothers. I give Leo and Dash a quick nod of thanks before returning my full attention to Luna. She meets my eyes, lowering her voice for only my ears. "The people I love have a bad habit of letting me down." She reaches up, her fingers coming to rest on the heavy pulse in my neck. "I'm worried if I love you, I'll get hurt again. And I am so fucking tired of getting hurt."

My hands shake with the need to disabuse her of this idea. But I'm not sure there's anything I can do to convince her. Not when life has proved how careless people can be with her heart.

"I love you," I say instead. Offering the truth. Offering me.

Luna sucks in a quick breath. Then her face slowly relaxes into a smirk. "You better. Because I decided even if you leave my heart bruised and battered in the end, being with you is worth it."

Is she saying what I think she's saying?

"Hell, Luna. Never. I love you so much. I never want to leave you."

Her thumb traces over my bottom lip. "That's the thing, Charlie Keller. I believe you."

LUNA

What convinced me?

Well, it doesn't hurt that yet again, he's showed up.

And maybe it's as simple as that. Charlie always makes sure he's here when I need him.

Yeah, he wasn't at the house when my dad abducted me, but no one can be around all the time. I don't expect my husband to be Superman. I just expect him to recognize when I need him and try his hardest to support me.

Like he did with this wild marriage idea.

Like he did the night I broke into Uncle Mike's.

Like he did with those perfect anniversary gifts.

Like he's doing now with his arms wrapped around me.

How could I do anything but trust this man?

"I love you too." There's no hesitation or doubt in my voice.

Charlie Keller is mine, and I love him.

He smiles down at me. The expression is soft and loving and warms my insides. Selfishly, I also want one of his giant, face-splitting grins, but I'm guessing the fear of what happened today steals the peak of his joy.

"I'm okay." I stroke my palm down his chest. "You know that, right?"

"Why are you wearing my mom's clothes?"

"Mine had blood on them."

"What?" The word whips out hard.

Well, that's new. Never thought my husband could get such a

dangerous edge to his voice. But here he is, glowering like the man is ready to commit violence.

And maybe I'm sick, because the sight has me hot and bothered.

"Dr. Millner already came by to see her." Regina strolls back into the kitchen, reclaiming her possession of the space. I want to learn that skill: wielding power over an area without a word.

Probably would involve me growing a few more inches.

"What did she say?" Charlie asks.

"She shined a headache-inducing light in my eyes and said I am the embodiment of perfection." I interlace my fingers with Charlie's, enjoying the way we fit together.

Regina snorts at my response, and I grin at the woman. I like her. A lot.

I think it's only a matter of time before I love her almost as much as I do her son.

Charlie settles his free hand on my neck and traces my chin with his thumb. "That's not news," he murmurs, before pressing a gentle kiss to my mouth.

Much to my consternation, he doesn't deepen it, opting instead to hold my eyes with a stern gaze.

"What did she say about your injuries?"

I sigh as if his concern bothers me, when really, I revel in the attention I'm not used to being afforded.

"No signs of a concussion, and the cut on my head isn't big enough for stitches. For now, I should ice it to keep from getting a huge bump, and if I start feeling funky, I should head to the hospital for more extensive tests."

"You don't want to go to the hospital just in case?" Charlie worries his lower lip with his teeth. I want to bite that plump mouth of his.

"I've gotten a concussion before, and this feels nothing like it. Just a bit sore. And pissed off. But I'm fine. Here." I hold out the ice pack I've been periodically pressing against my tender skull and sore cheek. "Husband privileges. You get to handle the ice."

His long fingers accept the cool compress, and he lays it on the area where I direct, holding it in place.

"Can you tell me what happened?" he asks in a low voice that has me complying, though I'd rather forget the whole mess. I run through the events that transpired after I woke up in my childhood bedroom. Charlie keeps quiet through the tale, but I watch his reactions in the tightening of his lips and burn of his eyes.

"I'll kill him," he says at the end.

And once again, his violent impulse comes off as utterly sweet to me.

"Come on. We both know if a guy needs killing, I'm better equipped on the follow through."

"Nah," comes a deeper voice to my left, and I realize Leo has stepped into the kitchen. "That's my job if it ever needs doing."

Again, I find it strange to hear my twin come to my defense. It's been so long since we were on the same side. But I'm happy for it even if we're both planning patricide.

Okay, I'm not *really* planning it. Just daydreaming about it.

"Well, now we have a waiting list. But with Uncle Mike in the know, I don't see Bill being a problem anymore. Harder to sneak around when your watch dog knows what to look for."

"He can't get away with what he did to you," Charlie growls.

Then there's a sharp cluck of a tongue from Regina. "Son, you listen to Luna when she tells you to let it go. She knows best how to deal with her family. Besides, she just told you she loved you. That's what you should be thinking about."

Charlie snaps his mouth shut, returning guilty eyes to me as if he thinks I'm about to rescind my love.

Not a chance.

"Sorry," he murmurs while carefully arranging the ice pack against the back of my head. "I'm dense. I love you too. You know that, right? Hell, I'm obsessed with you."

His words drive away all the darkness of the day, and I grin up at him so hard my face hurts. But Charlie is here to soothe away all my pain.

Leo shoves his hands in his pockets and ducks his head.

"I'll head out," he mutters.

"Oh, no you won't," Regina glares at my brother, and I watch his face go pink. "I told my husband to put a steak on the grill for you. You better stay and eat it."

"I..." He trails off as our eyes meet across the kitchen.

That's when I realize it's been over a decade since the two of us have shared a meal together. Leo used to be the person I was closest to in the world. The person I trusted more than anyone. It was his abandonment, more than our parents', that cut me so deep I never expected the wound to heal.

But he's here, and I have Charlie by my side.

Yes, Leo might leave again. He might choose the wrong road and not tell me he's going or why.

But I won't be alone.

"I want you to stay," I say. I've always wanted him to. And now if he goes, at least he knows the truth.

Leo presses his mouth in a tight line and offers a jerky nod.

Charlie keeps the cool pack against my bruise as he leans in to place a kiss on my forehead.

And I begin to know what it feels like to be settled.

Chapter Forty-Seven

LUNA

"I shouldn't be here." Leo stares around at the gathering in Paige and Dash's backyard. Everything sparkles with decorations.

"It's your birthday too. Just shut up and deal with it."

My brother grimaces down at me while tugging at the collar of his button-up shirt. A nice shirt I did not tell him to wear. Which shows me just how much Leo secretly wants to make a good impression.

"You're a fucking motivational speaker, you know that?"

I'm just about to snipe back at him when I catch sight of Dash across the yard. His gaze is on us. Part wary. Part hopeful. He may have pretended he gave up on his big brother, but I knew all along his softy heart still wanted to find the Leo from our younger days.

This Leo is different. But so am I. So is Dash.

We all got tougher over the years with and without each other.

But when the three of us stood outside our childhood home, a united force, I knew I'd been right all along not to give up.

"Let's mingle. Everyone here is nice, as long as you're not a dick." I quickly scan the party before amending my statement. "Well, Mr. Herbert will probably try to freak you out with his grim reaper stare." Leo raises his brows at me, and I shrug. "That's what Dash calls it. Also, the guy in the black T-shirt and jeans is on duty. He's my friend Violet's bodyguard, so he's not about to get cozy with anyone. But it's a good group."

My brother grunts, but he lets me push him off the back porch. I head Dash's way first. He watches us approach, his arm loosely around his wife's waist.

And it fully hits me. Our family is bigger now.

Paige is part of it. Charlie is part of it.

"Leo," Dash says in greeting. "You made it."

"I did."

Their voices are tight. I guess the truce they called when coming to save me is more tender without my life on the line to give it fuel.

"Paige, this is my brother, Leo. Leo, this is my wife, Paige." Dash waves between the two of them.

I notice a slight wince on my twin's face at the title. A reminder of the wedding he wasn't invited to.

Still, Leo doesn't mouth off something rude like he might have in the past.

"Good to meet you, Paige." Leo extends his hand.

The blonde grins wide, accepting the shake with enthusiasm. "You slashed my tire one time, remember?"

My twin stiffens as he retracts his hand. "Uh, yeah. Sorry about that."

Paige shrugs. "I'll likely seek revenge. Luna already promised to help."

Leo's mouth curves up in a hesitant smile. "Oh, really?"

"Yeah. Sorry in advance."

I groan. "No, Paige. You don't apologize for taking revenge. You rub it in mercilessly. That way they know never to mess with you again."

My sister-in-law's soft face glows with happiness. "Okay. I'll try to be more ruthless." She turns to Leo. "Prepare to suffer, Leo Lamont." The threat is not in the least bit intimidating and loses every ounce of warning when she smacks her forehead. "Oh crap. I forgot it's your birthday."

Then, surprising all three of us, Paige steps forward and wraps Leo in a hearty hug. Dash and I both hold our breath, waiting to see what our brother will do. But we didn't need to worry. After a moment of hesitation, Leo returns the embrace.

Paige steps back, letting her hands rest on his shoulders. "Revenge will come another day. You know you're my brother now, right? I've always wanted a brother."

Leo's mouth opens like he's going to respond, but nothing comes out. He's saved from coming up with words when our group grows by a member.

"I thought I was your brother." Charlie slips his hand into mine as he appears at my side.

"You are now! We did it! We're related." Paige holds up a hand, and Charlie gives her a high five.

I glare back and forth between the two of them. "That was your game all along? Seduce us innocent Lamonts just so you could have a familial connection?" I jab a finger into Charlie's belly, and he acts like the attack hit harder than it did. "Divorce! I declare grounds for divorce!"

"Too late. You already fell in love with me." My husband hugs me tighter to his side.

The tension from bringing Leo into the group fades as we all exchange light-hearted jabs. Doesn't hurt that there's plenty of drinks going around. Then Pig and Pumpkin sprint between us, racing each other around the yard in a game of chase that has everyone laughing. At one point, Paige's mom joins our group, and she ropes both of my brothers into a conversation about classic Chevys, which she restores as a career.

I duck away from the gathering to use the bathroom, giving Pig a loving pat on the belly when I pass by the spot where she's collapsed on the grass.

When I step back outside, I pause, surprised at how much I enjoy the happy buzz of conversation mixing with the occasional dog bark and some gentle music. Violet must have brought one of her guitars, because she's perched on a lawn chair with the instrument in her lap as Regina reclines next to her, humming a tune with her eyes closed.

A movement catches my eye, and in the shadows just beyond the glow of the party I see her.

My mother.

Vivian makes no move to come closer. She stands just inside the gate opening, arms crossed tight over her chest, her eyes not on the celebration but on the house itself.

She stares at the little building as if it confuses her.

I don't know her purpose for coming, but like I've done plenty of times in the past, I decide to head her off before she can damage my brothers.

"Vivian," I say in greeting.

She starts, just realizing I'm only feet away. Then her brows dip, and she reaches into her large purse, focusing on her hands rather than me. "When did I stop being Mom?"

I wonder what she's looking for. Maybe a birthday gift?

She pulls her hand out, holding a box of cigarettes.

Yeah, no.

"When did you start?"

Her eyes narrow at me, and I brace for the fight.

But then her shoulders sag, and she drops the smokes back into the recesses of her purse.

"I haven't done what mothers should, I guess."

Even as she wilts under my scrutiny, my mother is still a gorgeous woman. Her dark hair has a loose curl as the strands fall halfway down her back. The skintight dress she's wearing shows a body just as in shape as mine. Plenty of people would think we're sisters.

A connection sparks in my mind then. Thirty years ago today, this woman lay in a hospital bed screaming her head off as she pushed me and then Leo out into the world.

She was eighteen. Probably terrified.

I could almost feel bad for that young woman, suddenly expected to care for two new lives when she had barely lived any of her own.

But a tough situation doesn't excuse her neglect.

Someone can be scared and still do the right thing.

"Why are you here?"

Vivian doesn't answer my question directly. Just goes back to staring at the bungalow.

"My little prince in his little castle. Why is it so small? Her parents have plenty of money. Did they cut her off too?"

My mother says *too* like she and Paige are the same.

"No. He lives here because he loves it. And he loves Paige. Now why are *you* here?"

She flicks her eyes back to me, then across the yard. As I follow her stare, I realize it's landed on Leo. Every one of my protective instincts flares to life.

"Leave him alone." I step forward, wishing I had Dash's height, wanting to loom over her. "He's having a good time and doesn't need you to guilt him into leaving with you."

Her mouth twists, and she blinks as if I blew dust in her eyes.

"I have two hundred thousand," she says.

The statement rocks me back on my heels. I never kept precise track of my parents' income, but I know they don't have money like that.

"Dollars? How'd you get that much? Even if you pawned everything Dad ever gave you, that still wouldn't come close."

Her lips tighten, and she stares behind me. I glance back to see Paige talking animatedly to a bewildered Leo as Dash stands just behind his wife, arms wrapped lovingly around her waist.

"My mother did not forget me." The statement has me whirling to meet her eyes. Shockingly enough, there's a shine to them. "I received a letter. A check."

Of course.

"You're rich now? Great." I can't keep the bitterness from my voice. Vivian probably handed the money over to my father before the envelope hit the table.

"No. I came to tell you to keep your money. Leo's debt is paid."

"What?" I shake my head to clear away the fog of confusion. She can't have just said what I thought she did.

"Your uncle is in some trouble with the law. He trusted the wrong person, and now they're watching his every move. Apparently, someone in the organization was collecting info on the cars. Like they were going to move against him."

I keep my face blank even as a triumphant smirk threatens to curl my lips. What's wild is how easy the revenge was. All I did was print off the pictures of the VIN numbers I'd taken, stick them in an envelope with a note reading *Don't trust Nicky*, and then anonymously mail them to my uncle's home. Mike's paranoia took care of the rest.

It's on the tip of my tongue to ask what happened to the rat my father brought with him to kidnap me, but I keep the question to myself. No point in hinting at the truth. Nicky partnered with the wrong Lamont. He never should've broken into my home and bludgeoned me. He landed squarely on my revenge list that day.

Oblivious to my hand in the events, my mother keeps talking. "With the way your father treated you...well, Mike doesn't know who to trust." She examines her perfectly manicured nails. "Money is power, and he needed money fast, not over the next year like you'd planned. He accepted my payment in place of yours and agreed to cut Leo out of the business." She smooths her hands down the front of her dress. "It's a mother's duty to protect her children."

When have you ever? The question hisses from a still bleeding part of my heart, but I keep my mouth closed.

Instead, I let my eyes catch on Charlie as he trots out onto the deck with a pile of wrapped gifts in his arms.

And I think about what he would want me to say.

Damn it. I hate the high road.

"You could get out too. You've never been a part of the business. You could leave."

My mother smiles, but the expression seems to hurt her face. "No. I couldn't leave your father. Our love is not the fading kind."

That I believe. Though I've often doubted if either of my parents held any affection for their children, I've always known they loved each other. Maybe the emotion is a darker one, twisted because both are selfish. But it's there.

Still.

"Marriage doesn't have to be like what you have." Again, I seek out Charlie and realize he's found me too. My husband watches me intently. I wave, and he nods back, leaving me to handle this the way I want.

"The years will change that," my mother says, regaining my attention.

Keeping rash, defensive words from spilling out is a struggle. It's my natural defense with her. Instead, I let my mind soak in the memories I have of my husband. Of all the mistakes we've made, but also the ways we work to fix them.

My dad doesn't fix things.

My mother doesn't acknowledge when something is broken.

They never had a chance.

But telling her will only lead further into the darkness, and all I want is to step back into the light.

"We'll see." Then I move forward, placing a hand on her shoulder. The gesture is as much as I can give her. There's no hug in me. "You did right by Leo. This is what Wai Po would have wanted."

Vivian shrugs away from my palm. "My mother wanted Tsai Mei-ling. A perfect, well-behaved daughter. But that girl never existed."

I'd thought my mother's rejections couldn't sting me anymore, but I still feel the pinch of her dismissing my touch. Still, I stop myself from snapping back at her. Wai Po's memory solidifies in the air between us, the visions we hold of the woman vastly different.

Mine is full of hope and the beginning of acceptance.

My mother's holds something darker. Another generation of mother-daughter strife. A tradition I hope never to pass on if Charlie and I ever expand our family. My worry of that is small. With a husband like mine, how could a family be anything other than full of love?

"Make sure Leo doesn't screw this up." Vivian pushes through the gate and doesn't look back, strolling out of our lives as easily as she always has.

"You okay?" A familiar deep voice whispers the question in my ear, and I lean back against Charlie's chest.

"My mom paid off Leo's debt." Best to be blunt.

"Hmm." A soft kiss drags up my neck. "No need to stay married to me then, huh?"

"Nope." I tilt my head, giving him better access. Then, in a slow languid movement, I turn in his arms, reaching to clasp my hands behind his neck. "Charlie Keller, will you stay married to me?"

His heart-melting grin is the only answer I need.

Epilogue

LUNA

"You got your passport?"

"Yes, sir." I pat the pocket on my backpack I zipped the stiff little booklet into this morning.

Charlie continues naming off items on my checklist, waiting for me to point out the place I packed each item. All the while, Leo watches us from the couch with a roly-poly pit bull sprawled over his lap.

"You all ever heard of being over-prepared?"

I suppress the urge to flip my brother off. He agreed to dog sit while Charlie and I travel for two weeks. I can deal with a little snark.

"I'm not about to get stuck in a foreign country without the proper supplies." My voice comes out with only the smallest bite.

"It's not like you're going to the moon. I think they sell underwear and toothpaste in Taiwan," Leo taunts.

"But not passports." I turn a glare on him.

Leo rolls his eyes and smirks at Charlie. "Think your marriage will survive the honeymoon?"

"You're soooo funny." My voice could crumble to sand it's so dry.

Two weeks ago, Charlie and I had our one-year anniversary. This trip is the honeymoon we never thought we'd take when the union was a farce. But now we're going to the other side of the world.

And Leo is our mocking send-off party.

My twin lounging on my couch isn't a strange thing anymore. The sight is a common occurrence nowadays since he moved to Nashville shortly after our thirtieth birthday. He needed to get away from the city he'd only ever been a criminal in, and I got him a job with my old boss, Treyvon. Despite my worry about putting my reputation on the line for a guy who could blow everything up in my face, Leo didn't flake.

Much as I hate to admit it, the two of us are a lot alike. Other than the twin thing. For one, getting out of New Orleans and moving away from our toxic parents allowed us both to start fresh. Of course, I didn't have an arrest record behind my name, and I'm certain Leo's relation to me is the only reason Treyvon took the risk.

Turns out my brother has been kicking ass at the gym. He's enrolled at an online college to get a degree in business. One night we were hanging out, and after a few beers Leo admitted he wants to ask Treyvon about being a manager once he finishes all his courses.

I'm trying not to get too hopeful, but it's been eight months since he started, and nothing has changed.

Doesn't hurt that he's fallen in love with a beautiful lady.

The one currently sprawled across his lap.

"I'm going to give you so many treats when they're gone," he whispers loud enough for me to hear.

I scowl. "If you give her too many she'll puke. I better not come home to a house full of dog vomit."

Leo shrugs with an evil grin as he continues to rub Pig's belly.

"Better you worry about our overeating." Charlie grins down at me as he sets aside the checklist.

The man has a point.

We finally decided on a couple's activity: cooking classes. Charlie found a place where we could learn to prepare food from different cultures, including Taiwanese. He's still not the best in the kitchen, but my husband makes a pretty amazing sous chef, following my orders exactly.

And now we're letting our stomachs dictate our travel plans. Our trip coincides with Taiwan's annual beef noodle festival. Apparently, the dish is a big deal over there. Not only do they have a competition for the best recipe but also entire celebrations around it. Just the thought has me salivating.

Still, I bet if I get to sample the top-ranked dish, it won't hold a candle to my Wai Po's. The recipe that was so good my mother still made it for us from time to time even as she purged every other indicator of her past from her life.

I haven't seen Vivian since my birthday party. Maybe she and Leo are still in touch, but I get the sense they aren't. Maybe I should be sad or disappointed the bridge remains a crumbled heap, but I try not to dwell on things that won't change.

I've got my brothers, and they're enough for me.

When I add Charlie to the equation, my life is pretty fucking great. And that's not counting his parents, who are a bonus.

There was a time when I would have been satisfied if the people I loved were simply safe.

But now I know what it's like to see them happy and to feel their love and support in return. Some days I stare in the mirror and recite their names, just to convince myself I really have all of them and that they love me too. The idea is unreal.

"You ready?" The deep voice of my husband rumbles against my ear, giving me shivers of anticipation.

I nod.

"Get out of here. I want to raid your fridge." Leo shoos us away, his eyes fixed on the TV.

Charlie shakes his head, grinning all the while because he seems to think my brother's attitude is hilarious. He extends the handles of our rolling bags and drags them toward the door, stopping when he realizes I'm not right behind him.

"Did you forget something?" His thick brows curve up.

Charlie stands tall in the front hall of the house we share now, wearing a T-shirt with the logo of the guitar shop he now manages and looking hot as hell in the tight cotton. But what looks even better on him is the thick titanium band around his left ring finger. I bought the piece as an anniversary gift to replace the spur-of-the-moment one he got himself on our wedding day.

I wanted my claim on him. Because Charlie Keller is mine.

"Nope." I step between the bags, moving close enough to press my palm against his chest, directly over his heart. "I have everything I need."

***

Thank you for reading! Did you enjoy? Please add your review because nothing helps an author more and encourages readers to take a chance on a book than a review.

And don't miss more from Lauren Connolly with her steamy paranormal romance, **FIRE MAGIC & ICE CREAM**. Turn the page for a sneak peek!

And visit www.laurenconnollyromance.com to keep up with the latest news where you can subscribe to the newsletter for contests, giveaways, new releases, and more.

Sneak Peek of Fire Magic & Ice Cream

QUINN

My body is on fire and not in a good way.

"Door!" I screech, sprinting through the kitchen, my bare feet squeaking on the tiles.

Luckily, Cat doesn't hesitate. She jumps from her stool and whips open the sliding glass door.

I knew there was a reason she was my favorite sister.

The sun beats down, high in the blue Phoenix sky. Anyone else might find the intense rays uncomfortably warm. But most other people don't run around wrapped in a toga of flaming bedsheets.

Fortunately for me, a swimming pool sits a couple of frantic leaps out the back door. The water shimmers, its calm surface cool and inviting.

I wreck the tranquil scene with a self-serving cannonball.

Safely in the water, I hold my breath and stay immersed. The cool, gentle cradle helps soothe my racing pulse and clear my panicked mind. When I can think again, the only thing that keeps me from groaning in mortification is the fact that I would drown myself in the process.

I can only deal with one life-threatening event each day.

My lungs ache, demanding I stop pouting and give them some well-deserved oxygen. With a strong kick of my legs, I break the surface and breathe in deep.

"Hey, Fireball. You have an accident?"

Immediately, I miss the almost meditative silence of being underwater. Harley, my older sister, grins at me from her poolside lounge chair.

I do my best to affect a casual air, which is an impressive feat for someone treading water while clutching the charred remains of a bedsheet to cover her naked body.

"I wouldn't call it an *accident*. Merely a failed experiment," I say.

That does her in. Harley collapses back on the cushions, cackling like an evil villain. I imagine the red-gold curls spiraling down to her shoulders are Medusa's snakes.

As Harley shakes in mirth, the sunlight glistens on her gloriously tanned skin. She's one of those elusive redheads whose melanin decided to work right. The only reason someone might mistake *me* for tan is because I have so many freckles that they blend into a solid brown blur at a distance.

Big sisters suck.

Cat, who followed after my mad dash from the house, settles at the edge of the pool, dipping her feet in and offering me a sympathetic smile.

Baby sisters are much preferred.

Once Harley calms down enough to talk, she gifts me with a smirk. "Guess those flame-retardant sheets didn't work out like you were hoping."

"Not exactly." The blackened edges float wistfully in the water around me.

Not for the first time, I curse the means in which my Elemental gift chose to show itself.

Dad had told the three of us, once we were old enough to understand, that the Byrnes descended from one of the rare family lines who could trace their origins back to the ancient Elemental Gods.

Our ancestor being the Goddess of Fire.

"One day, your powers will reveal themselves."

"When?" Harley, the oldest and most demanding of us, asked.

"I'm not sure. But the magic is normally tied up with a strong emotion. And it will likely be different for each one of you. None of you need to worry though. I will help you. I'll teach you how to control the fire, like my mother taught me."

Dad kept to his word, helping Harley when she was thirteen and her fear of a rattlesnake ended up setting the whole front yard on fire. And again, when Cat was eleven and her anger melted the tires off the bike of a bully who was mocking her best friend.

Fear. Anger. Those were emotions my dad could incite in them enough to practice. He was mostly successful. I'd say, ninety percent of the time, my sisters were in complete control of their abilities.

But when I was fourteen and the sight of a teenage heartthrob singing about basketball on my TV had the couch underneath me going up in flames, we ran into a problem.

No way in hell was I going to try getting aroused when my dad was anywhere in the vicinity.

I insisted on practicing by myself.

Unfortunately, that meant no one was waiting to douse the heat if it got out of hand.

Fourteen years later, and I'm still setting furniture on fire.

"It's not fair!" My feet settle on the pool floor, my body having floated to the shallow end. "I can't even touch myself unless I'm in the shower."

"You could always hook up with a Squid," Cat supplies, her voice gentle.

If it were Harley who had made the suggestion, I would've snapped back. Instead, I groan in defeat.

"All the Squids are cocky bastards. *You* can barely stand to be around them, and you're one of the most chill people in the world. Last time you ran into one you melted his shoes to the ground."

Cat blushes at the reminder. Most people are shocked when they see a girl so sweet lose her temper. But I love it. She's glorious when she's in a rage.

"I'm not saying talk to them. Just...sleep with one."

The plan might appear good in theory, but reality is often a disappointing bitch. A Squid helped me pop my cherry.

Even in my brain, that sounds gross.

Correction: a Water Elemental was my first. And what a disappointing event that was.

Twenty-two and desperate, I caved. When the guy was finally naked, he spread his arms wide and raised a set of thick eyebrows, as if to say, *You're welcome*. Suffice it to say, I didn't have to battle my fire too badly during that drunken escapade. Whenever a little flame popped up, he'd just douse it with a wave of his fingers.

So I know what a dick feels like inside me, but I would've thought a Water Elemental would be better at getting a girl wet.

A repeat held no appeal, and I was back to practicing on my own.

And failing miserably at it.

"Forget Squids. Quinn runs so hot, she needs an Ice Elemental," Harley declares as she rubs on a generous coating of tanning oil.

I snort in response. "Sure. I'll go out and find one of those. And I bet he'll be riding a unicorn on his way home from tea with Bigfoot."

None of us have ever met a descendant of the God of Ice. Dad said they were rumored to have died off over a century ago. Elementals in general are rare. Phoenix is home to well over a million people, and there are maybe fifty of us magic wielders among that number. Possibly more, but it's not like we put our powers on display. That's a good way to get yourself dissected in some government lab.

No thank you.

We keep our abilities to ourselves and fit in with the humans as best we can.

Harley twirls a curl around her middle finger. "I fucked a guy with big feet. And I'm talking *mythically* large. Plus he had more hair than an entire waxing parlor could handle."

"Are you trying to tell us that you not only met Bigfoot, but that you also slept with him?" Cat asks, flicking water at our big sister.

Harley fiddles her own fingers, evaporating the droplets before they land on her sun-drenched skin. "I'm just saying you never know what's out there. Maybe you need to take a sex pilgrimage north. Search the wild, frozen tundra to find yourself an Icie."

"An Icie?" I tug the mostly disintegrated sheet around my legs as I head for the pool stairs. "Is that what we're calling them?"

At some point, someone made up nicknames for each of the Elemental descendant groups. Squids, Petal Pushers, Airheads, Stoners, and Pyros. They aren't the most flattering, but we all seem to have embraced them.

Harley shrugs. "Nah. I can think of something better. Give me a minute."

As I climb out of the water, dripping and barely covered by my singed bedding, a rush of jealousy overwhelms me at the sight of Harley, so relaxed and carefree on her lounge chair, and Cat, calm and rational while making gentle waves with her feet. Both of them are able to explore their sexuality, sleep with whoever they want, without worrying that they might barbecue their partners or turn their bedrooms into ashes.

"Why are you here? This is Cat's and my house. Ever think we might like our privacy?" I know I sound spiteful, but I'm strung tight and looking for a fight.

My big sister lies back on her chair with a smug smile. "My apartment doesn't have a pool. Plus, I like to be around when you turn into a fiery comet of lust."

"Why? So you can mock me?"

A flicker of something wicked flashes behind Harley's hazel eyes. "No, though that is a fun bonus." She holds a hand up to stop my angry growl. "I'm here because I know a perfect way to cool you down."

Don't stop now. Keep reading with your copy of **FIRE MAGIC & ICE CREAM** available now.

And visit www.laurenconnollyromance.com to keep up with the latest news where you can subscribe to the newsletter for contests, giveaways, new releases, and more.

Don't miss more of the *Forget the Past* series coming soon, and find more from Lauren Connolly at www.laurenconnollyromance.com

Until then, discover Connolly's steamy paranormal romance
FIRE MAGIC & ICE CREAM

🐾

When fire meets ice cream, will passion turn into a melted mess or dessert flambé?

Quinn Byrne is rare even among fire elementals, with her powers hard-wired into her arousal. She can't touch herself without setting the sheets ablaze. With an incendiary sex drive, Quinn's dating life is dryer than the desert that surrounds her hometown of Phoenix, Arizona. She'd give anything to have a normal romantic relationship. But she knows one thing for sure: human men are out of the question. No exceptions. Not even if the guy is trying to woo her with delicious ice cream.

August Nord is new to town, building a business that involves things staying cold. His whole life has been one, long icy stretch, until a fiery redhead saunters into his ice cream shop. Quinn is the hottest accountant he's ever met, and a small business owner would be dense not to hire a professional to review their finances, right?

As the two approach their attraction with wary steps, the sparks flying between them are all too real. Will the flames feed their burning desire or melt their chance of a happily ever after?

🐾

All reviews are **welcome** and **appreciated**. Please consider leaving one on your favorite social media and book buying sites.

For books in the world of romance and speculative fiction that embody Innovation, Creativity, and Affordability, check out City Owl Press at www.cityowlpress.com.

Acknowledgments

This book, like most I've written, couldn't have made it to the page without the loving support of my parents. Thank you for always being the best set of cheerleaders for my passion.

I want to thank my agent Lesley, and the team at City Owl Press for helping me get all the Forget the Past books out in the world. Also thank you to my insightful sensitivity reader, your willingness to read my story and give feedback on my work means so much to me.

And a final thank you to everyone who has ever fostered/adopted a rescue animal! You are a hero in your fur baby's eyes.

About the Author

LAUREN CONNOLLY is a Colorado Book Awards and HOLT Finalist and an author of contemporary and paranormal romance stories. She's lived among mountains, next to lakes, and in imaginary worlds. Lauren can never seem to stay in one place for too long, but trust that wherever she's residing there is a dog who thinks he's a troll, twin cats hiding in the couch, and bookshelves bursting with stories written by the authors she loves.

www.laurenconnollyromance.com

facebook.com/LaurenConnollyRomance

twitter.com/laurenaliciaCon

instagram.com/laurenconnollyromance

tiktok.com/@laurenconnollyromance

About the Publisher

City Owl Press is a cutting edge indie publishing company, bringing the world of romance and speculative fiction to discerning readers.

Escape Your World. Get Lost in Ours!

www.cityowlpress.com